How to Start
a Charter Airline

HOW TO START
A CHARTER AIRLINE

Susan Haley

Macmillan Canada
Toronto, Ontario, Canada

PICKERING PUBLIC LIBRARY

Canadian Cataloguing in Publication Data

Haley, Susan Charlotte, 1949-
    How to start a charter airline

ISBN 0-7715-9048-2

I. Title

PS8565.A54H6 1994   C813'.54   C94-930445-X
PR9199.3.H35H6 1994

Macmillan Canada wishes to thank the Canada Council and the Ontario Ministry of Culture and Communications for supporting its publishing program.

Cover Design: Kevin Connolly/Boyes and Connolly
Cover Illustration: Leo Scopacasa
Text Design: Joe Lobo

Macmillan Canada
A Division of Canada Publishing Corporation
Toronto, Canada

1 2 3 4 5   98 97 96 95 94

Printed in Canada

HOW TO START
A CHARTER AIRLINE

CHAPTER ONE
A Letter

HELEN CAME out onto the front steps of the Co-op reading a letter from her ex-husband. It was the only thing in the mail. She was still expecting a cheque for her work on the village census.

Paul wanted a divorce. But that was not all he wanted.

"Whoops!"

She lowered her letter and stepped aside just in time to avoid colliding with the pilot.

"Sorry."

Helen stood over by the porch rail and began to reread the letter from the beginning.

She became aware that someone was right by her elbow and put the letter down again. It was the pilot, and he seemed to be lingering with intent. She looked at him blankly.

"Wanted to tell you I'm going into Mountain River this afternoon—"

He was a stocky man: black hair combed straight back and sharp, humorous eyes. His name was Max Malkovski and Helen thought he must have slept with nearly every young woman in Island Crossing since his arrival in the summer. It was partly, she suspected, because he had no other form of accommodation. As the occupant of the nicest log cabin on the lakeshore, she regarded him now with reserve.

"—and I was wondering if you'd like to come with me."

Helen stowed the letter in her jacket pocket, considering this proposition. The two things in Mountain River that were not in Island Crossing were a liquor store and a hotel with a beer parlour.

"I don't have any money," she said.

He grinned. "But I do," he said. "Need to talk to you about something."

*

There were no other people standing on the village dock; evidently she was going to be his only passenger. It was a sunny day, a light breeze rippling the lake water.

Helen had never been in a float plane before, nor in any aircraft of this vintage. It was a Beaver with the registration WWW. A village joke had it that this stood for Whisky, Whisky, Whisky. She now heard him calling it this way on the radio, announcing his departure to the empty blue sky above.

He seemed inclined to chat, but the engine noise was too loud and Helen was a little nervous, looking between the bush passing beneath and the gas gauges, both of which read E for Empty with unwavering needles.

After a while she began to feel more comfortable and looked around her. It was an old model. The ceiling of the cockpit was covered with flocked carpeting in a raised pattern of fern leaves, while the floor seemed to be made of plywood. Undoubtedly the gas gauges merely didn't work.

She rather disapproved of the existence of this plane in Island Crossing. Like many of the isolated lakeland villages of the North, Island Crossing was not connected to the outside world by road. People travelled by boat in summer, skidoo in winter; the larger centre, Mountain River, had an airline that ran an irregular scheduled service.

A plane in Island Crossing was a quicker, more direct way of getting the inhabitants to and from the bar. This was why she was taking it now.

She had been living in the village for more than two years. She had originally gone there with Paul Ayre, her husband, an anthropologist doing research on the Indians of the subarctic. But he had left both her and the project after a bad weekend in March of the year they came, and she had stayed behind, finishing the log cabin on the lakeshore and no longer being or pretending to be concerned with anthropology. She supported herself with small contracts and part-time jobs, plenty of which existed in the village for a person with her education.

She had never gone to the bar before. She was there now, seating herself a little self-consciously at a table clothed in orange towelling, entirely as a consequence of her letter from Paul Ayre.

The pilot was ordering whisky for her. For himself, he ordered pop. Helen smiled. He was not entirely sure of himself, she could see.

"Well—cheerio," he suggested.

"Cheerio." She was not entirely sure of herself either. The letter in her pocket was making her proceed rashly. The pilot was attractive in a way, but what he was doing with her was what, so rumour had it, he had already done with every available woman in the village.

"I've been thinking quite a while I'd have to get to know you," he was saying.

Helen sipped, raising her eyebrows.

"People've been telling me you're the one to talk to."

She thought again of her house. Sometimes she put up transients, but she didn't think he was planning to pay rent. Seduction was almost built into his plans.

"Thing is, I've got this plane, see?"

"Is it yours?" she inquired.

"Nope. Belongs to some cockeyed crook down in North Winnipegosis. I fly the plane, send him all the money at the end of the week. What a deal, eh? I mean *all* the money," he added.

"It doesn't sound great," Helen agreed.

"Anyway, you know this air service here?" He indicated Mountain River with a gesture around the bar.

Helen nodded. She knew it by its terrible reputation.

"They're trying to throw the book at me."

"Is it illegal, what you're doing?"

He paused, seeming not to have considered this question before. Helen helped him out.

"I don't see how they can complain about competition, considering how bad they are. The door handles come off in your hands, I hear."

"These flapjacks think they have a monopoly. And some legal eagle in Ottawa keeps trying to call me up. Would have too, except I don't have a phone."

"Ottawa?" Helen began taking an interest. It was not surprising that Island Crossing people had pointed her out to him. She had had some dealings with Ottawa on their behalf. She regarded herself as a champion of lost causes.

He was ordering her another glass of whisky.

"The Air Carrier Act. Ever heard of that?"

She shook her head.

"That's the book they're trying to throw at me."

"Do you have a copy?"

"Could get one." He was looking at her intently. "I guess you'd know how to read a thing like that."

3

"I have a telephone too." Helen returned his glance, half-amused. "But if what you're doing isn't legal—"

"Look, if it isn't, then half the cowboys in the territory flying point-to-point and minding their own business ought to be in jail. That's the way it goes in this business. Man gives you an old clapped-out machine and says: go there. With any luck, there'll be some homesteaders there who want you to take them someplace. Keep flying, that's the main thing."

"But you have to have a license, don't you? What kind of license do you have?"

"Pilot's. Commercial," he replied.

"Don't you have to have something else?"

"Crook who owns the plane has a charter license, I guess."

"Is there something wrong with the plane? Could that be it?"

He paused, then shrugged. "Those crackers in Ottawa don't care about that," he said. "Airworthiness Division is in Winnipeg."

Helen laughed. "The plane's pretty old, isn't it?"

"Nothing a shave and a haircut wouldn't fix," he said, grinning. "So—you'll give me a hand?"

"Okay."

Helen took a drink. He lit a cigarette.

"Don't you drink at all?" she asked.

"Oh, I drink. Oh yeah, I do drink." He looked down at the innocent glass in front of him. "But you can't drink and fly, see?"

She smiled.

"So I was wondering," he went on lightly, "whether I had to take you home tonight."

CHAPTER TWO

People Starting Fires in the Rooms

THEY WERE in one of the airless rooms upstairs, jukebox sounds from the bar below blending with the buzzing of flies on the sealed windows.

But they were not getting anywhere fast.

Max was sitting on the bed drinking whisky out of one of the blurry glasses from the bathroom. Helen prowled beside the door. There was a management sign posted on it that read:

> People making a disturbance after hour's
> or setting fire's in the rooms will be
> persecuted.

He liked her well enough, she was sure of that. But he didn't seem able to get on with it. Perhaps he had some preconceptions about her character that made seduction difficult.

As for Helen, her being here at all was entirely due to the letter in her coat pocket. He was not her type; she had never slept with anyone in the least like him. The letter was making her do this.

He cleared his throat.

"Married?" he asked.

Helen nodded.

He poured her a glass of whisky and she went over to the night table to get it.

"You too, I guess."

"Not lately," he replied. "What happened to the man?"

"He left," she said.

She decided to take off her jacket and gain some distance on the pocket.

"Is that how come—" he cleared his throat again "—a lady like you ended up in Island Crossing?"

Lady. So that was it. She considered taking off her clothes but compromised by going over to sit beside him on the bed.

"It's a good place to stay."

"Was thinking of staying myself. Before all this came up." He lit a cigarette.

Helen now regarded him with slight hostility. They had come up here for sex and he, at least, was supposed to want it. Were they going to talk all night?

"A place with 200 people, most of them unemployed, can hardly afford to support a plane," she remarked.

"They're spending a lot more money getting this cockeyed outfit to send a plane over from Mountain River."

"To go to the liquor store and the bar."

"There's bringing in groceries. And tourists. They're talking about some kind of fishing lodge, aren't they?"

"Tourist fishing." Helen had been on the writing end of this idea for several years. "Have you talked to Henry about that?" Henry Woodcutter was the Chief in Island Crossing.

"Oh, he's all for it. Had him in here with some guys the other day. Just a question of loosening up the money."

Helen secretly hated the idea of tourist fishing in Island Crossing. They needed a hotel for crazy transients like him, she decided.

"Don't you think you're just exploiting them?" she said.

He regarded her in silence.

"I mean, using them to get yourself a job."

"Well—so are you."

There was some truth in it. As a consultant she was cheap, but he looked like a pretty cheap airline too.

"I'm not trying to make a million bucks," he said. "I don't know—there has to be some place to get started."

A party had been going on in the next room for some time. The partition that separated them reverberated with loud music. Now it began to thump in a suggestively rhythmic way.

They looked at each other. Helen put down her drink. Max stubbed out his cigarette.

They had both concluded that they could no longer postpone it.

6

Helen started to unbutton her shirt. He still was not making a move, and she felt she had to make her intentions clear. She exposed a naked shoulder and hesitated, holding the shirt closed across her breasts.

Max was watching this, his lips beginning to curl into a smile over his sharp teeth. He stretched out a tentative hand and let it glide from the rounded top of her arm down behind her back, taking the shirt with it. She could tell from his fingertips that he liked it. There was no going back now.

There was a lot of screaming next door, no longer in time with the thumps.

Max was lying on top of her now and he was kissing her. He had taken off his clothes and the rest of hers very quickly. They were both naked.

Then there was a gigantic crash, a glass-shattering noise. Someone had thrown something, possibly another person, through a window.

They lay against one another, their legs still intertwined. Helen could now only hear the thumping of her own heart. There was a long, frightening silence.

Had someone been murdered?

Wild shrieking began in the next room. Helen shot bolt upright.

An instant later there came a heavy knock on their door.

Max sat up too.

"Next room," he shouted.

"This here's the police!"

"Wrong room!"

"Open up!"

Max leapt out of bed and began groping for his clothes. Helen tried to jackknife under the bedspread.

"We're comin' in!"

Still pulling up his jeans, Max hobbled to the opposite corner of the room as the lock flew splintering off the doorjamb.

Two policemen in uniform entered the room with their guns out.

"Sorry to break up your party—"

"Next door," said Max.

"Oh yeah?"

There was now an unearthly quiet next door.

Helen sat up, clinging to the bedspread.

"Who's this?" One of the RCMP men, reholstering his gun, came over to look at Helen. The other one went into the bathroom. He emerged after a moment, tucking his gun away as well.

"No one in there."

The policeman standing over Helen had just lost the first round of their eye battle.

Max regarded them helplessly from his corner, his hands hanging at his sides.

"Hey you!" said the constable to Max. "Seems to me I met you last week. Wasn't your party actin'-in-such-a-way-as-to-cause-a-disturbance-of-the-peace-namely-settin'-fire-to-a-rug in this very hotel room? I ought to book you. Should of done it last Friday."

"Dave," said the first policeman, now staggering backwards from Helen's poisonous gaze. "Hey, Dave—"

"Yep. I remember you. Bringin' in all them drunks from Island Crossing—"

"Dave," said the first policeman more urgently. "I guess we got the wrong—"

"Wrong room," repeated Max. "Next door."

Dave went over to Helen and now in turn met the laser of her eyebeam.

"Next door?" he asked, momentarily disoriented.

"Think you should hurry," said Max.

"Oh." They began to back out. "Sorry, lady."

"Apologies, ma'am."

They shut the door behind them and it rebounded on its hinges, the lock hanging ragged in the opening.

There was still no noise from next door. Helen lay stonily, waiting for them to break the lock, but there was no sound, not even footsteps. The police had apparently tiptoed off down the hall.

She looked at Max.

He slumped into a chair beside the bed.

"What happened?" she asked, indicating the wall behind her head.

"Don't know." He looked up. "Want to find out?"

"Of course." She sat up and began to struggle into her shirt.

"Well, I guess," he said, "maybe this time it wasn't anybody from Island Crossing."

"That's true," she said in surprise. There was still no sound from the other room.

"Then—" he took her hand to help her up off the bed "—let's just go home."

CHAPTER THREE
Pancakes for Breakfast

THEY TIED up the plane at the boat dock. Helen took the path along the lakeshore. Her cabin welcomed her on its lawn of icy green grass. There was a dawn frost.

Max followed more slowly. When she turned around to wait for him, she saw that he was carrying a pack and a five-star sleeping bag she had noticed in the back of the plane. A suitcase had appeared out of nowhere.

"Got to do a trip at 9:00," he panted. "Want me to cook breakfast?"

Helen's dog was saying hello. He sniffed Max's leg and then, wagging his tail, turned to enter the house.

She began to open the door reluctantly. Her house was like a turtle's shell; the suitcase worried her. It was true that she had let herself in for this but the suitcase signified something more than she was sure she had bargained for. She had not seen a suitcase since her husband had left with hers.

While he set it down and unslung the pack, she went looking in the cupboards. There was some dry meat and a can of fruit leftover from Christmas. Like her Indian neighbours, Helen didn't keep much food on hand.

"Nice place," he remarked.

Helen turned around to share his appreciation. It was a nice place. Separated from the rest of the houses in the village by a tract of wasteland merging into muskeg behind, it commanded a little point going out into the lake. It had its own small grass plat stretching to the beach, its own paths, its own neat outhouse.

Inside it was very simple, even Spartan. Helen had finished the interior herself, eliminating all the features of Paul's design that were beyond her skill. It contained one large room with a bed in it. A simple set of steps, almost a ladder, led upstairs to a loft. The only other article of furniture was the stove, a wood-burning kitchen range, that stood in the middle of the floor. A picture window looked out over the lake.

Max wasted no time on the view. He was already approaching the stove in a businesslike way.

"There's nothing but this." She showed him the can.

"That's okay. Got some things in my pack. I always travel heavy." He was getting out a frying pan, which he set down on the cold stove lid. Then he disappeared out the door. A few minutes later, she heard him chopping wood.

Helen sat down on her bed. After a while, when he did not come back, she pulled up the comforter and put her head on the pillow.

Nothing that had happened so far committed her to anything. And if he had another flight in a few hours it seemed unlikely that any more serious development than breakfast was to be expected.

She fell into an uneasy sleep.

*

When she woke up, the cabin was warm. There was an appetizing smell in the air.

"Pancakes," said Helen.

"Coffee first."

She sat up.

Helen lived ordinarily on the kindness of her neighbours. In summer, she ate Sarah Woodcutter's fish and rabbits. In winter, she got a cut of the communal moose and caribou supply. Sometimes people gave her bannock but she never ate bread. Pancakes were something out of another life.

"God, how wonderful!"

He must have been waiting for her to wake up, for he brought a laden plate over to the bed. Then he sat down politely at the foot.

All he had done so far besides opening his pack was spread his sleeping bag on the floor. She was happy to notice that the suitcase was still out in the porch.

"What time is it?"

"About 8:00."

"Did you sleep?" She indicated the sleeping bag.

"Lay down, anyway."

"Was all this food in your pack?" She hunched over her knees, eating with pleasure. There was even strawberry jam on the pancakes.

"Haven't really had any place else to keep it," he replied.

"No. I suppose not." She remembered that he had been sleeping in a lot of different houses.

"Staying here a night, there a night," he continued. "Thing is, you've got to have breakfast. Might not eat again all day."

"I see."

"You know how people live here. Eat a bit of dry meat when they feel like it. Usually nothing much in the cupboard. I notice the kids like having breakfast, though."

"I'm sure they do." Helen put her empty plate down, and he instantly picked it up and took it over to the dishpan on the shelf where, to her astonishment, he proceeded to wash everything.

He certainly was domesticated, she had to admit.

"What's this trip you have to do?" she asked.

"Hunters and Trappers Association going in to Mountain River."

"Why?" Helen thought she knew all the movements of the Hunters and Trappers Association. She was their secretary, after all.

"Talk to the game warden about getting more money."

"What?" The Hunters and Trappers Association existed only to answer to a grant Helen applied for every year. "Whose idea was that?"

"Mine, I guess."

"Tourist fishing, eh?"

"Well, that's what they've got to offer." He shrugged, hanging up the dishtowel.

Helen threw back the comforter and sat up on the edge of the bed.

"Listen," she said. "I think you've already got a pretty good idea what people do in this place. If not, I'll tell you. They live here. They make a little money from this and a little from that, but what really keeps it all together is that they can hunt and fish here in peace. Do you know what a bunch of tourists would do to a place like this?"

"Fish," he suggested.

"A tiny one-season industry that will bring in booze, welfare, and the game laws."

"They've already got booze and welfare."

"Only when people go to Mountain River. For example, when those guys go to Mountain River today, how many of them are going to be sober by the time you get them to the game office?"

He smiled at her.

"Have to see about that."

11

"Well, it's not a good idea. You're just drumming up business for yourself."

"Trip's on me." He sat down beside her.

"Yes, but the next one won't be. That'll be when they run out of the whisky they bring back."

"Hey! You don't think much of these people here."

"I do," she said. "I do think much of these people!"

He was silent.

Helen suddenly realized how self-righteous she sounded.

Trying to control her annoyance, she looked down at her bare feet on the floor. They were small and narrow, reddened by the constant practice of wearing nothing but Wellington boots in cold weather.

She noticed that he was looking down at his feet too. His feet were large and square, clad in the bushman's heavy woollen socks, linsey-woolsey-coloured and much washed.

He didn't want to argue. Helen started to laugh.

He pounced on her instantly and pressed her back into the comforter on the bed. They exchanged a long, electric kiss.

"Holy Smokes!" said Max. She noticed that he was taking off his clothes as quickly as possible and began to follow suit.

There was no tentativeness in his approach this time and no particular finesse. He had given up on the struggle with his shirt. She tried to help him with her jeans. It was going to be a cold weather mating.

And then—she found it quite impossible to believe that this could be happening again—the door leading in from the porch opened and several people entered the room.

Helen sprang upward a couple of inches quite suddenly as Max rolled his weight off her, and pulled up the quilt.

It was Henry Woodcutter, the Chief, and two of his henchmen. This was the form of house entry usually practised by men and small children in Island Crossing. This type of situation was often the subject of stories told at Christmas parties and picnics. Helen remembered laughing at a few of these jokes herself.

Henry approached the bed and took a good long look at Helen. Unlike the Mountain River RCMP, he was in no way impaired by her annoyance.

Max was still pulling on his pants.

"Hi, Helen."

"Hi, Henry."

The other two men nodded to her, taking a good look as well .

Max now started to back all three of them towards the door.

"Just came by to pick him up." Henry eluded Max and dodged around to resume his conversation with Helen.

"I told him to see you," he explained.

"Thanks a lot," said Helen.

"Well, you're a woman, aren't you?" Henry asked.

"Yeah, she's a woman. Now would you please just—" Max succeeded in shepherding him away.

Henry was being reasonable. He was also plainly fresh from an all night drinking party.

"I thought maybe you needed a whiteman, Helen," he explained.

Max very determinedly pushed all three of them out onto the porch and followed, shutting the door behind him. There was a bit of arguing outside but it began to recede. Max had evidently driven them off the doorstep. She waited quietly where she was, expecting him to return.

He re-entered the room a moment later, snatched his jacket from the hook, and disappeared onto the porch, where she presumed he was finding his boots. Then he came back and stood in the doorway. Helen turned her head to look at him.

"Should I come back?"

It was a plaintive question.

Helen raised herself on her elbow.

"When?" she asked.

"Tonight."

He gave her another long, anxious look and then backed out the door.

A few minutes later she heard the roar of the Beaver's engine on the lake.

CHAPTER FOUR
Women's Fishing

HELEN ANSWERED the telephone twice that morning. Both calls came from people trying to charter an aircraft.

One was from Island Crossing: someone who had probably been at Henry Woodcutter's drinking party. The other call was from the headquarters of the trucking company in Mountain River. The man seemed to have spoken to Max already. Helen made an appointment for Max to bring in a ton of freight to the Co-op the very next day.

After noon she went out to sit on her front steps and observe the lake. Island Crossing folk spent a great deal of time looking at the lake. It was a way of getting the news. Village life centred around what happened there.

A pair of sandhill cranes lived off a reed bed about a quarter of a mile away from Helen's stoop. They were making a lot of noise in their harsh, mechanical-sounding voices; so were the gulls, picking up fish guts on the beach.

Sarah Woodcutter must have been to her nets that morning.

The sky of October, sere and cloudless, reminded Helen of the relentless blue of the coming winter.

Sarah herself now came around the corner, carrying two trout neatly split and draped over a section of peeled sapling.

"Been drying fish," she remarked, giving them to Helen.

Helen stood the sapling against the housewall and wordlessly moved over so that Sarah could sit down on the steps. It was clear that Sarah already knew about Max. There were two trout on the stick.

Sarah was Henry Woodcutter's oldest sister. Most of the village were Woodcutters or immediately related to Woodcutters. But Sarah was almost unique in Island Crossing because she had no husband, no man at all.

She lived in a cabin nearby, which, like Helen's, stood at some distance from the village. Sarah made her own way, and she supported herself quite well off fish, rabbits, small birds, and a little trapping in the winter. She was one of the remaining old women who knew how to tan hides, but she never did beadwork or crafts. To the men of the village, she was not like a woman; they ignored her. But Helen valued her above everyone else in the place. She loved her, she admired her, and she knew, with respect, that she didn't understand her.

Their acquaintance had begun only after the breakup of Helen's marriage. Sarah would have no truck with anthropology.

"You look tired," said Helen.

Sarah glanced at her, but did not smile. Helen knew that she looked tired too.

Helen's dog came over and stood by Sarah, and her hand dropped to caress his ears and his muzzle. He was an old dog, hers before she gave him to Helen. She had a puppy now, more useful for scaring up game.

"Want to go fishing?"

It was an odd request from a woman who had been up early to empty a net. But Helen had an insight into fishing now, after a few years here. There was fishing for food and for dogs, and there was fishing where fishing was not the point. Privacy, especially for women, was a hard-bought commodity in Island Crossing.

Sarah had had a client the night before.

It was not exactly a professional relationship. Helen knew this from personal experience. Sarah would receive some screaming, overwrought woman, drunk or half-drunk on homebrew or perfume, and turn her into a human being again overnight. She wiped off the blood, put wet cloths on the black eyes and the bruises, and listened. For this she exacted no fee and was not often rewarded with thanks.

They always went back to their husbands. Where else could they go? When Sarah thought there was some hope they might go somewhere else, she took them fishing.

She had taken Helen fishing too, long ago.

Helen followed Sarah down to the lake, carrying her fishing rod. Sarah also had a rod, but it had an unreliable reel.

The girl waiting beside the boat was called Rosaleen. She had been living with Eli Balah all winter. She had two bad black eyes.

"He broke her nose, I guess," said Sarah.

The lake was pure cerulean, almost unruffled. It was one of the last good days of the fall. The sparse spruce blended away along the line of the bay into the misty blues and browns of the leafless hardwoods. The colour of the ground was red, the colour of cranberry and bearberry, a muskeg colour.

Rosaleen had two children, one of them, a boy of seven, in the bow of the boat. The other one, a baby, was with someone in the village. Helen thought the girl herself was about twenty-one.

"I got a white rug at home," she told Helen.

They were trolling. Sarah drove the boat at a leisurely pace over the brown rocks below.

"He bought it in Mountain River last Christmas. When I seen that rug—"

Eli Balah was a troublemaker, and one of the people Helen had no use for at all. He was her own age, about thirty, and old enough to be through with mischief; but jail and perhaps some other things that had happened had left their mark on his character. Helen felt that Rosaleen was not the first woman he had beaten.

Helen began mentally writing up a case history as Rosaleen prattled on. Eli was not the father of the child in the bow. He had been very nice to her at parties. She was from Buffalo Neck, not Island Crossing, and she had met him there at a party. He was the father of the infant in the village. When he quit his job pumping gas in Buffalo Neck they had had a few fights, not bad ones. Now they were living here with his father, on his father's pension.

"So when he spill wine on the rug, I get a cloth, tell him to clean it up. Sure, he was drunk. But he give me the rug." She began to cry drearily.

Helen looked at Sarah. Really, when you considered that Rosaleen was the sort of girl who was attracted to Eli Balah, could there be any hope for her? He was a hopeless case, and did it not therefore follow that she was too?

Helen was suddenly ashamed of herself for this line of thought.

Her line snagged and she got a tangle. Rosaleen had her rod and she had the one with the unreliable reel.

Rosaleen continued to cry.

"Where did he get the wine?" Helen asked.

"He was in Mountain River with that pilot."

Sarah gave Helen a piercing black glance.

"You're his woman now, I guess," stated Rosaleen.

The snarl in Helen's line had become a bird's-nest. She tugged at it, making it worse.

16

The boat passed over the algae-covered rocks, the long tendrils swaying in the ripple of their passage. The gulls screamed overhead, yearning for them to catch something.

Helen had started out in Island Crossing as a learned observer. Since then she had been a non-combatant, a kind of neuter, not a woman, achieving nothing but a tenuous peace. It appalled her to realize that overnight she had become somebody's woman, the woman of that pilot.

Sarah spoke:

"That pilot, was he the one who pounded you?"

"No."

"Then be still."

Helen went on trying to untangle her line, hampered by her clammy fingers.

Sarah had brought them to a good place, the riffle of an incoming stream over a ledge. She shut off the motor and took Helen's rod away from her.

Rosaleen was fishing, sniffling a little. The child up ahead peered into the depths of the water, keeping his own childish peace.

Sarah retied the leader and cast. At once she got a fish. He came swimming up out of the clear water straight at them and dived under the boat just in time. The boy in the bow shouted. Sarah was playing it, letting the line run.

The fish surfaced again and they saw it was a pike, of a good size, long and lean, but with a major head.

Sarah began to draw in her line, slow and sure. The reel was not unreliable in her gnarled, skillful hands.

Helen held her breath, rooting for the fish as she always did at this moment. She lived off game just like her neighbours, but her culture had a different myth about animals, about animal pain, animal fear.

"Got him," said Sarah softly. She picked the fish out of the water.

The hook went through his upper lip only. Helen looked away, then looked again as Sarah held him up.

Sarah now nimbly unpicked the hook, holding the pike by the gills. Long, unattractively barred with yellow and the pale marks of growth, he seemed to bare his teeth at them.

"Now I let him go," said Sarah, and the fish slipped away under the water on a ripple of blood.

The child leaned forward, crooning to himself, and watched it glide off among the rocks. Sarah started the motor.

17

Helen was still wrapped in her thoughts. She stopped Sarah on the dock just as she was about to stalk home with her fishing rod. Rosaleen and the boy had already disappeared.

"Do you think—?" she said. "What she said about—?"

"He going to put skis on that plane?" asked Sarah.

"I don't know. I hardly—"

"Tell him: put skis on this winter. Tell him I say so," commanded Sarah. "Babies get sick in the bush every winter. Think Mountain River Air Service going to take 'em out? Cash first, they say. Where's your cash in the bush?"

"But Sarah," said Helen, taking her arm.

"No!" said Sarah abruptly. "You know something? It's up to you." She freed her arm.

It was a frank exchange, Helen realized, as she walked home. Was he going to put skis on the plane?

CHAPTER FIVE
Why the Dog Didn't Bark

WAS HE going to come back at all?

She thought it was 9:30. Helen lived by estimating time. Her watch battery had run down about a year and a half before. But the equinox had passed and dark came early.

And it was dark now. Surely it would not be legal for him to land on the lake after dark?

They had landed there that morning almost before dawn, but she was aware that this had been a desperate initiative on his part.

It had been an act of desperation on her part to go with him in the first place. But that was not the way it seemed now.

She liked him.

She wanted him to come back.

Helen pulled herself together. She had not waited for a man in years. Why was she waiting for one now? On the basis of what had passed between them so far, she had no reason to wait at all. She usually went to bed shortly after dark and that was what she was going to do now.

She lit her lantern. Helen had not put in electricity; she had had no money to pay an electrician, and there was none in the district in any case. Her house, unlike most of the houses in the village, was not supplied all complete by the government.

There were no dishes to be done as she had cooked Sarah's gift of fish on the fire outside at about the time when she thought Max might show up. She looked crossly at the frying pan and the pack, then went out to chop wood.

He had chopped enough wood for three days already. She stoked the stove.

The dog stopped clicking around on the floor and lay down.

Helen had grown up in the city without pets or animals of any kind. But this dog was perhaps her other true friend in the world. Sarah, who was not sentimental about animals, usually just called him Hey You or the equivalent in her own language. But he had been named Bootleg by Mrs. Henry Woodcutter's children, some of whom were still young enough to think this had something to do with his legs—which had, indeed, four handsome white boots. As a consequence, he was a village character. Helen was very fond of him.

Now he put his nose down on his paws with a sigh. He was looking wistfully at the door.

It occurred to her to wonder why the dog had not barked at Max. Perhaps that meant he was trustworthy, that the dog liked him too.

She estimated that it was 11:00. It was very dark. He wasn't coming. She blew out the lamp and got into bed.

Some hours later, she dimly heard the roar of an aircraft and the characteristic popping of the Beaver's engine. When she woke up fully it was later yet, and a thin, filtering daylight was coming in through the windows.

Max was standing just inside the door, his hands in his pockets, looking down at his bedroll, which was still spread out on the floor.

Helen jumped out of bed, making an inarticulate noise of surprise and fear. Bootleg had not barked again.

"You said you'd be back last night."

It sounded like an accusation. She went across to him and put her arms around his neck.

He hugged her lightly. He felt cold and slightly damp.

"Lucky I made it back. It's pretty foggy out there." He pressed his face into her neck. "You're nice and warm."

"Did they all go to the bar?" She was sure they had.

"Oh yeah." He laughed a little. "Had to get 'em out of jail."

He was walking her backwards towards the bed, lifting the heavy cloth of her nightgown up to her waist.

"Jail?"

Helen didn't like this at all.

He continued trying to move her backwards.

"It was okay. We called the game warden and he came over and got 'em out."

"Oh, for heaven's sake!" Helen tried to push his hands down. This was just what she had been afraid of.

"So he's coming in here the day after tomorrow."

Max had stopped trying to move her, but he kept his hands persuasively on her waist. Warm, firm hands; she remembered what they had been like when he touched her before.

"What is he coming for?" she cried. "Tourist fishing?"

"Well, maybe. Wants to see the Hunters and Trappers. Well-run organization here, he says. He's coming in with me, not Mountain River Air. Doorhandles fall off their planes, he says. But now there's a plane here—"

"Really?"

Instantly Max began to take off her nightgown again.

"But you have a flight for the Co-op too," she murmured. "A thousand pounds of groceries."

"Saw the guy. Gave him your number," said Max.

"But you're supposed to be there—" she had raised her arms co-operatively and the nightgown came off over her head "—at 9:00 this morning!" She laughed.

"It's only 5:00. And there's a fog."

He was taking off his own clothes now and she stood beside the bed, waiting.

Jail, fog, haste. Did it have to be? She had been so long a non-combatant.

They kissed and he pushed her gently down on the bed. He was in a hurry, but it didn't matter; so was she. She had been in a state of wild sexual excitement for over twenty-four hours.

After a moment, however, he rolled off her with a groan and began fumbling with something. It came to her that he was putting on a condom. She had forgotten about this necessity; it had been a long time since she had used one.

She leaned over him to watch.

"Busted it, I think." He went to find another.

"Here, let me help." She took it out of his hand.

"Holy Smokes!" said Max.

Her humble action had aroused him. It aroused her even more to see that she had had this effect. He seemed to think he should engage in foreplay but it was not necessary. She merely took him between her legs and rose to the orgasm with their first kiss. As she lay there in its aftermath, panting and sobbing, she felt him hesitate, a little bewildered by the force of her desire. Then he too, plunged into the wild and rocky sea that churned around them.

21

At last they lay still. The tears of pleasure were drying on her cheeks. He shifted to let her head rest on his shoulder and she relaxed blissfully. Something had begun at last.

Or at least for her it had begun. She raised her head to look at his face.

He gave her a peaceful smile.

"I wasn't sure you were coming back," she said.

They looked into each other's eyes.

"Thought you might lock the door on me."

"I never lock the door."

The dog snuffled slightly, some nightmare rabbit disturbing his sleep.

"Well, I did. After I came in."

Helen laughed.

"That was a very good idea."

She bent over him and he put his hand up beside her temple, pushing her hair back.

"You were crying, know that?"

Helen nodded, a little embarrassed. She was remembering her wildness. It was not a decent way to make love to a stranger.

"God, that was nice," he said.

The expression on his face was now wide-awake and lively. His eyes searched her face, taking in the ravages of her emotion with apparent pleasure. Helen felt a faint flicker of renewed desire, and knew that he saw this too.

She put her face down against his neck and he stroked her back and flanks with electric fingertips.

"Holy Smokes!" he whispered in her ear.

CHAPTER SIX
Fog

THE WATCH on the arm under her head said 9:00. Helen came to with a start. It was day again.

"Max!" She sat bolt upright and turned around to wake him up. "It's morning. Don't you have to do a flight?"

He did not open his eyes. Instead he put his other arm across her waist and clasped her bare breast in his hand.

"Can't go," he said.

"Hey, wake up! You have to go."

"Have to, but I can't. Look outside."

Helen jumped out of bed, overcoming a certain resistance on his part, and went to the big window to look out over the lake. The world outside was muffled in a dense fog. Not a thing could be seen beyond the pearly grey grass on the verge of the beach.

"Oh." Helen hopped up and down on the cold floor.

"What are you doing?"

She had gone to the woodbox. She took out some kindling and opened the firebox door of the stove. She was freezing.

"I'll do that."

She could hear him getting out of bed and she turned around. He was naked. So was she. She had forgotten about that. She hopped back into bed quickly. He was making the fire now.

Then she watched him. He was nicer-looking with his clothes off than on, muscular, smooth, a pale brown colour all over. He stoked the stove quickly and neatly; he knew how to make a fire.

Then he went to fill the kettle from the water tank in the porch. She was still admiring him when he turned around and approached the bed, picking some of his clothes up off the floor.

"Looking at me?" He smiled at her, pulling up his jeans.

He was not a very handsome man, about forty, strongly built, and of middle height. The skin of his body was hairless despite the black hair on his head, and his face was not heavily shadowed with a beard. What characterized him most was a look of alertness: a springy walk, sharp eyes, a long nose, a mouth that smiled quickly and easily.

He had gone outdoors and Helen remained in bed, thinking about him.

He liked her. He liked her a lot. She knew that; but it surprised her how much she liked him. The force of her desire for him the night before stunned her; and now she stayed in bed, wanting to have him again. It was remarkable that this was happening, that she was allowing it to happen.

He came back inside, carrying an armload of wood, which he put down in the woodbox. He started to make coffee. Then, suddenly, he turned aside and relocked the door.

There was no doubt that he had moved in.

At last he brought her a mug of coffee. He sat down on the side of the bed with his cup in his hand.

She took refuge from his scrutiny in her coffee. "You must be tired. You can't have gotten more than three hours sleep."

"Cops gave me a sofa," he replied.

"Oh?" Helen laughed. "I thought you might have been in a cell."

"Said they were sorry about the other night. Asked me to tell you."

"Really?" Helen spoke sarcastically. She had no use for the Mountain River police.

"Said they might come in here with me sometime." He was laughing silently.

Helen regarded him for a moment and began to laugh too.

"To go fishing, you think?"

"Sure."

He was looking at her closely again and Helen dropped her eyes. Perhaps she had developed something prudish in her personality during the time she had been alone in Island Crossing. He was taking very obvious pleasure in looking at her naked under the coverlet, setting off a sexual reaction she was fighting to conceal.

"I guess I should say I'm sorry about what happened in that hotel too," he said. "Didn't really have time yet."

"Oh, it's all right."

"Shouldn't have taken you there at all. Didn't have anyplace else to take you."

"Well, it doesn't matter."

"Sure it matters. Should do these things right." He leaned forward and took the nearly empty coffee cup out of her hand. Then he put it down on the floor with his own, setting them neatly side by side.

Helen sank down in the bed, looking away as he took off his clothes. It was warm under the comforter, but she was shivering as he slid in beside her.

*

She thought he believed they had done it right this time. It had been an old-fashioned three-act drama. As a lover, he was a little conservative. Perhaps it was because he thought she would like that. Her contented body was telling her that she did. And she liked him the better for caring what she wanted.

The watch on the arm under her head said 11:00. But for once he seemed not to have any plans. They lay there idly, curled together, listening to the faint crackling of the stove.

It was very still outside in the overcoat of the fog. On a day like this no one in Island Crossing got up in the morning.

"What are you thinking about," she asked at last.

"What do you keep the bathtub for?"

Helen had an old-fashioned cast-iron tub on the porch beside the water butt.

She rolled over energetically. "Having baths."

"Haven't had a bath in a month." He rolled over, too, and they lay facing one another. "Only got wet when I fell in. Not to wash."

"Well, you can even have hot water here." She prepared to get up at once.

"No, no." He drew her back down. "I was just thinking about it."

"Couldn't you have had a bath anywhere else you stayed?"

Helen had suddenly reminded herself of all the other places he had stayed. He ought to know she was aware of that.

He studied her face for a moment. Then he said:

"Couldn't get a bath. Slept on the floor too."

"Oh?"

He was silent.

Helen considered this for a moment. "Really?" she said.

25

"Could have had a couple of beds, I guess. But it makes trouble." He continued to watch her carefully.

"Yes, I suppose it was more convenient with me."

He regarded her a short while longer, then turned over on his back.

"Maybe you won't believe me."

"About what?" Helen knew he wanted her to believe him so far, but she wasn't sure that she did. She lay down on her back too.

"Day I came into town," he said, "I saw you behind the firehall picking berries. Big rubber boots."

That was true, at least.

"Thought you must be some guy's wife. But then I noticed there weren't any whitemen around." He paused. "Wanted to ask you once or twice. Didn't know what to say. So I asked around instead."

"What did they tell you?" She lay rigid. Henry. What had he really said?

"Nothing much," he replied. "Only about how you were in on this tourist fishing deal. Not what I wanted to know."

She relaxed a little. He rolled over.

"You don't know what you're like, do you?"

"No, of course not!" She smiled in spite of herself.

"You're a beautiful woman. Pretty face, blond hair, pretty body."

Her looks had ceased to matter to Helen a few years earlier. It was a shock to have him allude to them this way.

"So it took me a while to get up the nerve to do something."

"Nerve?"

"Yeah. I was hanging around whenever I could, but you didn't even notice. I'd wake up on some floor and think about it. Just say hello or something, I'd think."

"You can't be serious." Helen pulled the sheet up over her head and he began to pull it back down gently.

"I'm telling you the truth." He looked into her eyes. "I couldn't believe it when I got you to come with me."

"I wanted to go."

She remembered her motive. She had never thought much about him. Of course, she had known what was going to happen if she went with him, but that was all.

"Sleazy bar, stinking hotel room. Cops. And you were so nice. I wanted to ask a couple of times if you were real."

Helen laughed. "We were caught in flagrante delicto by the police. I thought that was reality!"

"Yeah. I really messed it up. How did I get to be here?"

She rolled over on top of him and lay there, smiling down into his face. Her hair fell in a pale cave around them.

"But now, at least, you know I'm real."

"No," he said. "Not sure I am either."

CHAPTER SEVEN

Last Ditch

FIRST THEY had breakfast. Max did the cooking. Then they began heating water for the bath.

It was possible to have a bath in two buckets of water, one for the soap and one for the rinse, but for the first bath in a month she felt he needed more water than that. And the water should be hot too.

Perhaps other people in Island Crossing were celebrating the autumn fog this way.

She herself had a sponge bath and washed her hair in the dishpan on the ledge. Max returned from the porch wearing a towel around his shoulders. He sat down with a sigh of contentment on the bottom step of the loft stairs.

He had a long scratch on one leg ending in a big scab. The other leg had a bruise on the shin.

"You look as if you've been through the wars," she commented. She sat down beside him.

"Got this one when I fell off the floats." He inspected the scab. "Happened right here. I was trying to get some drunk out of the plane."

"Was he resisting?"

"No, but he was heavy. Fell in between the pontoon and the dock. Thought I was going to drown."

"What happened to him?"

"Nothing. Staggered off, I guess. There was no one around when I came up for the third time."

"And what about this one?" Helen put her finger lightly on the bruise.

"That was the other time I fell in."

Helen smiled and began to dry her hair in the towel. He liked having somebody to talk to, she thought. He was an entertaining talker.

"Another drunk?" she asked.

"Nope. Stupidity. Dropped the barrel wrench. Had to go after it. Went in the wrong way, head first."

"It's kind of cold at this time of year, isn't it?"

"You bet."

Max now took the comb out of her hand and began to untangle the long strands of her hair.

"Do you like this—this life you lead? How long have you been doing it?"

"Flying, you mean?" Her hair was fine and hard to comb. He worked at it patiently, not pulling. "Learned how to fly when I was twenty. But I've only been doing this about five years now. I did a bunch of other stuff after I got married." He paused, comb in hand. "Trouble is, there's not much else I'm good at."

"Have you had this particular job long?"

"With Fly Spray?"

"Fly Spray?"

"North Winnipegosis Fly and Spray," he explained. "Since last summer."

He had only been in Island Crossing since early September.

"Been all over. Agaric likes to keep moving."

"Who is Agaric?"

"Owns the machine," said Max. "Stuff I was doing last summer was more or less agricultural," he went on.

"Do you mean spraying fields?"

"No. I mean hicks. Used to go into some little one-horse town and land in the back pasture. Stay a week and do anything. Aerial photos, stunt flying, take the kids for rides. Plane was a Piper Cub."

"I didn't know that happened any longer."

"It doesn't," said Max. "Whole thing didn't keep me in sliced bread. Turned what I made over to the boss and never saw it again. Then Agaric went to jail and I started driving a truck."

"Went to jail?"

Helen sat on the step in front of him, looking up. He prowled back and forth in front of her.

"It was some funny deal he had over a pair of DC-3 engines. When he got out, he got hold of this machine. Said I could make my wages back flying up North. I fell for it and here I am."

"You mean you're still trying to recover your wages from last summer?"

"Yeah. Only now I'm trying to get my wages from this summer too."

"But that must be thousands of dollars!"

"Ten, I figure." He grinned. "Well, make it eight. I'd settle for six, to tell you the truth."

"Couldn't you get, you know, a nice steady job with a real airline?"

"I'm forty," he said. "Besides, all I ever flew was crap. Broke down, thirty-year old, government-certified crap. Thing is, there aren't many of us around any more who can fly it."

"It sounds kind of dangerous. I suppose it's exciting, though."

"That's what I thought when I left the farm."

He went to get a cigarette.

Helen followed him over to the kitchen area. She wanted to hear more.

"Was that where you grew up? A farm?"

Max was now bending over the open stove lid, lighting the cigarette with a spill. His face was illuminated by the sudden blaze, and she found herself thinking he was not ordinary looking at all. The febrile light of the fire revealed the odd planes of his cheeks, his long, slightly hooked nose, the slant of his dark eyes.

"The farm belonged to my stepfather," he said.

"Oh, I see. Were your parents divorced?"

"No."

"Then your mother—?"

"She had me before she married him. She was about fifteen when I was born. But she never told anyone who did it."

He looked at her for a moment.

"But I think the guy must have been an Indian," he said.

That was what she had seen in the light of the fire. He was like and yet unlike the people she knew so well: his hair, his nose, his smooth skin, his brown colour, his alertness.

"Ma had Indian blood herself. Grew up near the reserve. Probably my step-dad didn't think he cared about that when he married her," Max went on. "Probably didn't think he'd mind me, either."

"But he did—did mind you?" Helen was nervous.

"She had four other kids with him. Married him when she was about twenty. But I don't remember much before I was twelve," he added.

"Why not?"

"She died about then." He paused. "Well, he killed her, I think."

"My God!"

He was merely thinking about it, looking at the end of his cigarette glowing between his fingers.

"I don't know what they said it was. Some sickness. Cancer. Too many kids. But what it really was was getting hit and hurt and beat up every day. Anyway, he tried to kill me too, after that."

He spoke quite steadily. But she knew he was telling her something he didn't usually talk about. The lightness of the tall tales he had been telling had gone out of his voice.

"Sure, he took the belt to them all. Especially when he was drinking. But when he beat me up, it wasn't for anything I did. It was for what I was. He usually took the trouble to tell me that."

"How did you get away?" Helen faltered.

"Ran away," he replied. "Call the place Last Ditch. I jumped out. Social services caught me on the run when I was fourteen. Put me in a foster home. That was a good place. Finished school. I still see those old people sometimes." He lifted the stove lid again to drop in the cigarette end. "I was lucky."

"You must hate him," she said.

"I did. I was going to grow up and kill him. But I haven't got any of his blood in me. Found out what I was like after I got married."

"What do you mean?" Helen was horrified. "What did you find out?"

"They say you get like that if you've been beat when you're a kid. You do it to your own kids. And your wife. But I never hurt 'em. Never hurt anyone—not that way. It was good to know."

A moment later, he looked at her and smiled.

"Jesus, I'm telling you everything, aren't I?"

CHAPTER EIGHT
A Table

THE EVENING began without there really having been any day. The thick fog still clung to the lakeshore.

They had been out in the late afternoon together to chop wood. Helen was very proud of her woodpile, which represented the summer's scavenging.

Max did not seem to be impressed.

"You're only cutting up the round pieces," she protested, as he knocked two neatly split halves off the chopping block.

"What's this?"

"A table I found at the dump."

"Yeah," he agreed. "It looks like a table."

"I thought I could burn the legs. The top is useless."

"But it's a table," he said. "You don't have a table."

"Do I want a table?" she asked.

"You want a table."

He began lugging it inside and after a while she went to help him. If he was going to stay with her, it was true, she would need a table.

He went back out to the woodpile and selected two thick rounds of firewood, sawed-off stumps Helen had been unable to split.

"Chairs, I suppose."

"Yeah. Chairs."

Chairs, two of them. Well, true again. He was used to chairs. They had been sitting on the loft steps and the bed.

"I was saving those to burn after Christmas," Helen remarked.

One of Mrs. Henry Woodcutter's children, the middle boy, Danny, entered silently on Max's heels and deposited a neatly skinned rabbit on the new table. He stood for a moment, looking around, his eyes flitting with interest from the table to the stump chairs to the rumpled bed.

"How much?" asked Max, reaching in his pocket.

"Sarah, she sent it." The child backed away, his glance now moving to the towels on the steps.

"Tell her thanks a lot," said Helen, stuffing the five dollar bill back into Max's wallet.

"She said you must be hungry." The boy was stalling by the porch door, looking down at the unopened suitcase. "They was all over at her place."

"I'm sure they were." Helen began to laugh.

"They seen you come out to chop wood."

"It was nice of them. Were they worried?"

"Oh, they weren't worried." The boy was backing out the door reluctantly. His eyes lingered over the bed again. "Sarah threw 'em out when they started makin' bets."

Max shut the door firmly and locked it again.

Helen sat down on the chair nearest her and rolled her eyes.

"Sure got neighbours in a place like this." He looked at the rabbit, whistling. "How come you got that for nothing?"

"In a way it's not for nothing," she said. "I help her out a bit too."

But it was, she knew, truly for nothing. There was nothing she could ever do for Sarah that could repay her for what she had done for Helen.

Max put an onion and two potatoes on the table. He had produced them like a conjuring trick out of his food pack. Now he began jointing the rabbit.

"Is that Sarah Woodcutter?" he asked. "Heard about her."

"What did you hear?"

"She hates men," he said.

"I can imagine who told you that!"

"Well, I saw her once or twice. Never said a word. Wouldn't even look at me."

"She's very independent," Helen explained.

He shot her a glance of amusement. She saw that he had her bracketed with Sarah. But she could explain Sarah to him somehow. He was not obtuse. In fact, he had demonstrated in many ways that he was a sensitive person.

"She lives all by herself. I know that's very unusual here." Helen drew her block of firewood closer to the table to watch what he was doing with the stew. He certainly could cook.

"Sarah is one of those people who have a function in a place like this," she continued. "In the old days she would have been a shaman."

"A witch?" He transferred the jointed pieces of rabbit to the frying pan and began peeling the potatoes.

"A good witch," Helen amended.

"You don't believe in that?" he asked.

"In magic? No, I don't. But if you do believe in it it makes a difference. It even works." Helen rested her chin on her hand. "I started out here as an anthropologist," she said.

"With that guy you were married to?"

So perhaps he had heard of Paul Ayre, the man she was married to.

"Yes, that's why I came. He was doing a doctorate on these people."

He was silent, turning the rabbit, his back to her. Helen wondered what else he had heard about her.

"Sarah and I got to be friends—no, it's not like that," she said. "She's my old woman. She's like my mother. Better than my mother. Anyway, she became my friend after he left."

He was still cooking. She looked at his back.

"She says you should put skis on the plane this winter," she said.

He salted the mixture in the frying pan.

"Because of the babies that die in the bush." They did. A baby had died of pneumonia in the bush last winter.

She was still waiting for him to ask her something about herself. But he didn't ask her anything. He was an intelligent person, this was clear.

He sat down opposite her, having adjusted the pan on the stove to suit him. They smiled at each other, surprised to be face to face.

"See? You needed a table," he said. "You're already using it."

"That's true," said Helen, taking her elbow off the table momentarily and then putting it back down again.

"Buy you a pair of shoes sometime too."

"That would be going too far."

He laughed. "Buy you anything you want tomorrow in Mountain River."

"Why don't you get me a copy of this—what did you call it? Air Carrier Act?"

"Oh that," he said. He grimaced, then paused a moment. "Don't need to worry about that."

"What? But—" Helen gazed at him, astounded. "I thought that was the whole point!"

"Can't win with those legal eagles. Just keep moving, it's the only way."

"But you said—!" She cast her mind back over the way she had been seduced. "You wanted me to find out what those complaints meant. I thought you—well, in a way—you hired me!"

"Oh yeah. I told you all about that garbage, didn't I?"

He stood up and took a turn around the floor.

"Got a letter that day. Guess it was on my mind."

"A letter?"

He had met her on the steps of the Co-op, coming away from the post office. Helen remembered her own letter.

"Want to see it?"

"Okay. Who's it from?"

"Agaric." He went over to his jacket on the hook and took a crumpled envelope out of the inside pocket. "Good thing I didn't throw it away."

Dear Freddy,

You remit last week $215 in cash and flew for $2,450. The outstanding amount is being taken off your wages. You should send same amount of cash you make.

Also, pay gas bill out of cash received. We won't pay your gas bill.

Last, it's giving me headache, all these calls from Ottawa, Air Transport, etc. It's giving my wife headache too. Last night God tells her this wickedness got to cease.

So come back. Pronto.

How are you doing anyway? Caught any new diseases we never heard of down here? Ha. Ha.

She read this missive twice, puzzling over the handwriting, which was not entirely illegible, but crabbed.

"God?" she said.

"Oh, yeah. His wife got religion when he was in jail. Some Reverend So-and-so tells her what God thinks. Takes the money too, I guess."

"So what does this mean." She looked again. "You owe him $2,235?"

"According to him, I owe him about $10,000."

"And that's what he owes you in wages, right?"

He nodded.

"Do you have the money?"

"What? The ten? Are you kidding? I'm paying all the expenses and sending the leftovers." He thought for a moment. "Except that gas bill. Didn't pay that."

Helen looked at the letter again.

" 'This wickedness got to cease'," she read. She looked up.

"Means when I take the plane back, I'm out of a job." He shrugged. "Could just leave her here to freeze in, I guess."

Helen put the letter down. A wave of desolation swept over her. She had approached this affair with cynicism. It seemed she no longer felt that way. It had been the beginning of something new, something totally unexpected.

"So all that stuff you were telling me in the bar—" She stood up. "That was just—"

She reviewed her presuppositions: that he needed her, her house, her phone, her help. As a matter of fact, he had just wanted to get her into bed. What she had imagined was a carefully laid set of plans was only common sexual adventuring. So this was the end of it? Or maybe a week or so longer till the lake froze.

"Got the letter. Thought I had to do something about you," he was saying. "It was now or never."

Again she thought of her own letter. The one she had received that day from her husband, Paul Ayre.

CHAPTER NINE

Talking in the Dark

"Hey! Where are you going?"

Helen was heading for the porch.

She had got it all backwards. That was bad. She had begun to make plans. But apparently it was just a one night stand, after all.

"What's wrong?" He caught up with her and she stopped, with her forehead pressed against the outer door.

"Damn," said Helen. There were undignified tears in her eyes. It was all very humiliating.

He tried to embrace her and she stood there stiffly, resisting.

"Look, that wasn't all just a line of goods I was selling you," he said. "Thing was, I got Agaric's letter and I was still thinking about it. Then I saw you coming out the door of the Co-op and—" He drew in his breath. "Well, I just had to find out. About you. About those rubber boots."

Helen laughed. Then she wiped her nose. "You must think I'm a fool," she said.

"No! I just want you to know I'm not a liar, that's all."

"But you said you wanted me to help you."

"The right person can always think of something," he said. "It seemed like my lucky day when I met you there."

Helen was feeling suffocated. She went back into her cabin, brushing past him in the doorway, and walked over to the big window. She peered out into the darkness. There was no sound but the faint, muffled washing of tiny waves on the pebble beach.

They had both had letters in their pockets that were somehow terminal. An impulse had brought them together. That was, perhaps, the kind of person he was. But he did not know the kind of person she was.

She knew she was not a lucky person. But she could solve problems. He had a problem and she had already started to think about it. She had been taking him seriously.

"The thing is, it's hopeless," said Max, behind her.

She turned around.

"Why?" she demanded.

He lit a cigarette. He was looking rueful, even sad.

"Couldn't you get another plane?" she asked.

"Maybe I could. Could even pry this one back out of Agaric, I guess. But I don't want to end up in jail. Who's going to handle all that garbage from Ottawa?"

"Me," she said. "Well, you asked me to," she went on, when he looked at her in astonishment.

"But maybe it's a bad proposition," he suggested. "All I know is how to lie and cheat and steal. You read Agaric's letter."

She regarded him stubbornly.

"And those guys in Mountain River too," he said. "They think I'm a haywire outfit."

"Except that they all want to charter your plane and go fishing."

He put his cigarette out in the stove. Then he approached her by the window.

"What did you think you could do?" he asked. "With that guy in Ottawa."

"Find out what's at stake. You think you're doing something worthwhile here, don't you? Tell him what it is."

"And you wanted me to stay on? Here? With you?" he asked carefully.

She nodded.

It was absurd. She had thought this was what he intended all along.

"Was that why you started to cry over there?" He pointed at the porch.

Helen nodded, ashamed.

"You cried," he said, "because I wasn't going to stay the winter?"

Helen was on the verge of crying again.

He was looking at her in a very peculiar way. She thought he was touched. Perhaps he was not used to anyone taking him seriously.

She now thought of half a dozen ways of qualifying what she had said. He shouldn't think it was anything other than what it was, a business proposition. For she could tell he thought it was something quite different from that.

He had taken her by the waist and was kissing her. This was a new kind of kiss he was giving her, a very passionate kiss, a kiss of love, even. She put her hands up to his face and pulled back her head a little.

"So as soon as you can you'll have to get me this Act—"

He was turning her around, drawing her towards the bed.

"And I'll have to see these, whatever they are, complaints—"

He took off the rudimentary clothes she was wearing and his own as well. Then he pulled her down beside him on the bed, kissing her in the same way as before, a passionate kiss.

She guessed that whatever was going to happen, he was now taking her seriously, and not just because of her pretty face, her blond hair, her pretty body. It was no longer a one night stand. Not able to analyse how she had brought this about or whether it was really what she wanted, she gave in and let him carry her along on the tidal wave of sex.

*

At last she lay reflecting, Max's head in the crook of her arm.

This last time had been a kind of seal on the intimacy of their day together. However mistaken they were about each other's intentions, and perhaps were still mistaken, they had truly met one another in the flesh.

It was strange how people came to trust one another. He had told her some things about himself that afternoon that had made her trust him. The horror of his childhood, the way he had been made ashamed of his parentage, the fears he had had about himself; these were not things that were easily told.

She realized that she had told him absolutely nothing about herself. But she saw that he was putting his faith in sex. What they had between them there was the real thing, no imitation.

"What a fantastic day." She was trying to put her thoughts into words.

"You think so too?" She felt his lips move in a smile against the side of her breast.

"We've made love four times. And the last time was ..."

"Got to take advantage of a fog like this."

She felt the stir of his lips again and looked down sideways at him.

"We did, I think."

39

"We did."

He was going to get up. She felt him moving now in a more purposeful way.

"Stay here a minute."

"I was just going to light the lamp."

"I know. I wanted to say something to you in the dark." Helen struggled with herself for a moment.

He put his head down on her pillow and she felt his warm breath on her cheek.

Whatever happened, even if he left tomorrow, she had to tell him a little.

"I just wanted you to know," she said at last, "that when I went with you to Mountain River, that was an impulse, it's true. I had a rotten marriage and I thought I was pretty well through with men, but I'd just got a letter from my husband when you asked me to go. The letter said," she continued, "that I am keeping things that he intends to take back—by force, if necessary. Also that I have no right to this house. I was feeling like shit about that, and then you turned up and told me you needed my help, and you were so nice, and this has been so nice, that I . . ." She faltered.

He took her in his arms and she saw his face dimly, bent over her in the darkness.

"While we're still in the dark," he said, "I'll tell you something. The way it was with me from the beginning. That zoo act in the Mountain River hotel. Telling you things just to get you interested. The whole day today too. I didn't even hear what I was saying half the time. Maybe you don't know, but I'm in love with you."

She touched his lips with her fingers.

"I can't—"

"I know. Just thought I'd tell you."

She put her arms around his neck and they kissed like children.

She spoke hesitantly. "I asked you to stay. I meant it."

"You did. I couldn't believe you really did."

He released her gently and began to get up.

He went out the door and Helen took a moment to be terribly afraid. She had no idea what she was getting into.

Max came back into the cabin and Helen lay in bed, soothed by the familiar sounds of the lamp base being shaken, the scrape of the match, then the faint click of the chimney being set in its socket. The soft, mellow light filled the room as he turned up the wick. A moment later she heard him lifting the lid on the pan. A warm gust of rabbit stew came to her nose.

40

"Did that son-of-a-bitch tell you when he was going to come and take the place over?"

He spoke casually and she looked across the room at his smooth, muscular back.

"No. And anyway, I don't think he will. It was just a threat. To bother me. To—to frighten me."

"Well, I was just thinking out there—" She thought he was keeping his back to her on purpose, "— that I'd like to be here if he did come."

Helen lay still, listening to a further succession of domestic sounds: plates going into the warming oven of her stove, cutlery clinking, water being poured out of a dipper into her kettle.

An unusual sense of peace enveloped her. She examined it curiously. It was not just the relaxation of her bodily self, although this also was blissful. Perhaps it was the peace of confession. For she had made a confession of sorts. He knew something about her now. How had she managed to tell him it so economically? She thought of what he had told her in the afternoon, and realized that he knew quite well what it was like to be unforgiving and afraid.

CHAPTER TEN

2,235 Is a Very Interesting Number

"DON'T GET up." He had brought her a plateful of rabbit stew. "Have it in bed."

"We're wasting the table," she protested.

He brought her the salt.

"This is delicious. Potatoes in it too."

"Get scurvy if you don't eat potatoes." He pondered this. "Can't you grow potatoes in this place?"

"No one does."

"Too bad. Growing potatoes might be a way to make a living here."

"You're already making a living here."

"No, I'm not."

"Don't you have any money? You said you had some the other day." She had seen that he had quite a lot.

He set down his plate and found his wallet in his jeans.

"Got about $2,000." He counted briefly. "$2,235."

Helen laughed. "That's a very interesting number."

"It is?"

"It's what you owe this man, Agaric—what he says you owe him. Remember?"

"Oh yeah." He smiled. "Yeah, that. Well, I thought I might need it."

"You do," she said. "I think we should write him a letter about that tomorrow."

"Write Agaric a letter?" He laughed. "All he wants to find in an envelope is twenty-dollar bills."

"You ought to put things in writing."

"Sure about that? Been trying not to put things in writing most of my life." He took her empty plate away and Helen sank luxuriously against the pillows.

"But you should be keeping account."

"What are you going to tell him, exactly?" asked Max.

"That you're taking out your wages, of course. How much have you already taken, by the way?"

He shot her a glance, a little shamefaced, but amused.

"About four, I guess. That's why I said I'd settle for six." He looked at the floor and pursed his lips for a whistle. "You're not going to tell him that?"

"Of course not."

He turned away to the washing up.

"Why does he call you Freddy?" asked Helen. She had been mentally composing the letter.

"Hate being called that. Thinks it's funny, I guess," Max replied. "Call him Agaric myself. Kind of toadstool."

"Oh, I see. It's not his name, either?"

"No. Here."

He came over, drying his hands on the dishtowel and got out his wallet again. He extracted a business card and gave it to her. It read:

North Winnipegosis Fly and Spray
Sam Garuluk, Prop. and Gen'l Mgr.

"No phone number?"

"Has to change it too often." Max went back to the dishpan. "It was the phone company that got him over that deal with the DC-3 engines."

"The phone company?"

"Had a $5,000 phone bill. 'Fraudulent use of a disconnected phone' was the actual charge. Got him a month in jail because he couldn't pay the fine."

"What's that got to do with DC-3 engines, though?"

Max lit a cigarette and leaned against the kitchen ledge.

"He had a lien on a piece of flying junk some sucker bought from him way back when. Stole the engines off it, finally. One of 'em was okay. Drank a little oil, that was all. Agaric leased them to some cracker up North who was doing a contract. Fellow was mad as hell when he realized the other one was timexed. Seized them both for the down payment on the lease. Agaric was quite a bit into the gas company at that point, what with keeping me in the air on that Cub. So he ran up a phone bill, arguing."

"It sounds as if a lot of people wanted him to go to jail."

"Yeah," agreed Max. "Even me."

Helen considered the card in her hand again.

" 'Prop.,' " she said. "Do you want to be Prop., Max?"

"Sure. Why not?" He sat on the edge of the bed, smiling.

"No, really," she said. "Didn't you ever think of starting an airline yourself?"

"Have to apply for the license, though. Takes ten years, I hear. Arguing."

"Well, you could do it. I'll do it for you." He was not taking her seriously again, she thought. "But I want a title myself. What other positions are available?"

"There's Ops. Manager."

"That's you, obviously. Chief Pilot is you again. Is there a mechanic?"

"See a guy over in Buffalo Neck. Mechanic's Helper, that's me." He took the card away and looked down at it. "General Manager, that's you."

"But I don't know anything about airplanes, remember? What's the General Manager's job?"

"Tells all the others what to do. You'd be good at it," he said.

She closed her eyes, comfortable under his smiling glance.

"I think I'd be better at it than Agaric. It's so much fun listening to all these stories. I've never heard anything like this before."

"What have I been telling you?" He took her hands. "Haven't been listening myself, that's for sure. This has been some kind of a day. Fantastic, that was what you said, wasn't it?"

"Yes." Helen laughed, her eyes still closed. "I'd like to know how the betting is going out there."

"Some poor sucker lost his shirt when I lit the lamp."

"Maybe he'd get it back if you blew it out."

"Don't know whether I'll do that yet. Like looking at you too much." He drew down the coverlet slowly, and Helen felt him looking at her in the soft light.

"But I like to talk to you in the dark," he said, and got up to blow out the lamp.

CHAPTER ELEVEN
Sarah

THERE WAS a wind the next morning and the fog was gone.

Rotting potatoes and thawing meat were on Max's mind from the moment they got up; he had the Co-op flight to do. He was almost businesslike for a change. Helen found this reassuring.

She went down to the dock with him and helped him lift a five-gallon can of oil into the cockpit.

"She's a good old bird." Max patted the plane absently. "But she drinks a bit."

"How do you put it in?"

"Inside there." He indicated the cockpit. "There's a filler cap between the seats. I like to keep some by."

"You mean you can put oil in while you're in the air?"

"Yeah. Had to do that more or less all the time when I brought her up here. Dropped in at Buffalo Neck and got a man to patch her up. But I just like to keep it handy. Don't like surprises in this business."

"I should say!"

He laughed at her expression. Then he ducked under the fuselage and began to pump water out of the off-side float with a bilge pump. The water gushed out the spout, wheezing and spluttering. He was counting the strokes.

" ... 99 ... 100 ... 101 ..."

Helen walked up to the front of the left float, treading cautiously, one hand on the bulbous nose of the machine.

" ... 201 ... 202 ... 203 ..."

She peered around behind the propeller at the radial engine pillowed in the doughnut of sheet metal.

" ... 261 ... 262 ... 263 ..."

A moment later, he stopped and straightened up, panting. The bilge holes, she noticed, were plugged with halved rubber balls, the blue and red ones that small children play with.

"Is there a hole in that float?"

He looked at his watch. "Got to go."

The plane lurched on the water as he ducked back under the fuselage. Helen grabbed the dock and scrambled up.

"Shall I push you off?"

He was untying the ropes, thick nylon ones tied around the struts and bollards in loops and figure eights.

"No need." He saw that she was disappointed. "Okay. Sure. Then turn the tail around like this." He demonstrated.

Helen got into position.

He jumped up into the cockpit.

"Goodbye!" she called.

He nodded. The door was already closed.

There was a cough and a splutter. The engine roared, then quit.

Helen divined that she was making him nervous. His lips were moving. She thought he was probably saying, "Holy Smokes!"

He started the engine again. The plane rocked on the water, a yard from the dock. Helen had forgotten to keep holding the tail. Too late, she stretched out her arm, balancing on the edge of the dock. Max taxied off in the wrong direction and disappeared beyond the point into the reed beds.

A few moments later he reappeared again out on the lake, speeding into the wind, the unearthly noise of the aircraft reverberating down the shore.

Helen stood watching the plane disappear. She felt a major revolution in her consciousness.

She was already looking forward to him coming home that night.

It was not just her consciousness. It was her whole body. Every inch of her skin was telling her that it had been used tenderly for a true purpose. Her bones ached from the pressure of his weight; the flex of her muscles reminded her of his shape, his size. And there was a hollow place under her breastbone that was right now full of aircraft noise.

He was by no means a proper mate for her. Helen was an American with an urban background: her father, a surgeon, her mother, a country club socialite, her sister, a psychoanalyst. She had been an intellectual; she had been married to an intellectual. There was an absolute separation of experience, taste, interests, class, life history. She mentally tried him out in her home, in the city apartments where she had lived when she had been at university. He fitted nowhere.

It was, of course, impossible. But this was Island Crossing. They had met here.

She took the path by the lakeshore towards home. The village sprawled in a ragged line off to her right, a collection of small brown houses standing on the windswept barren ground behind the beach. The Catholic Mission was the only building that presented architectural variation. It was built like a barracks or a hospital and was bright blue in colour.

Island Crossing looked isolated and monotonous, but she knew it to be full of life and variety, rich in itself, more interesting and mysterious than any place she had ever lived before.

She had been studying the people here once, but she was no longer studying anyone. Helen had somehow dropped out of her own culture without actually joining another. She was not one of the pioneer white civil servants, teachers, nurses, doctors, agents of the Department of Indian Affairs, who ruled the community. And since she was not a part of that white officialdom, she was treated with indifference or friendliness depending on what people actually thought of her, and she responded in kind. It was her first experience, rare anyway in the modern world, of having village neighbours.

And she had one real friend: Sarah.

She met Sarah halfway along the path. The older woman had a shotgun open at the breach over her arm and a packsack on her back. She had been hunting grouse and ptarmigans in the muskeg.

Her half-grown dog, some kind of Labrador-Husky cross, bounded over to greet Bootleg, who was a more basic Heinz 57 type, black and tan on top and white on the undercarriage. They touched noses and then the old dog looked intelligently at Sarah. He knew she had something in the bag.

"It's a nice day, isn't it?" said Helen, falling into step behind on the narrow path.

Sarah nodded. She was always a little taciturn. Helen was not alarmed, as she continued to follow her friend up the slope to their houses. Sarah was going home to make tea for both of them, she knew.

Sarah's house was small and neatly kept. She had opinions about things. Water was not delivered; she had a rain barrel. She also had a birch tree growing right out of her housewall. It was not a sapling but a real tree. Its wiry fingers enveloped the roof and fell almost to the ground on one side, obscuring the window and tapping end-lessly at the panes.

The effect was organic, almost as though the house had grown there. It was a strange house, and in many ways it resembled its owner.

Helen sat down on the steps outside and examined the catch in the bag, while Sarah went in to boil a pot of rainwater. There were three ptarmigans, unlucky in their premature winter whites. In addition there was a small hoard of wild carrots and a knob of spruce gum.

Sarah used spruce gum for all her ailments: colds, flu, recurrent winter bouts of pneumonia, arthritis, and the after-effects of TB in childhood.

The older woman emerged with a knife and began skinning the birds.

"The pilot has gone to Mountain River for groceries," said Helen, clasping her knees and looking at the sky. She was trying to make it clear that she was willing to volunteer more information.

"Why don't he bring in the mail?" said Sarah irritably. "The mail never come for a week."

"Are you expecting something?" Much of the economy of Island Crossing revolved around cheques in the mail. Helen was waiting for one herself.

Sarah merely grunted, turning the small bird in her hands artfully.

Helen now began thinking of her letter from Paul and started to tell Sarah. Sarah knew all about Paul Ayre. Sarah put down the knife and went into the cabin to put the tea in the pot. Helen went on talking to her through the open door.

"I got the letter on Tuesday," she said.

"You went to Mountain River with the pilot on Tuesday."

Helen laughed unhappily. The connection was quite clear to Sarah too.

"Paul says he's going to take the house away from me."

Sarah put the teacups down on the step between them and resumed skinning the birds.

"He says he's going to come and throw me out."

"He's tryin' to scare you."

"That's what I think. Kind of a mean impulse." Helen took up a tailfeather and began to smooth it between her fingers. "But there's something else. He wants the notes. And the diaries."

Sarah was now looking with interest at the bird entrails. Helen had never been able to decide whether she was divining the future or merely looking into what her neighbours, the birds, were eating this fall.

"I couldn't give him back the diaries." Helen spoke flatly. "Why should I give him anything? I don't want him to think I'm afraid."

Sarah looked at her keenly and took up her teacup.

"You got another man now," she said.

"He's nice," said Helen. She felt shy, telling Sarah about Max. "He cooked the rabbit."

"I like to be alone, me," said Sarah.

"I know. Maybe I'm not as tough as you." Helen smiled at her friend. "Anyway, it just happened, that's all."

"Think he's a good one?" Sarah spoke rather as if Max were a Northern pike.

"Yes, you know, I really do," Helen replied. "He told me a lot about himself. He's got Indian blood," she added, knowing that Sarah would approve.

"Is he going to stay the winter?"

"I don't know. But I told him what you said about the skis."

"Tell him about the mail too."

"Okay."

She knew that Sarah was not altogether pleased with Max—or with her. But the mail seemed to be more on her mind than anything else. Helen wondered why. Sarah would not accept welfare.

"Henry told me he seen Delilah," said Sarah.

"Really?" Delilah was Sarah's long lost daughter. Helen had never met her. She was Sarah's only living child. But she had left Island Crossing a long time before.

"He seen her in Mountain River the other day."

"Maybe she'll come home, then?"

"She's going to send something first," said Sarah.

"You could write to her there yourself. I'd help you," Helen added.

Sarah sat still, her gnarled hands on her knees. "She's been gone since she was sixteen," she said.

Helen thought about Delilah. She had heard about Delilah constantly from Sarah. Delilah could trap and fish and tan and sew like no other little girl that ever lived. Sarah had been wont to compare Helen's fumbling attempts to make dry meat to the achievements of Delilah when she was ten. But there was a secret, sympathetic relation between Helen and Delilah that existed in Sarah's mind. And they were the same age now, thirty.

Sarah was looking out over the lake with her keen eyes. A lot was going on out there in the bay. A boat was speeding across to the nets. There were whitecaps now on the water.

"Fourteen years is a long time," said Helen, breaking the silence. "What do you think she's been doing in the meantime?" And why did she leave so young, she wanted to ask. Not for the first time, it occurred to her that Sarah had once been young and beautiful and passionate, and that she might have been cruel too.

"What I think?" said Sarah. "I think she's been a whore."

She stood up and hung one of the ptarmigans on a hook under the eave. Wordlessly she handed the other two to Helen. Then she went inside her house, and without actually closing the door, indicated that she was by herself again.

CHAPTER TWELVE
Telephone Calls

Helen walked back to her house and sat down on her own doorstep. She patted Bootleg, who sniffed longingly at her hands, still stained with the raw bird-meat.

The phone rang. Helen ran for it, startled.

"I'm looking for a Freddy—er—Alfred, or possibly Frederick, Malkovski?" It was the voice of a bureaucrat, clipped and well-modulated.

"He's not here right now."

"I see. This is his office, is it?"

"I suppose you might say so."

"Then this is Air Transport in Ottawa. Charles Fish speaking," he continued. "We got your number from an outfit called Mountain River Air. Can you give me an address for service?"

"Service?" Helen felt she was not completely in the picture.

"To serve the complaints," he explained. "We've been serving them on a man named Garuluk but he says he has no relationship to—er—your pilot."

"My pilot?" Helen stifled an impulse to laugh. This was the legal eagle, apparently. "Oh yes, my pilot," she said. She became as businesslike as possible. "What are these complaints about, anyway?"

He began to tell her, but she had no way of understanding what it was that he was saying. He was talking in impenetrable bureaucratese. He also read aloud to her several sections of the Air Carrier Act.

"So what do I have to do?" Helen asked finally. She felt a little swamped.

"Why—" The voice of Charles Fish was astonished. "Reply to these complaints."

"Well, I'm very glad Canada doesn't have the death penalty," she remarked.

Fish laughed cordially.

"But we can't afford to go to jail either. Couldn't you tell me what this is all about, really?"

There was a pause.

"Do you truly want to know? So few of you people ever ask."

"Just explain in English."

"It's very simple," he said. "You're really an operator without a license. We're the licensing authority. And there's no such thing as an operator without a license."

"But the owner of the plane has a license, hasn't he?"

"Oh yes." He sighed. "But you are 800 miles from his base. It's difficult to handle from an administrative point of view."

"We don't exist—from an administrative point of view?"

"You're a wild card, if I might put it that way."

"But Charles, this can't be so unusual. After all, you can take a floatplane just about anywhere."

"Yes. The other operators are always shouting at us. Hours on the phone—being shouted at."

"Good heavens! I'm sorry. But how can we even answer the complaints," she said, "if we don't exist?"

"Oh, you merely use Garuluk's number. Quote it at the beginning of your letter."

"I see. This happens all the time?"

"Indeed. So—we'll be hearing from you?"

"Oh yes. Yes, you will. It was nice of you to call."

He had a coughing fit.

"I'm sorry," he said. "I'm having trouble with my asthma. It was pleasant talking to you, Mrs. Malkovski."

"Oh no, it is not—" she began, but he had rung off.

She put the phone down pensively. She had an extensive acquaintance with civil servants. She kept the names of all Department of Indian Affairs bureaucrats in a private mental listing, with stars, Rorschach ink blots, and some skulls and crossbones beside each name. She liked Fish. She liked his asthma.

The phone rang again. Helen picked it up, surprised. This was another busy morning in Island Crossing.

"Did they find you?" a hoarse voice inquired at the end of the line.

It was Agaric. She guessed at once.

"He's not here," she said.

"Oh yeah? Who're you? Tell him to come home, will you? Just tell him that. Bring the plane back. Say I said so."

"Have you been talking to a man named Fish, Mr. Garuluk?"

"Fish? Who's Fish? Leave me alone. I've got problems, see?"

"Fish is in Ottawa," said Helen. "I just had a chat with Fish."

There was a stunned pause.

A thought struck her.

"Is this an illegal call?" she asked.

The phone went dead in a histrionic series of clicks. Helen put down the receiver. She needed a copy of the law just as soon as she could get it.

CHAPTER THIRTEEN
A Wild Card

MAX MADE three trips to and from Mountain River that day. Helen saw him coming back the first time while she was still sitting on her porch with the dog. The second time she was picking frostbitten rosehips on an eminence about a mile out of town. She could see the dock from there, and the boxes of groceries he was unloading. But she had escaped to think a bit and to regain some equilibrium. Things were moving much faster than they usually did.

When he arrived that evening for the last time, she met him on the dock. He was already tying up the plane. Remembering her failed attempt to help him that morning, Helen stood by, saying nothing.

"Hi," he said.

The Co-op truck drove down onto the dock to pick up the groceries. The Co-op manager was a sleazy whiteman Helen had repelled at a Christmas party. She stood off to one side while they loaded the truck.

There were two trucks in town, the Co-op truck and the water truck. The other vehicle was a D-7 caterpillar which was supposed to maintain the airstrip.

Max had brought in three loads of groceries. She had seen Max lifting them onto the dock, box by box.

"Two thousand pounds?" said Max. "That was more like four." He was looking after the retreating truck.

Then he took her arm and they began to walk down the path, the short way around to her house.

"Brought you something," he said.

"That looks like a bottle of wine."

He gave her the paper bag. "Cops sent it. Said it was for you."

"Good God!"

"Gave me a lift into town too."

"Why did you go into town?"

"Tell you later."

They entered the cabin.

Max looked around, sighing with contentment. Then he went over to the bed and plunged down, face forward, still wearing his jacket and boots.

Helen was simmering the ptarmigans in a poor imitation of the way he had cooked the rabbit. She usually just boiled them, but there had been a spare onion.

She sat down on a sawed-off stump, feeling pleasure in his pleasure at the bed.

"Would you like a glass of this wine?" she asked.

The bottle had a cork. Helen began operating on it with the blade of her pocket knife.

Max came over and took away the bottle. He opened it with his own knife, then set it down on the table and took her hand to draw her up in front of him. She looked into his eyes, an inch or so above hers. He was, somehow, just right.

He kissed her, but she could feel his fatigue.

"You were going to tell me why you went into town." She pushed him gently down on her stump and went to get coffee mugs for the wine.

"Went to see that Mountain River flapjack. Went to his office. I asked him to give me the Air Carrier Act."

"Did he have a spare copy?" Helen was astonished. He was unzipping his jacket and pulling it out from the front of his shirt.

"Nope. It was the only one he had. Charged me $100 and laughed. You know that guy? Brutson is his name. Shouts a lot."

"You paid him $100 for this?"

Helen took the document, thick as a telephone directory, and free in Ottawa.

"Wanted to get it for you."

Helen had already opened it on the table.

" 'Animals means poultry, mammals, birds, fish, snakes, and worms,' " she read.

"This is good," said Max. He passed her an enamel cup full of wine.

Helen took an absent sip. She was looking for an index. Fish had used a lot of terms to explain the complaints against Max: route protection, positioning charges, tariffs. She was leafing through the back pages. It was more horrible than she had thought. There was no index.

"Don't read it now."

"Oh, sorry. Cheers."

Max lifted the lid of the simmering pot.

"What's this?"

"Ptarmigans. Sarah shot them this morning."

"You live on her, don't you?"

"Yes," said Helen. She was now looking in the front for the table of contents. It was there but it was unintelligible.

Max added salt to the stew. Then he sat down, pulling his chopping block around to her side of the table.

Helen was sifting through the Act, letting the pages drop as she read swiftly a bit here and a bit there. There was a lot to it. This was Charles Fish's life, after all.

"Do you like it?" Max asked. He was puzzled.

"I wish I could understand it. It's written in gibberish," said Helen.

"Why Brutson laughed, probably."

"I'll just have to read it through from the beginning."

"Why would you do a thing like that?" he asked.

"My middle name is Boring Paperwork," she said. "You don't know me yet. I had a call from Ottawa today."

"Oh boy!"

"No, no. A very nice man. He has an asthma problem. You're a wild card, he said."

"Sounds bad."

"Not necessarily. Jail isn't in it apparently."

"What is in it?"

"A lot of writing." She was still a bit distracted. She had found a section on positioning aircraft and began to read.

He groaned, looking over her shoulder.

"This wine even comes from France." He put the cup firmly into her hand.

"It's good," agreed Helen. She prevented herself from turning the page. "Oh, yes, I also got a call from Garuluk."

"What'd he say?"

"He wants the plane back."

Max had evidently not had time to digest this information fully.

"Wait a minute. He called here? Agaric?"

"Well, no doubt he got the number somehow. Everyone else has it. I asked him whether it was an illegal call and he rang off."

Max began to laugh. Helen looked at him, surprised. It was funny, but she didn't see why he was laughing so immoderately.

"Agaric? Got you?"

"I had just finished talking to Ottawa," said Helen. "Why do you think it's so hilarious?"

"Agaric's got to meet you," said Max. "He doesn't guess there's anyone like you in the world."

"I think you've got that backwards, frankly," she said.

"You're right."

He stood up and Helen looked up at him, somewhat offended.

"Well, I talked to your employer and to Ottawa, and I've made some kind of dreadful stew for supper," she said.

He got down on his knees beside her.

"Remember yesterday?" he asked.

Helen had been remembering yesterday all day: sitting on the porch with the dog, picking rosehips, waiting by the dock.

She looked down into his face.

"The world is full of people. Agaric. This flapjack in Ottawa with asthma. Brutson. They didn't have yesterday."

"No."

"Take Brutson. Know how he remembers yesterday? Nothing happened yesterday. He drove down to the dock, spat in the water, and then probably went home and drank himself to sleep. Doesn't remember yesterday."

Helen was still looking down into his face. It was a very interesting face when you came to know him, a lively face, full of expression.

"Know what really happened yesterday?"

"To me?" Helen smiled, entering into the spirit of this. "Well, we made love. Then we made love again. Then we had breakfast. Then we made love ..."

"I got you in my bones. Could feel you running through my blood this morning like fire."

"I thought about you all day," she said softly.

He put his arms around her waist and buried his face in her lap. Helen stroked his hair and rubbed his neck, remembering the 4,000 pounds of groceries he had lifted down into the plane, then up out of the plane.

"Thought about you all day too. Soft skin, long neck, pretty breasts, long legs. The way you kiss. The way you feel in my arms. The way you laugh and cry. I was going to come home and eat you up."

He groaned, pressing his face into her thighs.

"You're exhausted, Max. You'll probably feel better after supper," she suggested.

"Supper," he said. He hugged her more gently for a moment, then got to his feet.

"I put an onion in it." She watched him a little anxiously as he went over to the stove again and took the lid off the pot.

"But you didn't cook potatoes."

"Were there some?"

"Sure. And a bay leaf. You've got to put a bay leaf in something like this."

He had begun to stir and peel.

But Helen was already looking forward to after supper. The future was opening up before her. Before yesterday, there had been no today; before today, there had been no after supper.

There might even be a winter. She turned back to the Air Carrier Act. What she really needed to find was a section titled: "How to Start a Charter Airline."

CHAPTER FOURTEEN
Violating Route Protection

H ELEN NOW spent several happy afternoons sitting cross-legged over her typewriter at the foot of the staircase with the Air Carrier Act and the Mountain River Air complaints disposed up the steps. The deductions she made from their contents were very interesting.

What the Air Transport Committee in Ottawa cared about was that Max was operating a charter airline out of Island Crossing without a license.

A charter airline was supposed to be a monopoly on a base. The base of North Winnipegosis Fly and Spray was 800 miles away. Max was covered by Garuluk's license number, but this was purely a formality.

Meanwhile, Mountain River Air Service was only 100 miles away. And from their point of view, Max was poaching.

Their complaints accused Max of a host of strange crimes, couched in the highly legalistic style of the Act: violating route protection, tariffs not filed for the zone, failing to charge for positioning.... But it all seemed to come down to poaching.

The good thing about the complaints was that they lacked concrete detail. They were written by an Ottawa lawyer, a specialist probably, and they were long on the law but short on fact. Helen speculated that Brutson didn't want to run up his telephone bill assembling the evidence. Fundamentally, he just wanted Max to go away. He was trying to intimidate him.

She usually told Max about this after supper and conspiring over the artful letter of reply Helen was composing added a strange new dimension to the sweetness of their physical pleasure.

It was just the kind of thing she was good at, as she had anticipated.

There were a great many rules. The airline business was heavily regulated, and airlines had monopolies on everything they were licensed for, not only bases, but even the routes they flew over. Charter services were not supposed to compete with scheduled services. Helen had been puzzling over an arcane rule about route protection all day.

"Tell me about something. Mountain River Air calls that plane of theirs *the sched.* Does this mean that Mountain River to Island Crossing and back is the route of a scheduled airline?"

"I guess so," Max replied.

He was lying relaxed on his back with Helen on her belly beside him, her hip touching his hip, his arm curved around her with careless possessiveness. Helen had been peacefully memorizing the front of his body with her fingertips. Now she sat up energetically.

"But that means you're not supposed to fly between here and there."

"Have to," he said. "I brought in the mail today. And two guys. Could hardly get them in the plane. The back was full up with sliced bread."

"There's something in these letters about it." She got out of bed and went over to fetch the complaints of Mountain River Air. They had arrived only after Max started bringing in the mail.

"Anyway, who's going to fly all that stuff if I don't? Brutson's plane's got a cracked cylinder. He fired the engineer last week."

Helen sat down on the edge of the bed, drawing her long legs unself-consciously up under her chin. Then she began to read aloud:

"'Condition Respecting Route Protection. The Licensee is prohibited ... .' That's you," she explained. "You are prohibited, well, blah, blah, from flying on a route, except, hmmm ... ." she studied it for a while. "All right, it seems to be saying you can fly on a route only if you have:

'a) ... a Class 1 or Class 2 license'—you don't have that; or—my God!—

'b) where in respect of a route the distance between any two points on the route as served, and between which the charter flight is intended, is greater than one and one half times the direct distance between such points; or ... '"

"Hold it! Wait a minute!" said Max.

"I know, I know, but it gets much worse. You have to read the whole thing. Listen to this:

'c) where the Class 4 charter flight originates or terminates at a point not included on a route if no local traffic is carried by the Licensee between any two points on such route; or ... ' "

"God! What is it?"

Helen set the document down on the bed.

"I'm trying to figure that out," she said. "There are ten of these conditions, and each of them is supposed to tell you when you are allowed to fly to Mountain River."

"Brutson wrote that? In a letter?" He was bewildered.

"No, no." She laughed and bent over him, putting her hands on his shoulders. "It's the law, Max."

"Well, I sure didn't know I was breaking that one!"

He made a sudden clever move, pulling her down onto his chest and rolling her over onto her back half underneath him.

"What I can't understand is how it could be saying—what it appears to be saying."

She put her arms up around his neck co-operatively.

"What I can't understand is how I got you for a lawyer. A beautiful, naked lawyer," he said in her ear.

*

Sarah was behaving more and more strangely. She was always withdrawn, but now she was positively absent. She appeared from time to time, but only to bring food. She would no longer come in the house.

Helen was sadly inclined to attribute this to the encroachment of Max into her domestic life. She now had real chairs, four of them, brought from Mountain River. There was fruit and bread in her diet; a calendar with a picture of a DC-3 had appeared. She had a new watch battery, and at the end of the week he brought her a white rug made of petroleum sheepskin, to put beside the bed.

She had learned how to push off an airplane. Max was very busy, and it was true that he needed her help, for the weather was getting colder, and it took a lot of physical effort to get the plane ready, pumping gas, and emptying the freezing water out of the floats. She knew her help was nothing though, when she saw him come in hours later, cold and exhausted, and throw himself down on her bed.

She was resolutely shutting her mind to the danger of the flying. He obviously wanted to fly for that very reason.

Coming back along the path from the dock, she saw that Sarah's door was open. The dog trailed her gladly up the lawn. Sarah was sitting inside by the stove and there was a spruce scent in the air: liniment made of pitch boiling in a pot.

Helen was a little uncertain. She had lots of news, but all of it came from Max. She was sure that Sarah would perceive this at once. There was a hint of jealousy in her stand-offishness.

She sat down beside Bootleg in the open doorway, propping her back against the jamb.

"I'm getting old," said Sarah.

Helen happened to know from reading the Indian Band list that Sarah was fifty-five. But Sarah often pursued this theme when she was annoyed or off-colour.

"I've been an orphan all my life. Never had no mother."

Sarah's mother had died when her brother Henry was born. She had been sent to a convent school in Buffalo Neck and she remembered the cruelty of the place with bitterness.

"I'd have been better off dead."

"Good heavens, Sarah," said Helen with energy. "You wouldn't have been better off dead."

"You ever want your mother? Lie in that bed and cry for her? Can't cry out loud because them nuns'll come and beat you? You never miss your mother like that."

Helen didn't miss her mother at all. But she was silent out of respect for Sarah.

"At least you still got one." Sarah spoke sharply.

"Someone to blame, I suppose." Helen spoke ruefully. She did not hate her family, but they were as remote and bleak to her as the possibility of life on Pluto. Her parents had finally divorced when she went to college, having waited politely for the last child to leave. "Some mothers are more useful than others."

"*Useful. Blame.* Now I tell you what. Nothing ever happened to you. Nothing bad ever happened. You don't know bad. Me, I remember bad."

"Yes." Helen was startled.

"I sit here and sometimes that's all I remember. Them nuns. My stepmother. Dead children. Being pounded by my husband. Hard work all my life."

"Poor Sarah. I'm sorry." Helen stood up and went inside. She patted her friend's shoulder a little awkwardly. Sarah put her hand over Helen's and Helen was touched.

"Make tea," Sarah ordered.

Helen began making tea, reflecting. Family was everything in this out-of-the-way society. Sarah mourned her mother forty-five years later. On the other hand, she scarcely spoke to her brother, who was alive and kicking, not among the saints. And Helen herself was something like a daughter to Sarah, kack-handed but dutiful.

"I got a letter from Delilah," said Sarah.

Helen paused, teapot in hand. So that was it.

The older woman went over to the bed and got an envelope out from under the mattress. She held it out to Helen.

"She's calling herself something else now," she said. "Read it."

The envelope was interesting. It was good paper, and so was the letter inside. Helen was used to reading mail to people here that was written on the cheapest kind of paper. Delilah used stationery. The handwriting had personality too. She read:

> Dear Mother,
>   I am in Mountain River and now I hear you
> are still alive.
>   Could I come home? There is a reason.
>   Your daughter,
>   Dallas

Sarah nodded. Helen folded up the letter. There was something else in the envelope: a $100 bill torn neatly in four.

"Maybe you shouldn't have done this, Sarah." Helen was looking at the money.

"Don't want money. Not from her or nobody."

Helen put a cup of tea down beside Sarah and went to sit on the bed. She tucked the letter back under the mattress.

"She writes good English," she said presently.

"Went to school ten years."

"Don't you want to see her?" Helen thought about the earlier part of their conversation. "She seems to want her mother. You ought to think of that."

"I think of it."

"What you said about her the other day. Is that the trouble?"

Sarah looked at her blankly.

"Do you believe she's bad?" Helen could think of no other way to phrase this.

"No," said Sarah. She pushed away her teacup. "Trouble," she said. "Me, I'm trouble. I sit here, think bad, bad, bad. She knows how I am. When she sees me, she'll know I'm still that way."

"What was it?" asked Helen. "What did you do that was so bad?"

63

But Sarah had begun to pray, or think, her eyes closed, her lips moving minutely.

Helen sat with her for a while, finishing her cup of tea, then tidied up and went home. The faint sound of an approaching aircraft was in the air, and she felt like a traitor as she left, as though she were abandoning Sarah, in spite of the fact that it was plain she was not going to be allowed to help.

CHAPTER FIFTEEN
Agaric

THE ICE was coming. There were hard frosts at night and the plane had to be scraped and brushed every morning. Max often brought the plane back to the dock wrapped in a carapace of ice from the spray kicked up by the landing.

Then it began to snow.

Helen was sitting cross-legged on the floor, typing placidly. The door flew open and Max staggered into the cabin, both legs glittering with ice. He was wet to the thigh. And he was in a hurry to get to the stove.

"My God!"

He was stripping, not too efficiently. Helen went over to help.

"Did you fall in again?"

"It was the wind." His teeth were chattering. Helen dropped his boots and ran to get a quilt. "Got her stuck in the ice. Had to get out quick. I got wet. Pushing her off."

The fall was trapping season and Max had been unloading gas at the bush camps dotted over the country. It was now nearly time for the great freeze-up when flying on floats would cease to be possible, but people had suddenly realized that they could use this plane to get first the gas, then the supplies, then the children and the grandmothers out on the land.

"Got warmed up in the plane. It was all right. Had to run home, though." He was toasting his feet one after the other against the warm side of the stove.

"But you could have frozen your legs!"

"Yeah. I wasn't too sure I was going to get out of there. It was okay once I got her in the air." He sighed. "Got to get out of here now."

There was an east wind. Helen thought of ice on the lake, blowing their way.

"But where are you going to go?"

"North Winnipegosis. Got to get the floats off. Take her south for change-over. Time to put the skis on."

So his plans really had changed.

He was going to try to bring the plane back on skis. Perhaps he now believed that she could handle the paperwork. They had sent Helen's letter replying to the complaints.

His eyes roved around the room. "Pack up," he muttered. "Wonder if I've got enough gas."

But they had heard nothing at all from Garuluk. What if Max couldn't persuade Garuluk to let him bring the plane back? Helen began to feel miserable. She might not see him again.

"We'd better take food too. You never know. It's a long way."

"We? Am I going?" She had a contradictory feeling of apprehension.

"You've got to come," he said.

"I do?"

"For a start, what am I going to tell Agaric? Besides—" He laughed. "I'd like to see his face when you get out of the plane."

*

Helen was sick. She threw up in a boot.

They had a lot of trouble getting out. The wind overnight had cast the ice into their bay, and they had to carve a path through it to the main lake. Then they were out in the open, fighting the icy spray and bucking the white-whipped waves on their take-off run. The Beaver did not want to rise out of the water; it was becoming coated with ice. But at last it was tossed on a particularly high wave, and Max twisted first one float free of the surface tension, then the other.

Terror didn't make her sick. She threw up only after they had been in the air for several minutes.

Now they were flying low over the swampy bush and it was snowing hard. Max had a map spread out on his knees but, Helen couldn't see what use he was making of it. They seemed to be flying through a dense, lumpy medium like porridge, the definition of the landscape below restricted to treetops and muskeg, the occasional sluggish river winding on to nowhere.

She closed her eyes again. They had a long way to go.

The weather improved by noon and they began to fly higher. She was feeling better.

Suddenly the engine went bump and quit. Her eyes dilated with fear, Helen turned and gazed at Max.

Whistling through his teeth, he reached to adjust a dial labelled Fuel Tank Selector. The engine popped feebly, then sprang to life again.

She sat bolt upright for some seconds, gripping her seat, but the plane was going quite steadily again. Max seemed to notice her reaction, for he leaned over and shouted cheerfully:

"Had to let a tank run dry. We're going to need all the gas we've got."

They made a gas stop on a lake in the early afternoon. Max refuelled with the remains of a forty-five-gallon drum he had in the back of the plane. The bush around the lake looked taller to Helen, who was eating a sandwich on the float; it looked like forest, not like taiga any more.

But the overcast did not let up and the landscape below continued to be completely meaningless: no village or road or camp broke the monotony of trees. The vibration of the engine contributed to her dullness. It was getting on for dark.

Max folded up the map.

"Know where we are?" he shouted. He put the map on her knee.

Helen looked out. A river coiled beneath them. In the hazy distance she could see a lake, grey sky, grey water.

She unfolded the map and saw that it was covered with pencil notations. They must be getting close to somewhere he had been before. Looking between paper and earth, she tried to find a landmark.

He pointed to a lake on the map and gestured ahead. A moment later he shifted the whole steering mechanism in front of him over to her side.

"Just keep her going."

Helen grasped the stick gingerly and the plane lunged.

After a minute of rather alarming experiment, she discovered that the plane tended to fly itself. She didn't have to tell it what to do all the time.

Max smiled. He had been watching her attentively.

"Got to do something with the radio."

He leaned across her and began to fiddle with the large grey instrument in front of her knees. It was in a most inconvenient spot.

After a while, he gave up, and merely rested his head on her lap.

"Are we very far away?"

"Better not be."

The gas gauges were, as usual, steadily fixed on empty.

He swung the steering mechanism back and peered intently forward. The engine noise changed and Helen looked down, relieved to see the large lake below.

"Where are we?" The noises the plane was making frightened her.

"North Winnipegosis."

The wings tilted and Helen craned her neck to see out his side. There was a farmhouse, a flying field with a windsock, and a ramshackle yard full of equipment. Some ragged fields stretched beyond and then there was a road, the first she had seen.

Max went in low over the house and then pulled up slightly, announcing his arrival with an earsplitting burst of sound. Then he banked over the lake and came around to land.

A gaunt figure in American Gothic-style striped overalls waited for them on the dock. Max jumped down on the pontoon, rope in hand, but the man caught the strut and pulled them to a stop.

"You again? Ha! Ha! Thought you were goin' to let her freeze in up there."

"Ha! Ha!" echoed Max, busy with the rope.

Agaric opened his mouth to speak again, then caught sight of Helen manoeuvring her way out. His mouth remained open for a minute until, recollecting himself, he shut it with a click of false teeth.

"This is Agaric, Helen," said Max, enjoying himself.

"How do you do?"

"Boy's always makin' a joke of my name," muttered Garuluk, staring at her.

Max got out a cigarette, watching Garuluk's expression with interest.

Agaric reluctantly dragged his attention away from Helen and clambered down onto the pontoon, where he began peering into the gas tanks.

"Empty, huh?"

"I'd have gone somewhere else if I'd had any more."

"Too bad. Oh, I'm glad to see her all right. The plane, that is." Garuluk kept his eyes off Helen. "But she ain't safe here."

"Got some bills, have you?"

"Sheriff keeps tellin' me he's goin' to come out."

"Oh great. Got to take her away before he gets here, I guess."

Garuluk seemed torn between assent and denial. He nodded slowly, mouthing the word Nope.

"I'm not going anyplace tonight, that's for sure," said Max. "Except to a hotel." He stretched.

"Hotel?" Agaric was alert. "Can't afford no—"

"Helen here's not sleeping in your barn."

"Oh yeah." Garuluk nodded sarcastically. "One of them flea-bitten rooms at the Rosebud, you think that's better than my barn."

Helen got the suitcase out of the back of the plane while the two men retreated, arguing, to a truck in the yard.

Garuluk drove them into town, droning on about his troubles. He was trying to sell a pair of skis to pay off his overdraft. He had a gas bill. The telephone had not only been cut off, but the line had been removed as well this time.

"Problem is, those skis are mine," Max pointed out, leaning around Helen, who was in the middle.

"Yeah, but considerin' what you owe me now—"

"And we're putting those skis on WWW tomorrow, you and me," Max concluded. He sat back again and Garuluk had another horrified moment of eye contact with Helen.

They were in some kind of town. It did not look very prosperous. Farming at this latitude was marginal, the fields clawed out of the living bush within the last generation. The hotel was not much of an improvement over the one in Mountain River, although it had a proud neon sign announcing the presence of TV in every room.

Garuluk followed them into the lobby. Max had taken charge of the suitcase. He was talking to the Chinese clerk at the desk and now he pulled out his bulging wallet.

Garuluk stared at the wallet with popping eyes.

"I'm paying for this out of crew expenses," said Max. He selected a fifty-dollar bill.

He took Helen's arm and led her towards the stairs. Helen turned around to wave at Garuluk, who was still dumbstruck by the sight of the wallet. When they turned the corner of the landing, she heard him exclaim:

"Crew expenses! What in tarnation—?"

Helen went looking for a shower. The bathroom contained only a conventional tub, so she turned the taps on full blast, the noise of the water drowning out the bells in her ears from the Beaver's engine.

Max appeared in the bathroom doorway.

"I'll wash your back," he said.

About halfway through their bath the phone rang. Max got out of the tub and stomped dripping into the bedroom.

"Where'd I get her?" she heard him cry. "Tell you what. I'm taking her back there too, just as soon as we get those skis of mine on the plane!"

Helen got out of the tub and began to dry herself serenely. The bath had settled her nerves and now she felt merely tired. She took a spare towel into the bedroom for Max. He was staring with disgust at the phone.

"Says he's not paying for your half of the room."

"Well, you already made him pay," she pointed out.

"Flapjack!"

"By the way," asked Helen, dropping her towel and beginning to coil up her hair in front of the mirror, "which half is my half?"

"I don't know, but whichever half it is, that's the half I'm sleeping in tonight!"

CHAPTER SIXTEEN
Notice of Seizure

HELEN HAD not known quite what to expect in North Winnipegosis, so she had brought a dress and a pair of shoes with her, unearthed from her old wardrobe. She wore them to supper, which they ate in the café of the Rosebud Hotel. She was not yet aware that she was going to be news, however.

Max seemed to be recognized, she noticed. The old farmers nodded to him, then pretended to look into their coffee cups, staring covertly at Helen all the time. The waitress called him Freddy.

"This is a far cry from what we eat in Island Crossing." Helen leaned back in her chair. "Apple pie. I'd almost forgotten what it tastes like."

"There's a dance at the Legion," remarked the waitress.

"Want to go?" Max also leaned back, regarding Helen with pleasure.

They were watched all the way out the door. When Max paid for her meal, this was noted. When Max helped her into her parka, a frisson swept the cafe. She preceded him outside, feeling the eyes boring into her back.

"Do you notice that everyone seems to be watching us?" she asked.

"Yeah, but you're the one they're looking at."

They walked down the road to the Legion Hall. Max immediately deposited her at a table and went off to get their drinks at the bar.

Trying to appear nonchalant, Helen took in the musicians, a pimply guitarist and his octogenarian colleague, the fiddler. They were the only two people in the place who were not staring at her.

"Excuse me." Someone put his arm confidentially on the back of her chair and squatted on the floor beside her. Helen turned to look into a grin arranged like a car grille below a set of headlights.

"You taken for this dance?"

"No, but I—" Helen glanced at Max's back.

"Oh." The man also looked over at Max. "Are you shacked up with him?"

"Shacked up?" It was, perhaps, the term for it.

"Well, that's okay." He stood up. "I just didn't know you were shacked up with Freddy."

They were all looking at Helen. But what interested them about her was that she was with Max.

Max turned around and walked purposefully towards her, carrying a glass in each hand. The man behind the bar was gazing after him.

Then the fiddler's chin went up, and, addressing his blank eyes directly at Helen's chest, he produced the first notes of the dance. The people in this place danced the jig, and the dust soon began to rise in clouds out of the wooden floor.

"Got the hang of it yet?" asked Max, and she went to dance with him, trying to catch the stomping rhythm of the music.

It was a country pleasure. Watching Max, she realized he must have been born to it. Last Ditch, Saskatchewan, was not very far from here. They were dancing the ache out of their bones, just like all the truck drivers and farm wives and road allowance people around them.

Helen knew that Max was proud of her. Here in this place, back on the edge of the world, he wanted to show her off, and not just to Garuluk. He thought she was beautiful.

She had been amazed to see in the hotel mirror how pretty she actually was. Helen had not cared what she looked like for years. She did not even have a mirror in Island Crossing.

She was surprised and even a little scared that her looks seemed to matter so much all of a sudden. She had been alone a long while, and her solitude had seemed to her a kind of freedom. She was afraid of the way her relationship with Max was beginning to change her, making inroads on her independence.

But he was a loner too. Solitude and independence were his lot in life. He had probably been alone most of the time, even when he was with other people.

Without her, he still would have come back here to North Winnipegosis and gone to this dance, and probably ended up in bed with a woman too, but there would not have been much joy in it.

"What'd that guy say to you?" he asked.

"He wanted me to dance with him." Helen smiled at Max; his eyes were sparkling. "I told him I was shacked up with you."

"Sure are." He swung her around into a new battery of stares.

*

The next morning, not too early, they hitched a ride with one of the poker-faced farmers in the café back out to Garuluk's farm.

Garuluk was sitting idle on a trestle beside the dock, chewing a straw. There was no sign of the winches and cranes that would be needed to get the plane out of the water and off its floats.

Max walked briskly towards him, Helen trailing behind. It was a nice day. She saw no reason to participate in a quarrel.

"Where's my skis?"

"Over there." Garuluk pointed to the long grass with the straw. "Should've sold 'em. Feller was out here just last week—"

"So what's the hold-up?"

"Seen the sign?" Garuluk again pointed the straw, giving Max a poisonous smile.

Helen now noticed the sticker on the door window of the Beaver. DO NOT... it began. Max jumped down onto the float to examine it.

"Just wanted to be here when you was readin' it. Ha! Ha!" Garuluk stood up and strolled away.

> DO NOT MOVE
> This property is in the custody of the
> North Winnipegosis District Sheriff's Office.
> It is forbidden to alter the position of
> or otherwise interfere with this property.

Helen sat down on Garuluk's trestle and looked with concern at Max's back. Life with her husband had trained her not to speak at such junctures, so she waited in silence.

He was reading the sticker slowly. Then he turned away and walked down to the front of the float. He began to whistle.

Helen waited, hugging her knees.

Max jumped up on the dock and sat on one heel beside her trestle.

"What do we do now?" he asked.

73

Feeling that this question was rhetorical, Helen preserved her silence.

"Could punch Agaric in the nose. Could drown myself like a cat. Tell me."

"Well, he did warn you." Helen could have bitten her tongue after she said this. It was essential not to give advice or say anything that could be construed as a reproach. Either one always brought down a hail of invective on her head.

Max turned up his face to look at her.

"Did he?" he asked. He laughed bitterly. "Bet he phoned the sheriff himself."

"Why would he have done that?" Helen pressed her hands together, squeezing the blood out of her fingertips.

"You want to take a look around this place?" Max sprang to his feet and helped her up. "Take you for a walk."

They went out behind the house and barn and walked through the field to the grassy airstrip. Every yard of their progress was marked by a wrecked and deteriorating airplane.

"It's like an elephant graveyard," said Helen at last, looking at the rusting hulks surrounding them.

"He loves failure, see? He's an expert at it, a real pro. So why do I have to help him out?"

Helen was now very tense. She felt that she had got Max into this predicament by persuading him that she could deal with the bureaucracy. But she had been more than a little naive.

This thing wouldn't go at all without the airplane, and Garuluk wasn't going to let them have it. That was a brute fact. You couldn't ignore brute facts. Max had known it was hopeless from the beginning. And now, not only did he have to swallow more failure, but he had her on his hands as well.

"Hey, what's the matter."

She was white-faced and trembling, trying not to cry. Crying always made everything much, much worse. He had not said any of these things yet, but he was sure to now that he had noticed the state she was in.

And it really was all her fault. She saw all her grand talk in Island Crossing for the nonsense it was.

Max was looking into her face acutely. After a moment, he led her to a derelict Beech 18 in the bushes and sat her down on a pontoon. He stood in front of her, lighting a cigarette. Then he sat down beside her and put his arm around her waist.

"So what are we going to do? Tell me," he said.

"Oh Max! It was all just a pipe-dream, I see that."

But Helen suddenly grasped that he did not blame her. For a short while her reflexes had been telling her that Max was her husband. But he was in no way like her husband.

She blew her nose on a poplar leaf.

"I was a fool to imagine—" she began.

"What?" said Max. "Think I'm going to let him get away with this?"

He was vehement, even a little angry.

"Look, he thinks I'm a crook. But I know he's a crook. And only one of us is right!" He pressed her back against the float strut of the airplane and looked into her face. "See, what he thinks, he'd rather have the plane taken off his hands by the sheriff than be robbed by me. He thinks I've got his money!"

Helen nodded. She had grasped that Garuluk was getting his revenge.

"But what we're going to do is, we're going to put skis on that old bird and take her back to Island Crossing for the winter. And then we're going to take some more of his money!"

He was pressuring her to agree. Helen wiped her eyes with her fingers and nodded again.

"Well then, all you've got to do is think of how we're going to do that."

"Me?"

"Like I said, the right person can always think of something."

"And you really think I am the right person?"

He sat smoking in silence, his head turned away, giving her time to think.

Helen leaned against the float strut and closed her eyes, trying to calm down.

If Max had been her husband they would have progressed from screaming insults to physical violence by now. She travelled back four years in time and 1,500 miles away to a bathroom in the basement of the Social Sciences building of the University of Iowa, where she had had a serious nosebleed. She had believed her nose was broken, although in fact it was not. It had not hurt enough, as she now knew.

"Who do you suppose was responsible for the seizure?" she asked, not opening her eyes.

"Oh, the gas company, probably. Could be a lot of other people, though."

"And what happens to the plane now?"

"I don't know, really. Think this just hangs it up in hell till he pays."

"It's your gas bill, right?" She opened her eyes. "How much do you think it is?"

"About four," he said. He smiled, a little shamefaced. "I took my wages, remember?"

75

"So we—you have the money?" she asked.

"My wages. Yeah." He shrugged.

"But Max, don't you see?" Suddenly she was excited. She leaned forward and touched his shoulder. "If you pay the debt, you become Garuluk's creditor. You take over the—what do you call it?—lien on the plane."

"Yeah, but then the money's gone. Agaric's never going to pay me."

"Yes, that's true. But in a sense you'll own part of his plane. It's all written down. And he can't sell it without paying you."

He looked at her and she could see that he was thinking: Do I really want to own Garuluk's airplane? But he did want to own it, she was confident of that. She remembered him sitting on her bed in Island Crossing, looking down at Garuluk's card. He wanted to be Prop.

"And then," she went on, "we could take the plane and you could fly it all winter and maybe you'd make enough money to start buying him out."

It was the pipe-dream again. But really, she considered, it was much more his idea than hers.

Max began to laugh.

"Agaric's not going to like this," he said. "Like you say, it'll all be written down."

He jumped up and held out his hands to her.

"C'mon," he said.

"Where are we going?"

"To see the sheriff."

"But how are we going to get into town?"

"For a start, let's steal a truck!"

They ran across the yard, Max pulling her by the hand. The truck was standing in front of the house and Max pushed her in ahead of him on the driver's side. Too breathless for comment, Helen perceived that he knew this truck well. It lacked an ignition lock. Perhaps it had been stolen before.

The front door of the house opened and Garuluk stepped out on the porch. But Max had finished tinkering with the starter and they were off in a spurt of gravel.

There was an explosive cracking sound behind them, and Helen realized, astounded, that someone was firing a gun. Max had his foot down on the accelerator and they careened up the road at the top of second gear.

"My God!" Helen ducked as there came a second blast from the shotgun, but it was all right, they were out of range.

Max was laughing.

"See what I mean?" he cried. "He'd rather shoot up his tires than lend us his truck."

They had a busy afternoon. They started with the sheriff, who suggested they get in touch with the gas company. Max made an uneasy telephone call from another office.

"He says we can pay the bill," he reported, coming back.

Then they went to see the bank manager.

"But we don't just want to have a lien. We really want to buy the plane," Helen explained.

"Go on paying Garuluk's debts and you'll be in a fair way to do that," said the bank manager jovially.

"We couldn't get a loan?"

"Come back in six months and show me a wallet like that again, you can!" He roared with laughter.

"Oh well." Helen was resigned. "At least that takes care of the seizure sticker."

"Got a thinker here, Freddy." The bank manager slapped Max on the back.

CHAPTER SEVENTEEN
Wife

THEY WERE in the café eating a sandwich. Max still had a few hundred dollars.

"Everyone around here calls you Freddy."

"Hate it," said Max. "Always did."

"But it is your name, is it?"

"Yeah, for what I used to be. Trying to sell insurance. Cheating on the wife. Freddy, that was me."

"Where did Max come from, then?"

"My old people," he said. "You know, the ones I told you about, my foster parents. They thought I'd be better off if they called me Max. So I put it on my pilot's license. Always thought I'd use it if I could get a job flying."

A booted and helmeted motorcycle cop entered the café and strode over to their table, his steel-toed boots clacking on the linoleum.

"That Chevy truck out there yours?"

"Nope," said Max.

The cop regarded him solemnly, pushing up his goggles.

"Sheriff sent me over here to remind you to return it," he said.

"No problem."

"Wish we'd get some good clean theft around here. Nobody in this district but weirdos," the cop remarked, snapping down his goggles again. He strode out, lifting a hand to the waitress.

*

They went to the bar of the hotel that night.

Garuluk had been surprisingly tranquil when they brought back the truck. He seemed almost co-operative.

"Think he's still got something up his sleeve," said Max, pulling out a chair for Helen.

"Why on earth? We did him a favour. Your wages are paid too."

"He'd probably rather go to jail."

A handsome blond woman wearing a barmaid's uniform now approached their table.

"Hi," she said to Max. She put her hands on her hips.

"Hi," he said. He looked annoyed.

"I heard you were in town."

"Who told you?"

"Mrs. Holy-boly Garuluk. Who do you think? Who else wants to make everybody unhappy." She now glanced casually at Helen. "Still, I guess the kids would like to see you. Or had you forgotten about your kids?"

"I hadn't forgotten about my kids." He began to stand up, then sat down again, looking at Helen. They were both looking at her now.

"Why don't you introduce us?" said the woman dryly. "I heard about her too."

"This is my wife," Max said to Helen. He hesitated. "Her name is Helen," he told his wife.

"Helen Ayre," said Helen.

"Make that ex-wife." She drew out a chair beside Helen and sat down. "My feet are killing me. It's no treat serving in a bar like this. Especially on Saturday night."

Max was looking for a means of escape. His eyes rested longingly on the men's room door.

"You could see Freddy for a start," suggested his wife. "He's helping out with the dishwasher. I guess her and me can get along pretty well without you." She was taking off her high-heeled shoes.

He glanced at Helen. She merely raised her eyebrows at him. It would be impolite to make a face under the circumstances.

"Missy's the name," said Max's wife, turning her back on Max and raising one shoulder to exclude him further. "Used to be Malkovski, but I'm calling myself Johnson again."

"Pleased to meet you," said Helen.

Max rose furtively and made off towards the bar.

79

"Bet he wouldn't have bothered to see them if I hadn't caught him." They were both looking after Max.

"Is the other one here?"

"Oh, so he told you there were two, did he? Must be serious then. I like to know who's getting my $200 a month."

Helen began, very unfairly, to dislike this woman.

"Not that that's enough to support two kids, anyway. Or were you thinking that he married a barmaid?"

Max now reappeared from behind the bar and went to the men's room. He was trailed by an adolescent boy, who looked sulkily in his mother's direction.

"The payoff in front of the urinal," said Missy.

"I really don't—"

"—have anything to do with it. I know, I know. But you're sleeping with him, aren't you? You must think he's something."

"I must," said Helen sadly.

"He probably told you what a lousy time he had as a kid," Missy went on. "So why doesn't he care about them?" She glared at the bartender, who was frowning at her from his post behind the taps.

"Maybe he's just afraid of making them as unhappy as he was." Helen remembered what he had said about this.

Missy was putting her shoes on again.

"Boy, you're smart!" she snarled. "You must be some kind of psychologist. I wish I'd thought of that. Never would have married him."

"Sorry."

"Well, like you say, you've got nothing to do with it, so why worry?"

Max returned, the boy still on his heels. "Are you okay?" he asked Helen.

"No," she said.

"This is my son Freddy," Missy told her. "How much did he give you?" she demanded.

"It's going to be for my bike, Mom." He was about seventeen or eighteen, Helen guessed.

"Sure. This year, your motorcycle. Next year, a new toilet. Damn you, Malkovski!"

Max followed her to the bar and Helen was afraid they were going to quarrel. With relief she noticed he was reaching for his wallet.

The boy, Freddy, was examining her with interest.

"Are you Dad's girlfriend?"

She nodded.

He appeared to be aware that she was distressed.

"My mom always gets like that when he's around," he remarked. He sat down. "I just wish I had a place of my own where I could see him sometimes."

"You'd like to see him?"

"He's my dad, isn't he?" Freddy was now also attending to the bartender's scowl. "Got to go."

He departed abruptly, and Helen thought about his resemblance to Max. He had an alert, anxious manner and his features were sharp under a thatch of mousy blond hair.

Max came back to the table and stood over Helen.

"Let's get out of here."

"Okay. Do you think that will help?"

She stood up and let him lead the way out. He took her around the corner and pressed her into a dark doorway. She heard him groan. He was holding onto her by the open front flaps of her parka.

"What about the other one," she said coldly. "I guess he ought to get something too."

"Got to go out to the farm."

"Are you going to stay the night there?"

"She says we'd better. She told me to bring you."

"What a fun idea!"

He looked into her face, their noses only a few inches apart. "You don't have to do anything. I'm not asking you to do anything."

"Didn't you know they'd be here? Weren't you expecting to see them at all?"

"The kids? Yeah, I was going to see the kids. Oh boy!" He put his head down against her collar bone and Helen allowed herself to feel a little sorry for him. This situation was certainly all his fault. But at least he seemed to know it.

"So how are we going to get there?"

"Freddy'll take us."

A car backed around the corner and waited for them at the curb. Freddy was the driver.

He spoke through the open window.

"She said to get you."

Max opened the door and looked over his shoulder at Helen.

This was all going too fast.

For two years she had kept herself at a distance from any personal relationships, aside from her friendship with Sarah. Max's life was obviously in a mess. And if any more nasty or difficult things occurred this evening, she wasn't sure she could cope.

He had never told her his life was so complicated. He still had a wife. His kids were not grown up yet. And he somehow seemed to expect her to be his ally in this situation when she wasn't sure she was on his side at all.

CHAPTER EIGHTEEN

And Kids

HELEN WAS sitting in the front seat between Max and the boy.
"What about your job?" she asked Freddy.

"She'll get me off. It was only to make money for the motorbike anyway," he explained.

"Mickey's home?" asked Max.

"Yep."

They drove in silence out of town and into the dark countryside.

"Mickey's been sniffing," said Freddy.

"Sniffing gas?"

"Yeah, that. And glue. Things like that."

"Does your mom know?" They were both looking straight ahead.

"She'd hit the roof. Told him to stop or I'd have to do something."

"Did he stop?"

"I dunno."

"How old is Mickey?" asked Helen.

"Sixteen," said Max. He stretched his arm across the back of the seat behind her head. She leaned forward a little and he instantly put it down around her shoulders. Helen felt his arm as an oppressive weight. But she did nothing about it.

"Going to school this year?" Max cleared his throat.

"Yeah."

"How's it coming along?"

"Pretty good. Taking Grade 11 English over. But I got a different teacher this time."

It was as though they were back in the plane again, droning through the thick snow. Nothing was to be seen outside the car but the frostbitten verges of the country road. Trapped inside the capsule, Helen let her mind rove backwards and forwards over their banal conversation.

"Brought back Garuluk's plane for change-over," said Max.

"Goin' to go again?"

"For the winter, I guess."

"Where?" asked the boy.

He didn't know where, Helen told herself mechanically.

"Up North. Trying to get started. I'd take you with me, but maybe you'd better finish school."

"I'll give you the address," said Helen. "And the phone number."

"You live there too?"

"Yes."

The boy nodded thoughtfully. He didn't seem to hold it against her.

He said to Max:

"Remember when you took me up in that Cub?"

"Old enough to drive, you're old enough to fly."

"Yeah," said Freddy.

"I showed 'em how," explained Max.

"Showed us loops and barrel-rolling. You ever seen him do that?"

"No," said Helen.

"Not in a Beaver," said Max.

"Guess you can't on floats," agreed Freddy.

He turned off the road down a steep incline and Helen had a moment of vertigo. Then they emerged out of a tunnel of trees into a brightly lit farmyard. The house was dark, but Helen saw a blue flicker in a back window.

"Mickey's watching TV," said Freddy. "He wants a VCR."

He spoke baldly. It was not a demand. But Helen felt he was anxious to give information.

She watched Max open the back door. He twisted the knob sharply to the right and gave it a slight kick at the base of the jamb, obviously a familiar homecoming routine. She realized with surprise that her dominant emotion was no longer annoyance. It was jealousy.

Freddy turned on the kitchen lights and Max disappeared at once into the room beyond.

"Want anything?" asked Freddy. "Want a beer?"

Helen shook her head. He took away her coat kindly and she sat down at the kitchen table, looking around.

It was a modern kitchen in a homely, farmhouse-like way. Missy was plainly a good housekeeper; a good mother, too, thought Helen dispassionately. Hockey equipment was stacked in the porch. A clutch of photographs in magnetic holders were stuck to the fridge. All the pictures were of the boys, none of Max, she was relieved to see.

"Hope Dad's talking to Mickey about sniffing," remarked Freddy. He got himself a can of pop.

"I hope so too."

"Somebody's got to talk to him."

Helen was looking at the light fixture over the sink, a kind of plastic or metal egg box over a fluorescent bulb. It was absolutely clean, no dust.

She shivered. The house was cold.

"Sure you don't want anything?"

Helen wanted nothing, but she saw that he was still trying to be hospitable. The conversation in the other room was important.

"Could I have some tea?"

"Sure. I'll make it." He put the kettle on. "Do you live with Dad?"

"Well, he lives with me, as a matter of fact. We just met about a month ago."

Freddy continued to look for the tea things, but she felt he was interested.

"How'd you meet?" he asked.

"It's quite a small place, only about 200 people. There really wasn't anywhere else for him to stay."

"I guess he's the only pilot there." Freddy liked Max being a pilot, this was clear.

"He's the only pilot I ever met."

"I thought about being one. But I dunno." Freddy sat down opposite her. "Maybe Mickey'll be one. I get sick in planes."

"Me too."

"Girls like it, though." He looked at her inquiringly.

"Like flying, you mean?"

"Like guys who can fly." He went back to the teapot. "Mickey told a couple of hundred girls about going up with Dad."

"Have you got a girlfriend yourself?" He was very nice, she thought. The resemblance to Max faded and reappeared.

Freddy put a cup of tea in front of her.

"Maybe when I get my bike."

Max now came back into the kitchen, trailed by his younger son. This one was more like his mother, tall and bonny, with a sullen, high-coloured face.

"This is Helen," said Max.

"How do you do?" she said.

The boy looked at her for a moment, and then asked Freddy:

"Why'd you bring her?"

"Mom said to."

Max was looking in the refrigerator for beer, another old familiar habit, she saw.

"She's Dad's girlfriend," Freddy told Mickey. "Came down from up North with him."

"Hey, what's the matter," said Max. "Where's your manners?"

"Hi," said Mickey briefly.

"I made Helen tea," Freddy remarked.

Max no longer looked evasive or sheepish. In this masculine company he was relaxed. He sat down at the table with a can of beer and smiled at Helen.

"We were talking about flying," said Helen. She began to relax too. "I was telling Freddy how I got sick."

"Got sick in a boot, at least," said Max.

"Not like Freddy," contributed Mickey. The glower was fading from his face.

"I'd have got sick into a boot if I'd had a boot."

"You were white as a ghost."

"You were green as a fish," Max said to Freddy. "It's like that sometimes."

"It is? Did you ever get sick?"

"Sure."

"When did you get sick?"

"Got sick all the time. Worst was some kind of hurricane out by Teddersfield. I threw up all over the cockpit."

They were both hanging on his words.

"Got into a cloud," said Max. He lit a cigarette. "Some of those prairie thunderheads could tear a jet in half. Went up. Went down. Couldn't see how to get out."

"When was this?"

"What were you flying?"

86

"Flying a Howard. Kind of learned how to fly on a Howard. I must have been about twenty at the time. I was going on a cross country just for the hell of it. Looking for clouds, really."

"So what happened?"

"Came out on the other side. Landed in a field. Cleaned up the puke. There was puke on the ceiling. Had puke in my ears. Lucky there wasn't any hail in that cloud or I wouldn't be here now." He drained his beer can.

Of course it probably took this kind of bravado to want to be a flyer in the first place. And he was not exactly bragging, after all.

"Did you ever fly a jet, Dad?"

He shook his head, going to the refrigerator for another beer.

"Never even been in a jet."

"You haven't?" Helen was startled.

"Have you?" The boys were both looking at her. "Fly it yourself?"

"Well, no, of course not. I don't know how to fly. But I've been all over the place in jets. I went to Greece once in a Boeing 747."

"What was it like?"

Helen tried to recall.

"Long," she said. "I got sick a couple of times. Not in a boot. They give out bags."

"Could you fly a jet, Dad? If you ever got the chance?"

"Sure." He looked at Helen and she saw again that he was enjoying himself. "All there is to flying is wings."

"Because of lift," said Freddy.

"Airstream," said Mickey.

"Engine is only thrust. Somebody's got to tell you how to start it, though."

There was the sound of a car pulling up outside. A long, dull silence followed. They sat like conspirators waiting for the thought-police to arrive.

CHAPTER NINETEEN
The Night Before

"CHRISTOPHERSON'S bringing her home," Freddy said to Max. "I forgot to tell you."

The way they all called Missy *her* struck Helen.

After another long, harrowing pause, a car door slammed, then another one.

"He's sleepin' with her," Mickey spoke hurriedly.

"So what? Dad probably knows that already," said Freddy.

Missy entered the kitchen, followed by a massive person whom Helen recognized as the bartender. She put her large purse down on the table. Christopherson stood by the door, looking across the room at Max.

The temperature in the house, whch had risen to normal on Helen's private thermometer, sank again into the frigid zone.

"Well, well." Missy looked pointedly at the beer in Max's hand.

"Dad's giving me a VCR," Mickey announced.

"Santa Claus comes home. Want a beer, Chris?"

Christopherson said nothing. He came a little farther into the kitchen, still gazing at Max. He had the size and weight of a bouncer and a mean light in his eye.

"Mickey, go to bed and no argument," Missy said briskly. "Likewise you," she added to Freddy.

"She told you I went to bring Dad home? She said it'd be all right if I—"

"I told him," said Missy.

Christopherson nodded.

"Just leave us alone. I'm tired." Missy sat down and Freddy left reluctantly, eyeing first Max, then Helen.

"What's this—tea?" Missy looked into the mug on the table.

"Freddy made me some tea," Helen said.

"That was nice of him, don't you think?"

"It was." Helen's hackles rose. She saw no reason why she should be persecuted in the presence of Christopherson. She had obviously been invited to fill out this foursome. She drank a bit of cold tea out of the mug.

"We've got a hotel room," Max said to Missy.

"What a waste. No one's going to drive you back there."

"Well, I've got to get up early, that's all."

"Fine. I'm going to bed too. You can take the guest room. With her." Missy jerked her head at Helen.

"My name is Helen," Helen said to Christopherson.

He nodded. She wondered what was going on in his mind. So far he was just a physical presence. He obviously filled space in a very satisfactory way from Missy's point of view.

"The toilet doesn't work," said Missy. "Go outside if you have to. God, I'm tired," she added. "Let's just go to bed, Chris."

She left the room, ignoring Helen, and after a pause signifying some brain process on his part, Christopherson followed her.

Max got up and locked the back door mechanically.

"All right, let's go to bed too." Helen was angry at him, but the behaviour of the others made her anger less acute. He had not arranged this, after all.

Max opened a door beside the one to the living room. They were going to sleep in the basement, it seemed.

There was a couch in the half-finished family room.

"Does it fold out?"

He unfolded it.

"Good." She sat down on the mattress. "Our hostess didn't provide us with bedding."

Wordlessly, he went upstairs and reappeared a few moments later with some folded blankets. She helped him to spread them on the bed.

Your wife appears to hate you, I must say."

The bedding was old and pilled. There was a patched sleeping bag underneath. Helen turned back the top blankets and sat down to take off her shoes and stockings.

"Do you hate me?" he asked.

"No, I'm just mad," said Helen. "I don't know what you did to your wife to make her so nasty, but I suppose she has a right to be, whatever it was."

89

Max sat on the edge of the bed.

"Couldn't you steal another truck or something? I'd almost rather die than sleep here."

He didn't answer.

Of course, she was trapped unless she was willing to make a fuss. Getting back to North Winnipegosis would involve taking Missy's car or waking Freddy up to drive it.

She was angry at Max for this too; he didn't seem able to cope. He was not even getting ready for bed now. He just continued to sit there, saying nothing.

"Aren't you going to get undressed?"

The light switch was at the head of the stairs. She turned it off and then groped her way back to the makeshift bed.

Max had finished undressing now and he lay down on the other side of the bed, not touching her. They lay stiffly, side by side. He was tense, and Helen realized that she had been responding with irritation.

He had not tried to apologize. But what was there to apologize for? Forcing her to know things about him that she didn't want to know?

For she had had a glimpse of Max as he really was, as he had been. In Island Crossing he was a kind of bird of paradise. When he had told her that he had a family she had simply not understood, or chosen not to understand, all that a family entailed. Now she had seen for herself.

His wife was bitter, even mean, but this was his fault too, wasn't it? He was weak; evasion was his only strategy. He allowed himself to be humiliated. And he was allowing her to be humiliated.

On the other hand, she reflected, she couldn't stop herself from being on his side. He was good; he was truly gentle. She remembered him that morning at the float dock. He had not dreamed of taking his frustration out on her. And this situation too: he was in a mess, but he wasn't trying to hurt anyone.

She trusted him. And that was something. She had not been willing to trust anyone for a long time.

"Let's talk a little," she said.

"Okay."

"Do you still live here?" She had been wondering.

"No."

"When did you actually leave?" He had been up North only one season, after all.

"When I started working for Garaluk. But I took off—more or less—a couple of years before that."

"Aren't you supporting her—them—at all?"

"Give 'em what I can."

She thought he had probably given them everything he had by now. But she knew Missy did not find that good enough. Was it the money, then, or was Missy angry for other reasons?

"Your wife seems to want revenge for something."

"I wasn't much of a husband."

"How do you mean?" Helen raised herself on her elbow, slightly alarmed. There were some very bad ways of being a bad husband, she knew.

"Her folks were well-off—rich, really. Bought the farm for her. But they never saw much in me. Just a welfare kid who got their girl in trouble. Couldn't be a farmer. Couldn't keep a job. Pretty soon she got their point of view. I couldn't even screw after that."

He lay there, making no move to touch her, and she knew that this last part, above all else, was now on his mind.

"Well, I guess she's got Christopherson in her bed now," he said.

"Does that bother you?"

"No."

She knew he was lying.

"What do you mean, no? I'd be furious. This whole scene—" The whole scene had a planned look to Helen, as though Missy had set it up to humiliate him.

"She can do what she likes," he said shortly. "As long as he leaves the kids alone."

Helen lay down again, flat on her back. She could feel an electric vibration of misery coming from his shoulder, an inch away from her own. She guessed that this confrontation in the dark with her was the worst part of the evening, as far as he was concerned.

She lay still for a moment, thinking.

"I don't know anything," she said at last. "I was married but I never had any children."

He did not say anything and she turned her head.

"I've been acting like a judge," she said. "But the truth is that I'm scared."

He moved slightly and she reached over and felt for his hand, finding the wrist first, then clasping his fingers.

"I had a terrible marriage. That's why I—I got into such a state this morning at the dock. And now I've met your kids, your wife. I'm afraid of getting involved in your problems. Frightened that I am involved, really."

The fingers curled around her own.

"For two years now I've been like the walking dead. But when you came along I began to feel as though I wasn't such a bad person after all."

"I know what you mean," he said in bitterness.

"But in this situation I can't help at all. It's not as though I'm in the middle. I'm really on the outside." She spoke slowly. "Even though I'm jealous."

"Jealous?" He was surprised. He rolled over and tried to see her face in the dark.

"Well, this is your wife. You've been with her for eighteen years or so, whatever it's been like. I'm just a kind of episode."

"You aren't an episode." He let go of her hand and took her soulders.

"But what does it all depend on?" She spoke with melancholy. "Some sweet nights in Island Crossing..."

"Sweet nights," he repeated.

Helen realized now that she could seduce him and she wondered whether she should.

Her husband had suffered from the type of impotence to which Max had alluded. That, too, had been her fault.

Max was hanging over her, still trying to see her expression. She put her arms around his waist, slid her hands up to his shoulders and then back down over his smooth, narrow flanks.

He was going to make love to her. But Helen intended to do this her own way.

What was always a desperate ploy with her husband turned out to be merely a gentle and playful game with Max. After a moment or two, he lay back with a delighted groan and Helen gave herself over to imaginative abandon.

She leaned forward at last and lay down on top of him. He embraced her. A moment later, he was trying to roll her over.

"Max! What's this? Again?"

She pressed him back into the lumpy mattress.

"But this time I want to—"

"No, no!"

She began making love to him again. And again he submitted. Her power over him was intoxicating.

But she was not invincible this time, and the mounting waves of excitement lashed her until finally, blind and incoherent, she lay back and let him take her over the top to drown and be saved in the back-rushing shallows of a distant beach.

Max was holding her tightly and they lay clasped together for some time.

He released her at last and sat up. He found the shabby blankets and pulled them up over her. Then he went looking for a cigarette. At last he lay down, smoking quietly, with an arm under her head.

"I used to wonder," he remarked, "whether I did that the way other people do. Used to worry about it."

Helen laughed. "I remember thinking that. What you read in books doesn't help. And movies make it seem—" She waved her hand to indicate hyperbole.

"That was the closest I ever came to a movie, I guess."

"Me too." She laughed again.

But the bitter taste of the evening was out of her mouth.

"I've slept with quite a few people," she said. "About ten, I guess. I got married when I was twenty-four. But I had some affairs after that, too."

"Well, I got married when I was twenty-two. And everything I did was after that."

"Everything?" Helen rolled over on his arm and they assumed their usual Island Crossing position for discussion of the Air Carrier Act. "How many women do you think—" she began.

"Oh, about fifty."

"Fifty!"

She heard him laugh, his guilty laugh.

"Think that's a lot?"

Helen thought of the woman upstairs. She really did have her reasons.

"But you said, you know, that you couldn't. Not with your wife."

"Yeah. Not with her."

Helen rolled her eyes.

Max leaned over to put out his cigarette and she saw his profile against a square of moonlit window. He was smiling, although he looked a little haggard.

"I wasn't counting you," he remarked. "If I counted you, that would make it about a hundred."

"Including tonight as how many?"

She heard his guilty laugh again and put her hand up against his lips.

He bent over and kissed her, then assumed his usual going-to-sleep position, curled into her back, with his arms around her waist.

"You're not going to find out anything worse about me tomorrow, Helen. I guess you know the whole works now. He pressed his face against her shoulder blade and she felt his lips move in a smile. "Jesus, nothing's going to happen tomorrow."

CHAPTER TWENTY
And the Day After

H ELEN DID not find it easy to sleep. She lay awake for long stretches of the night listening to Max breathing and sometimes snoring, and wondered what she was doing with him and why.

The interminable dawn began to penetrate the basement room and she finally dozed off. When she awoke the house was still silent, but it was definitely morning. She needed to go outside quite badly.

Feeling gritty and sweaty and sniffing the dense odour of sex on her body, she pulled her crumpled dress over her head and went up the steps to the kitchen door. There was an outhouse across the lawn.

She lingered there for a while, even though her feet were bare. It was cold but pleasant, and the early morning sun shone in through the half open door.

The outhouse had a nice prospect of the house with the pasture beyond. Nothing much was being grown on this farm any more, but the scene was familiar and civilized.

She was a long way from Island Crossing.

The landscape, so barren by American standards, seemed lush and rich to her now. She remembered the apple pie, the simple assumptions of the people around her last night and the night before, even the music. This was not her home, but it was, identifiably, her culture.

Then she began to think about what had happened the night before. She was no longer upset, merely thoughtful. It was interesting that she did care enough for Max to put up with this situation. For whatever else he was, he was certainly in the wrong here.

She found Christopherson in possession of the kitchen. He was making a pot of coffee, lumbering heavy-footed by the sink.

"It's going to be a nice day," remarked Helen, careless of what he might think.

He glanced at her, frowning.

"It doesn't feel like winter here yet," she continued. "Do you farm at all?"

"I manage a bar."

"Oh yes. I forgot. Still, you come from around here, don't you? Probably you grew up on a farm like this."

He finished his coffee-making arrangements and turned around to contemplate Helen by the door.

"What the hell is he doin' here?" he said heavily.

"I guess he wanted to see his children," said Helen, and realized that this was the truth.

"I'd like to cook his liver for him."

"Why?" Helen shrugged. She could understand why the boys didn't like this man. What did Missy see in him?

He was probably jealous, she thought. The politics of the situation were definitely sexual. Perhaps he had also come ponderously to the conclusion that he was being used as a pawn in Missy's game.

Max emerged from the basement.

"Oh, you're there." He seized Helen in his arms. "Woke up and didn't know where you'd gone."

He looked as awful as Helen felt. She was suddenly amused by the spectacle they presented to Christopherson. He was shirtless, she was barefoot and naked under her dress.

She put her arms around his neck.

"After last night—"

"It's okay," she said, smiling.

Max was looking into her face worriedly. Then he apparently remembered last night more fully. "Oh yeah, last night," he said, and began to smile back.

Helen was feeling wonderful all of a sudden. At the same time she realized that she was looking wonderful. The rich oxygenated blood was flowing in her arteries. Her skin coloured delicately, her hair sprang forth, her eyes sparkled. Even the arches of her feet felt springy.

She looked at Max. He was physically perfect to her, not very tall, but with the muscles and flat belly of a man who did hard work. The skin of his face was smooth and brown; his eyes were shining.

He was looking wonderful too.

They inspected each other with pleasure and amazement.

Christopherson made a noise somewhat like a growl.

Helen bethought herself. She turned around and Max let go of her reluctantly. But Helen felt they had already put on enough of a performance for Missy's lover.

"Mr. Christopherson made us some coffee."

"Made it specially for me, I bet." Max folded his arms and leaned back on the doorpost.

Christopherson regarded him blackly. He was huge, five or six inches taller than Max and fifty or sixty pounds heavier. But Helen sensed that Max was not afraid of having his liver cooked by Christopherson.

Max unfolded his arms and opened a cupboard.

"Heard you got kicked off the force last winter," he remarked, taking down two cups. "Christopherson here used to be a cop," he told Helen.

"Cutbacks," muttered the big man. "What'd you hear, anyway?"

Max poured out the coffee and handed Helen her cup.

"Never said you robbed a bank, did I?"

"Got a good job now."

"Pouring booze? Too bad I didn't know. Would have gone to another bar." Max raised his laughing eyes to Helen over the rim of his cup.

"What're you doing here, Malkovski?"

"Drinking coffee in my wife's kitchen."

"You got no right being here at all."

"Funny thing, I was just thinking that about you."

Helen began to worry that they might actually start to square off at each other. Max was showing no fear at all, even though he would be the obvious loser in any physical contest.

"You want to know what I heard?" Max was saying. "Heard you got nailed for assault, that's what I heard."

"Never went to court yet," said Christopherson angrily. "Nobody nailed me with nothing."

"Maybe they dropped it when they fired you." Max shrugged. "I don't like to see you in my wife's kitchen, just the same."

Helen was wondering how she could break this up when Missy spoke plaintively from the living room doorway.

"I thought I was going to get a cup of coffee." She came farther into the room and the tension between the men quavered and failed. They both looked nervously at her.

She was wearing a very attractive nightgown. She had plainly taken the time to comb her hair, as well.

Christopherson lumbered to the coffee pot. Max retreated to the opposite corner. He was not attending to Helen at all now.

"Jesus," said Missy, sitting down. "Saturday nights. And I don't even get to have a hangover in the morning."

There was a silence. Missy's presence appeared to strike Christopherson dumb.

"Guess that's the way it is, working in a bar," said Max. But he did not sound confident, no longer unafraid of having his liver sliced up and fried. He was right too.

"Too bad I *have* to work in a bar," Missy snarled. "Or was that what you meant, Mr. Casual."

There was another numbing pause.

"Someone's got to fix that frigging toilet. I'll be damned if I'm going to go outside all winter."

Christopherson moved slightly. It might just have been his eyes rolling.

"I'm not talking about you, Chris. For one thing, you don't have the brains to turn off the TV, let alone plumbing." She smiled at him nastily.

Max cleared his throat.

"Got to go to work on an airplane this morning," he said.

"How are we going to get into town?" asked Helen. She felt they should plan their escape as soon as possible.

"Freddy'll drive us."

"Freddy'll drive you in *my* car," said Missy. "Just remember that, will you?"

"Thought of taking both the kids."

"Great. An outing with Dad. This must be some kind of holiday."

"I could use the help, really."

"If you go putting any more ideas into Mickey's head about flying airplanes, I swear I'll get a court order."

"He's still just a kid."

"That's what I mean. And while we're on the subject, why the hell did you tell him you'd give him a VCR? We could buy groceries for six months on what it costs."

"Yeah, but he wanted it. I had a talk with him." Max was trying to be persuasive.

"I guess you think giving him a big present will convince him you care about him?"

"Well, I do. Care about both of them. Care about you too." Max pushed back his hair in desperation.

"The difference is, I don't need it." Missy drank some of her coffee. Then she leaned her cheek on her hand and made a wry face. "Shit," she said briefly.

"Sure, I'm a swine."

"You want me to disagree with that?" She looked at Helen. "I bet she thinks I'm a bitch."

Helen did think this. But she was not going to be carried away by frontal attack. Missy was just too articulate, that was all.

"Well, I guess pigs have some rights too," continued Missy. "How's it going, anyway? I see you made a little money."

"Gave it all away, though."

"That's too bad." But Missy was pensive. "Glad you're doing it, aren't you?"

"Doing what?"

"Working for Garuluk. Flying up North. Must be romantic."

"It's not romantic."

"Sure it is. It's like in a book. Look at her. That's what she thinks too. I could probably have gone for you myself if I hadn't married you." She smiled at him, a real smile, and he smiled back. Helen felt a twinge of jealousy.

Freddy now entered the room and looked anxiously at both his parents.

"Go get your brother," ordered Missy. "Your father wants to show him another airplane."

Freddy retreated and she looked after him.

"Jesus," she remarked. "I bet he hasn't seen 9:00 on Sunday morning since he was ten years old. Usually it takes a block and tackle to get him out of bed."

She stood up and yawned. "Let's have breakfast."

"Can I help you somehow?" asked Helen.

"No, you can't. It's my house. I said you could come here. The least I can do is cook a decent meal. Go powder your nose." She spoke briskly but not rudely.

The confrontation seemed to be over. They had breakfast, a silent Sunday morning breakfast of pancakes and more coffee. Freddy was the only one who attempted to talk.

"Going to take the floats off the plane, Dad?"

"Yeah."

"I guess this is when you got to weigh her."

"Yeah."

Missy passed a package of sandwiches to Helen through the back window of the car. "Take these. Make 'em all eat some," she directed. She paused, her hand on the door. "Too bad, but you know, we weren't going to be friends anyway."

Helen nodded. It was an honest assessment.

"Take care of yourself," said Missy to Max.

"You take care. That guy—"

"Yeah, I know. I know all about him. But he won't mess around with me."

Freddy started the car with a jerk, then stalled it.

"For Christ's sake, kid!"

He started again and they drove off up the driveway through the avenue of trees.

CHAPTER TWENTY-ONE
Float Change-over

T HEY WORKED on the plane all day. It had to be dragged out of the water. Then it had to be hung from a crane while the pontoons came off. After that, they spent a long time tinkering with the skis, which were not in top condition after a summer in the long grass.

"How are we going to take off on these?" Helen was looking at them. These were straight skis; they wouldn't work on Garuluk's grassy airstrip.

Max looked into the clear sky. "Pray for snow," he said.

Garuluk was filling out the weight and balance sheet, sitting on the discarded floats, the stump of a pencil in his greasy hand.

Helen retreated to the toolshed to read a book that she had bought in North Winnipegosis the day before. It had been a long time since she had read a novel and she was horrified by the amount of sex in it. It was entirely about sex, even though it was ostensibly about something else.

Bored, she put it in her pocket and began to reflect.

She was still so unaccustomed to being with other people that she felt rather bruised. Only a month ago she would have found talking to a stranger or even casual contact of any kind, like a meeting of eyes, almost invasive—intimate and unusual. She was getting used to having Max in her life now. But what had happened to her in the last twenty-four hours was overwhelming.

Her jealousy, which was slight but ongoing, made her compare herself to Missy. She was undoubtedly prettier, softer, gentler than Missy; she saw how this seemed from Max's point of view and did not like herself the better for it. For the fact was that Missy was tough. She was defending two children like a wildcat, from Max, from other people. Helen was just on his side simply because that was the side she was on, not because it was the right side.

The boys had been enjoying themselves. They had slipped back to a younger age, a state of innocence where motorcycle gangs and substance abuse were not yet in the offing. Helen heard them playing together in the graveyard of wrecked airplanes, making engine noises.

Freddy came into the toolshed where Helen was meditating and began sorting through a tray of jumbled nuts and bolts.

"Got to find another screw like this," he told Helen, showing it to her.

Helen went over to help him hunt.

"Dad's in a good mood," he said shyly.

He continued to chat as they sorted through the oddments on the floor, and she perceived that he was treating her like someone of his own age, although not, of course, a girl of his own age. It was an awkward situation, but he seemed to be a sensitive boy. In many ways he was handling it better than any of the adults.

Mickey joined them and began adding to their little heaps. But he was restless. Plainly he was the rebel.

"Chris's got to go to court next week," he remarked.

"Yeah, I know, so shut up."

"Broke a guy's jaw," Mickey told Helen. "In the parking lot of the Legion."

"Good grief!" Helen sat back on her heels.

"Hope he goes to jail."

"He'll get a fine, you dope. Guy was a drunk Indian, anyway."

Helen thought of Island Crossing people going to the bar in Mountain River. The bar, but not the Legion.

"Where I live the people are all Indians," she said.

"Oh yeah? Is it a reserve?"

"Dad's mom was part Indian," Freddy told her.

She began, as well as she could, to explain what Island Crossing was like. She could see that they were interested. They were beginning to forget the adolescent shyness and anxiety they felt towards her as their father's girlfriend.

Suddenly Max appeared in the doorway. They all three looked up quickly, almost guiltily.

"Having a good time?" he said.

He smiled at them. Mickey glowered. Freddy looked apprehensive.

Max went out again. But the moment of unself-consciousness had passed.

"You know what?" Mickey said to Freddy. "I dream about killin' him sometimes."

"Not Dad!" Freddy was as alarmed as Helen.

"Cripes, what's the use of telling you anything! I mean Chris."

"Oh."

"Yeah. I'd like to mess him up." Mickey stretched, and Helen saw that he was going to be a big man. He was already bigger and taller than Freddy. "Sometime, when he's throwing his weight around like he does—"

"You shut your mouth!" exclaimed Freddy.

Almost instantly, they began to wrestle. The little grey tool shed trembled on its foundations. Helen jumped up, feeling that she ought to intervene. But then she saw that they were not hurting one another. They were just acting like young male animals, cubs of a certain species.

Mickey had Freddy down and was knocking his head against the soft splintery wood of the floor. But Freddy had seized his thumb and was bending it backwards. Mickey yelped, and they changed position suddenly.

Max appeared in the doorway, holding a greasy clamp in a greasy rag.

"Hey! What's going on?"

They leaped up and jumped him, both at once. He went over backwards into the grass.

Helen watched for a moment, then set out in search of a good place to read. Males had few ways to express affection; she felt they were better off without a witness.

It was getting colder. She had her parka zipped up. She replaced her shoes with mukluks. It might snow.

The boys left when it began to get dark. Helen stood beside Max, waving, as they drove off.

She felt guilty about the sandwiches, uneaten on the back seat of the car. She was hungry now and realized that they had no money and no place to stay.

Garuluk materialized beside them.

"Guess you figger you're all ready to go now, Freddy," he said.

"Sure." Max looked up at the occluded sky. Helen looked up too, and a tiny flake landed on her nose and melted there.

"My wife sent me down to say you want some supper?"

"Real nice of her," said Max.

Mrs. Garuluk did look like the sort of woman who got headaches, very severe ones. She had made a large country supper, which they ate in the kitchen, the four of them, together with a shy, mentally handicapped man, who served as some sort of farmhand. Helen was not introduced. Mrs. Garuluk was a woman who ate livers regularly on toast.

She began the meal with grace. The prayer included curses at everyone in the room, but she singled out adulterers as her main target.

Thereafter they ate in silence. Garuluk was fighting a losing battle for nourishment with his false teeth.

Max looked tired.

After Helen's attempt to help with the dishes had been repulsed, Garuluk got his flashlight and delivered them to the barn. Max went to get the sleeping bag out of the plane.

"Are you an aircraft engineer?" Helen asked Garuluk. She had been worried about the log books for some time. It seemed that they had to be signed out by a licensed mechanic.

"Nobody knows I'm not." He laughed—Ha! Ha!—and Helen nodded, annoyed.

Max returned and took the flashlight. They went into the barn and climbed up to the mow, where a pile of old straw looked as though it had been used as a bed before.

It was not snowing hard but it was very cold. Helen got into the sleeping bag wearing all her clothes, even her parka. Max, also thickly clad, squeezed in beside her.

"You okay?" he asked, after a moment. "There aren't any rats or anything. I slept here plenty of times."

"Oh yes. It was the Third Commandment at suppertime that finished me off, I guess."

He yawned. "Don't worry about Mrs. Holy-boly."

Helen was freezing and she moved closer to him. He put his arms around her and intertwined his legs in hers.

"Saw you talking to my boys today. It was nice," he said.

"They're all right, you know. Do they always fight like that?"

"Means they've got each other, anyway. Missy's a good mother," he added.

Helen thought of telling him what they had said about Christopherson, but realized he already knew, at least in essence. His own history was never very far from his mind, she guessed. She tucked her cold hands inside the front flap of his parka.

"Wish it was warmer," he complained. "We can't do any of that stuff she was describing in that prayer of hers."

Helen was too burnt out to wish for sex. She unbuttoned his shirt to warm her hands on his underwear-clad chest, and he moved to enclose her as much as possible. He was very warm.

"Hard to believe, but the world is full of girls who turn out to be like Agaric's wife," he remarked.

"Maybe that's because they have husbands like him."

"But you had some kind of a husband," he said. "And you turned out to be an angel."

Helen was silent. Her husband, his wife. But perhaps there was something holy between them, a bit of trust and honesty that neither of them had known before.

A moment later Max began to snore softly. But Helen was already asleep.

CHAPTER TWENTY-TWO
Dulce Domum

THERE WAS a skiff of snow on the ground the next morning. The weather, or perhaps some god not of Mrs. Garuluk's imagining, had decided to co-operate with their plans.

They packed the plane. Helen shivered, looking at the clouds. She was going to be sick on the way back too.

Garuluk came hobbling down from the house.

"The wife says you could get some breakfast."

"No thanks," said Helen quickly.

Max had been brushing snow off the plane. He climbed up over the nose like a mountain goat, then sat on the wings with his legs dangling while he worked with a broom. Then he climbed nimbly down and leaned on the strut.

"You're off, are you, Freddy? Don't you think you're forgetting something?"

"Need gas, Agaric."

"Ha! Ha! Those wings don't flap. Too bad."

Max whistled.

"That was a neat trick, the way you paid your gas bill. Now we're all broke—or aren't we?"

"Why didn't we set fire to his barn last night?" Max asked Helen, his eyes on Garuluk.

They started a staring match. Helen waited, uncertain what was at stake.

"Maybe we could get gas on credit," she suggested at last.

"Well now, I don't know that the gas company would be as stupid as that." But Garuluk seemed to have lost the contest. He stumped off into the high grass with

Max on his heels. A moment later they emerged between the barn and the outhouse kicking a couple of forty-five-gallon drums.

Garuluk pumped in fuel while Max loaded a barrel in the back of the plane.

"Don't ever say I didn't give you a start, Freddy."

To Helen's astonishment, the two men shook hands.

"Get in, Helen."

They were going home.

*

She began to feel better about 700 miles out of North Winnipegosis. Max folded up the map. He was looking happier too.

Then they were home.

There was still snow in the air, dimming the twinkling lights of the village. They came in over the unploughed airstrip, taking a look and going around again before the landing.

Helen saw a straggling procession coming up the road on their first overpass. But when they actually got out of the plane, she was amazed to see that the whole village had come out, men, women, and children.

It was like arriving on Santa's sleigh. People were kissing them and shaking hands, pounding Max on the back.

"Hey, Helen! Seen the big city?"

"Bring back any whisky? Or did you drink it all on the way?"

"Aren't you glad you're back up North?"

"Look at this here, you guys. We got a skiplane for the winter!"

Even Sarah was there, with her old-fashioned barn lantern. Helen went over to shake her hand.

"So you came back."

"There's no other place for me, Sarah."

Behind her back, Henry was concluding a speech. There was a chorus of cheers, and Max was pushed out in front. He was looking a little embarrassed.

"Spent all the money. Brought back the plane. Thanks a lot for coming out. Got to go to bed now. Long flight."

"No way!"

"Going to have a party!"

"Go get the drums."

The crowd was moving them down the road.

"Go get the brew pot too!"

"No, no, got to go to bed."

"You can't go to bed."

"Lost a lot of money the last time you did that!"

"Goin' to have a dance!"

"Go to bed tomorrow."

Looking longingly down the shore towards her house, Helen saw that the lamp was lit and a puff of fresh blue smoke was coming from the chimney. Sarah was nowhere to be seen. Her welcome was being prepared.

"This year we're really goin' to go trapping."

"Got our own plane this winter."

"Paws on the dog say this one's goin' to be a cold one."

They were dragged, still protesting, to the community hall. The close-packed bodies began to warm the room even before the oil drum stove heated. The drummers stood up. Mrs. Henry Woodcutter, poker-faced but festive in a print dress and moosehide leggings, led off the dance. Dim bulbs above illuminated the jostling lineup behind her. Henry seized a drum from a child, who brought it freshly warmed from the stove, and the singing chant began to raise the rafters. It certainly was a homecoming.

They got away at 3:00. Max was a little drunk on homebrew.

"Oops!" He had stumbled into Sarah on the stoop.

"It's okay, Max." Helen grabbed his arm to prevent him falling down the steps. "Sarah's been stoking the stove."

Sarah stood stock still, her head turned away, while Helen manoeuvred him in the door.

"Good night, Sarah." The joyful dog danced on his hind legs between them, leaping to lick Helen's face, to kiss Max's hands. "Thanks for everything. You looked after Bootleg too."

Sarah nodded and stepped down into the snowy darkness.

"Came down on the last gallon of gas, had to drink some kind of poison, danced with a person in whiskers," mumbled Max. "Then there's a witch on the doorstep." He took off a boot laboriously.

"Well, you're a hero in Island Crossing, anyway."

"Water!" he pleaded. "What do they make that stuff out of?"

"There's tea on the stove."

Helen was rediscovering everything. It was all so small, barren in a way, but hers. The tea kettle, the table and chairs lined up with the little rug, their bed, the Air Carrier Act on the bottom step of the stairs with her typewriter.

"This isn't tea. This is something that witch made."

Helen sniffed. "Labrador tea."

"Some kind of drug?"

"No, it's good. Drink up. No hangover."

"Hangover?" He groaned. "I'm taking about 800 people to the bush tomorrow."

Helen was skimming out of her clothes. She made a flying leap into bed and snuggled down between the sheets, still faintly cold and damp.

She held out her arms. "Come on, hero."

Max was undressing.

"How can they tell what kind of winter it's going to be from the paws on the dog?"

"I'll ask Sarah."

"Still doesn't talk to me. Doesn't even see me."

Helen thought of telling Sarah about meeting Max's wife and giggled. She knew what Sarah would think of Max, and of Missy too. But she was not altogether sure, she realized, what Sarah thought of her. Sarah was acting very strangely these days, in spite of the way she had come out tonight. Helen wanted to know more about that.

CHAPTER TWENTY-THREE
Henry

Dear Helen,

This time I think he really is serious about getting it done. I don't know what he wrote you, but he's been wandering around the Dept. like a poor lost soul all fall. (He has a part-time sessional, teaching Anthro 101, did he mention?) I have told him that I can stir up the money to send him out in the spring term. I know that this may not be perfectly all right with you, but he does have a Ph.D. in him and everything else he could do seems to be waiting till he finishes.

I'm going to Columbia next year. But I may see you in the spring myself. In the meantime, keep your chin up. These things have to be lived through, you know. You can't just go off and join another tribe the way they did in the good old days.

Love,
Marion

Helen read this, leaning against a shelf of canned beans in the Co-op. Marion was Paul's dissertation supervisor. She had once been a powerful guru of Helen's too. She was an anthropologist of international renown. That Columbia was getting her away from the midwestern university where she taught and where Helen had been a student was a striking piece of academic gossip. Was she intending to take Paul with her to Columbia? It was possible to speculate. No doubt they were sleeping together. Marion had a personal life like a female wildcat's.

Thinking these fine, mean thoughts, she dislodged a couple of cans with her elbow and the whole shelf began to come down on her.

Henry Woodcutter came around the corner and jerked her back as a triangular edifice of fruit juice cartons tumbled forward.

He beckoned and she followed him into the Co-op manager's office. Then he shut the door.

He didn't have an office of his own. The community hall was used only on ceremonial occasions like the night before. Henry used any office that happened to be available, a fallen tree trunk or a couple of gas cans on the beach would do him in a pinch. He looked fine now, leaning against the Co-op manager's desk, rolling himself a cigarette.

He was quite an attractive man, a little older than Max, longish hair, a slightly weatherbeaten face, good teeth, and a pair of piercing black eyes. He also had a wife and five children who managed without much help from him.

Helen felt a faint stirring of sex in the air. It was always this way with Henry.

"So," he said now, and grinned at her, his teeth gleaming fiercely.

She smiled, and shook her head, no. Henry wanted to know whether she was back in the running again. She had slept with him in the past. She supposed he had some cause to wonder whether she was going to again.

"Why not?" He put down his burning cigarette in an ashtray and approached her frontally, stopping about two inches away.

"I already have a man, Henry."

"Yeah, but you had one before too. I don't see that ever stop you."

"Well, it does now."

She put the flat of her palm against his chest and he backed up, but only a short way.

It probably had not occurred to Henry that she had told her husband about him. But Helen was more than a little ashamed of this fact. At the time she had told Paul to make him angry and jealous; to torment him, in fact. To make him impotent, she admitted to herself.

"I guess you like this guy? He's not like the other one." Henry spoke dismissively. He had never had much use for Paul.

"No, he's not."

Helen backed a little farther away. The time they fired the Co-op manager, she and Henry had performed a rash act in this very office. She had realized even then that Henry was finding out far more about her than she ever would about him. He had certainly enjoyed it.

He was following her thought now, she could tell.

She laughed.

He made a move towards her immediately and she again put out the flat of her hand.

He shrugged.

"Whatever you say, Helen. I kind of like this whiteman myself."

"That's good. But Henry—" Helen had nearly made it to the door. "All this stuff about tourist fishing. You know as well as I do—"

"Just between you and me—" He removed her hand from the doorknob and held her back with it. "We kind of need a plane here this winter. And if the guy wants to believe there's something more in it—"

He grinned.

Helen gave him a wide-eyed stare, simultaneously working her hand out of his grasp. But she was not displeased. It was, perhaps, not quite so clear that Max was the exploiter in this situation. At least Henry did not see it that way. The reverse, if anything.

"Okay." Henry was still not letting her open the door. "You want to do a little job for me? Here?" He indicated the office with a sweep of his hand.

"Again?" Helen had heard that the Co-op was in a mess. She didn't like this manager any better than the last one.

"Why I wanted to talk to you. Only it kind of reminded me—of something else."

"Well, okay. What is it then? Where's the manager?"

"Oh, he took off yesterday. Took the cashbox too. Funny thing, I thought he was going to do that. So I came in here the night before and filled it up with all kinds of junk: stones and bones and stuff. So now we've just got to see how much else he stole."

Helen nodded. Henry wanted her to present a carefully edited account of what had happened to the Co-operative Association. It was necessary to keep everyone strongly of the opinion that a Co-op was vital to Island Crossing, even if the manager was a thief.

"I guess you want me to do something about this too." Helen looked around the disorderly office. "I'll come back after lunch. But this time I'm going to do most of the work at home," she announced.

"This time," he echoed, grinning.

Helen began to open the door again.

"Hey, wait a second." Henry took a folded envelope out of the back pocket of his jeans. "Goin' home? Give this to my sister."

She recognized the high quality envelope, the same characteristic handwriting.

"From Delilah," said Helen.

"Yeah. Met her in Mountain River."

"What is she doing there, Henry? It's really bothering Sarah." Helen shut the door and looked at him earnestly.

Henry sat down on the manager's desk, his hands in his pockets.

"She's in a movie," he said. "CBC is there making some kind of documentary drama. Said she was an actress. Payin' her and everything."

"Really?"

"Pretty damn nice-looking too. Now, if she weren't my niece—"

"Yes, yes," said Helen absently. She had not seen Sarah since the night of their homecoming. She could take her this letter; maybe it would break the ice she felt was forming between them. Maybe Sarah would even take Delilah's money this time.

"Why doesn't Sarah want to see her?" she asked. Henry knew, she was sure. He might not tell her, though.

Henry rocked thoughtfully on the edge of the desk, his hands in his pockets.

"I dunno," he said presently.

Helen nodded. She had come to expect this and to understand it. These people were all related; they all knew each other intimately. There was really nothing they didn't know about each other. But they kept it to themselves—not only to protect them from the outside world, but to protect them from each other. Not thinking about the things you knew made village life more bearable.

Still, she felt that even though Henry knew everything about Sarah, he didn't understand her at all. None of the more conventional people in the village, a group that included all the men, liked Sarah. Her role as a therapist for battered women kept her an outcast. Helen decided to present her own point of view on this to Henry.

"Sarah saved my life," she said. "I might have committed suicide."

He made no comment, merely continued to regard her with intelligent eyes. He knew, of course, about the way her marriage had finally come apart. Everyone did.

"She's saved a lot of people—women, girls. You know perfectly well how common it is, Henry." Look at me, a case history, she added silently.

Henry cocked his head. He didn't beat his own wife; he merely ignored her. But he knew what Helen meant.

"You still doing that university shit?" he inquired.

"No."

"Keeping notes, stuff like that? You used to."

She shook her head.

"I thought you were writing a book. Used to wonder if I was in it."

She smiled at him.

"No."

You're in Paul's diary, she thought. But he'll never get that back. That's something besides his Ph.D. he'll never get.

Then she recalled Marion's letter and shuddered.

"Well, Sarah's got a book. Only she don't write it down," he said. "It's got a lot of stuff in it. About men. Me, I'm in that book."

"Oh." He was right about that, she thought.

"I don't like being in her book," he said.

Helen could understand why not.

"But I'll tell you something. You don't know nothing about her, what she was. She killed a man."

"What?"

"Like I say."

He gave her a bland look; he obviously felt he had said too much. It was Henry the man, not Henry the politician, the Chief, who was afraid of Sarah's book.

She had always imagined a younger Sarah, a beautiful woman, powerful and magnetic. But who could she have killed? Not her husband: he had died of TB along with her four children. It was someone else. Someone who came later. Someone connected with Delilah.

She wanted to ask Henry, but he had now turned away and was beginning to go through the credit files in the office, ignoring her. He was as skillful as his sister at letting her know she was not there any longer.

Helen went out, pondering. Sarah had killed a man. Was this what had turned her into a wise woman?

There were some things for which you could never forgive yourself, as Helen knew. Murder was certainly one of those things.

CHAPTER TWENTY-FOUR

Some Things You Could Never Forgive Yourself For

THE FIRST episode had taken place when her marriage was really falling apart. Helen had already started to take small community service jobs: "doing good" Paul called it with scorn. He was a scholar, not a social worker, he said.

But the truth was that these jobs gave her an insight into the place that he wasn't getting. He used to question her eagerly, then make fun of her efforts.

One night she had been working on the Co-op books. It was basically the same story: the manager had left hurriedly and the accounts were a mess. Henry had hired her to figure out what was missing and write a whitewashing account of events to the Co-operative Association.

Helen had been flirting with Henry for months, but it had never occurred to her that she was going to let him do anything about it. She had been working hard all night and it was about 4:30 in the morning when he suggested, "Why don't we quit?"

Helen nodded, then stood up to stretch. She didn't have much to look forward to at home. Paul would be up—he hardly slept now—reading and making notes in his tiny, perfect handwriting. In her mind's ear, she already heard him sneering at her.

Henry placed a determined hand on her diaphragm and she turned around, thinking: yes, why not? He had plainly been waiting for hours, smoking quietly, knowing this moment would come. And there was something particularly forceful about the placement of his hand; she would not get away easily.

"Yes, why not?" she said aloud, looking into his narrow, brilliant eyes.

And then, to his delighted surprise, she proceeded to back him up on the desk and seduce him, reversing his evident expectation that he was going to do this very thing to her.

She left him there, sleeping peacefully on the desk. He had been awake for the previous forty-eight hours, escorting the Co-op manager off the premises and trying to clean up the mess in the store, so he was not as alert as Helen. She was still full of energy, so she went straight home and told her husband.

That was the beginning of their violent quarrels in Island Crossing, although there had been violent quarrels before.

But Paul was interested. He was very interested indeed. Possibly this was what spurred her on to meet Henry again. It was a change to have Paul interested in anything she did. He was not jealous, he maintained. He merely despised her.

So she did meet Henry again; not often, for Island Crossing was full of snowdrifts, spies, and Henry's wife. It was a cold March.

They were both very curious about each other. Her impulsive action the first time had aroused in Henry certain expectations about white women in general. Meanwhile, Helen was playing anthropologist, her husband always in the back of her mind. For she answered all Paul's questions and he questioned her relentlessly.

She had been using Henry, of course, to torment Paul, to make him jealous. To make him impotent, she admitted to herself.

Still, she liked Henry. Her affair with him was really quite explicable, even though his occasional drunkenness, his carelessness about precautions against venereal disease and conception, and his extreme disregard for the feelings of his wife soon began to annoy her.

But what she found unimaginable now were her detailed descriptions of each episode to her husband. And he took notes, very detailed notes, and wrote them out in his diary.

Did he ask for it? Yes, he did. But why had she done what he asked? Why had she told him all about it?

After their last explosive quarrel, Paul had left. And then, somehow, through some chemistry, perhaps because of the intervention of Sarah, it had become simply apparent to Henry that she was no longer available. He had not made any kind of approach until now. They had worked together on various projects amicably enough, but Helen was simply a neuter as far as he was concerned.

Now she was no longer a neuter. Henry's delicate sensors had picked that up at once.

*

She was going to see Sarah with Delilah's letter.

115

She was surprised to find Abe Balah outside Sarah's house. He was squatting on the ground, his back to the housewall.

Abe Balah was one of the older men in the village. He was monolingual, and therefore Helen hardly knew him. He belonged to a group of men she thought of as "the uncles": they were unmarried or parted from their wives, and they usually lived by mooching on older sisters and other relatives, running errands and working at odd jobs, most of the time doing nothing. Helen knew they were the last remnant of that leisured gentleman of the woods, the hunter-gatherer, but the village took a thoroughly modern perspective and regarded them as bums.

What Abe Balah could be doing here she could not imagine. Ordinarily, he would not have come within a stone's throw of Sarah's house.

"Is Sarah home?"

He looked up but made no sign, so she proceeded to the door.

Sarah was in bed and the strong smell of spruce liniment hung heavily in the little room.

Helen was used to ill-health in Sarah. She had been truly sick as a child with TB, and she had seen so many people die of TB and flu and measles and pneumonia that she was a thorough hypochondriac. Usually Helen bore her monologues about arthritis and other more imaginary ailments, tedious though they were, like a dutiful daughter. Now she was alarmed. She had never known Sarah actually to go to bed.

"It was nice of you to light the stove for us the other night," she began, looking anxiously down at her friend.

"For you, not him," said Sarah shortly.

She was lying down flat, but she heaved herself up to a half-sitting position, looking at Helen with her hawk-like eyes.

"Henry gave me a letter for you," said Helen. She sat down on the bed.

Sarah put out her hand.

"From Delilah," Helen said. She watched Sarah open it slowly and fumblingly. Her hands were not used to paper.

She looked at the letter for a moment, then gave it to Helen. With the same uncertain movements, she took the $100 bill out of the envelope and tore it into four pieces.

"Really, Sarah," Helen began.

"Read it."

Helen opened out the letter and read:

Dear Mother,

116

I wrote last time and I thought you would send something by Henry Woodcutter or another one. But I did not hear.

Remember I am a Woodcutter too, and it is my home. Besides, there is a reason.

Your daughter,
Dallas

Sarah grunted.

Helen stowed the letter and the four pieces of the $100 bill in the envelope. She hesitated as Sarah made no motion, then she put the envelope on the blanket beside Sarah's folded hands. Sarah seemed to have been expecting this letter, like the last one. How had she known? And was she actually preventing Delilah from coming?

"I'm sorry you're sick," said Helen. "Should I make tea or anything?"

Sarah shook her head.

"Maybe I'm going to die soon," she said.

"What? No, you're not. What is it? Do you have the flu?"

Sarah stared at her impassively. There was a short silence.

Helen said:

"I got a letter myself. From Marion Karnagowski-Weagle, you know, the anthropologist, Paul's supervisor. She says he's coming here in the spring. She may come too."

Sarah's gaze seemed to become a trifle impatient.

"I don't know what I'm going to do if that happens."

"Nothing," said Sarah.

"But somehow I should make things clear to him. If I wrote him—"

"Nothing," she repeated.

"Nothing? What do you mean?"

The old woman pulled her shawl closer around her shoulders.

"He's your husband." She spoke in a rusty voice. "You can't do nothing."

"Surely I can!" Helen was startled. Sarah would never have said such a thing before.

"I had a husband," Sarah went on. "He pound me up too. Then he died."

Helen knew that Sarah's husband and four of her children had died of TB.

117

"It begun like this with the last one too," said Sarah. "He stay in bed coughing. Then came the blood. We carry him to the doctor. There was one in Mountain River then. Doctor say he got to go to the hospital. I say no. I knew he was goin' to die."

"Your husband?"

"The last one. He was only three. The baby die, then him."

Helen looked at her sympathetically, helplessly.

"Whiteman took 'em all to hospital except that one. I keep him and he die in my arm. I never forget."

"Poor Sarah."

"You never see your baby die. You haven't got no baby."

"No."

"Think I killed him?" she demanded. "Because I keep him."

"No."

"When I got Delilah I begin to believe in God again. God give me Delilah. Nothing goin' to make up for the others, but I got a baby in my arm again. I thank God. Go on my knees to him every day for givin' me another baby."

"Then let her come home."

"No."

"Sarah, you love her. Whatever she did. I can't understand why you won't let her come home."

"You don't understand. You got no child. You can't understand nothing."

Sarah was angry.

Helen stood up, hurt.

"I still don't see—"

"No!"

"But Sarah, I'm just trying to help. And she is your daughter. If you're sick, then surely—"

"Go home now," said Sarah. She looked at Helen fiercely.

Helen put on her coat. She was very hurt, close to tears. Sarah was trying to alienate her, saying things that she knew would upset and offend her, things that she did not believe, Helen was sure.

She went over to the bed and looked down at the old woman, trying to be submissive. Sarah's strong will was formidable if you got on the wrong side of it.

Sarah said again: "I'm going to die now." Then she closed her eyes.

Later on Helen went to check Sarah's net. Sarah would not die of starvation. Not while Helen could return that favour, at least.

118

There was now a great deal of ice on the lake and she went along the shore watching the play of sunset light on the remaining open water. Nets would have to come out soon, probably in the next few days.

She had been anticipated. Someone was already working on Sarah's net on the beach.

"This isn't your net," said Helen, astonished.

No one stole from nets in Island Crossing. Fish were as free as air.

He again gave her his uncomprehending stare. It was Abe Balah.

After this meeting it was Abe Balah who brought Helen food from Sarah. It appeared every day as it usually did, and Helen knew that Sarah was sending it. But there was no sign of the old woman herself.

Helen was afraid that Sarah was quite sick.

But she did not want to visit Sarah. She was even afraid to. Sarah was in some trouble from which she had resolutely, even cruelly, shut Helen out. Something had changed forever and there was no going back.

CHAPTER TWENTY-FIVE
Delilah Comes Home

IT WAS December. They had made quite a lot of money in the late fall because of the trapping. It was an unusually good season in Island Crossing. More people were going out on the land because of the plane, and they were going farther afield. By the middle of the month Helen and Max had $4,000, and all of it was in Max's wallet. Helen was looking forward to putting money into a down payment on WWW.

She had ceased to worry about Marion's letter. She was enjoying her life these days. Sex, uncomplicated by guilt, hurry, or conflicting emotions, was new to her. It was also plainly new to Max.

They seemed to be making up for lost time. Helen was thirty. Max was forty. The joy they were getting from each other surprised and delighted both of them.

Max was working hard. Women, children, and old people went to the bush with the men. The camps were full as far as 200 miles away. Even the bachelor uncles bestirred themselves and gave up making homebrew and playing poker to run traplines. It seemed that the same plane that had taken them to the bar in the summer was now driving them to work in the fall.

But Garuluk had one more card up his sleeve.

Max came in one evening from Mountain River, where he had been on a gas-buying expedition. He took off his boots, his parka, his down overalls, and withdrew his log book from the front of his down vest. Then he embraced Helen and gave her a document that he had kept between the pages.

ORDER OF THE AIR TRANSPORT COMMITTEE, it said.

Helen sat down, already reading it, her mouth dropping open in protest.

Garuluk's charter license was being suspended "for failure to file certain documents." The suspension order came into effect in thirty days, after Christmas.

"Saw Brutson," said Max. "He gave it to me. Pointed out I'm going to be chisel-chartering next month."

"Chisel-chartering?" Helen looked up at him. "Operating without a license? But what does it have to do with chisels?"

"Has a lot more to do with haywire, I'd say." Max shook his head.

" 'Failure to file certain documents,' " she said, thinking about it. "What documents?"

He shrugged. "Whatever they are, he won't file 'em now. Agaric gets stubborn."

Helen laughed. "So I saw." She sat for a moment, still thinking. "What are we going to do, I wonder?"

"You'll figure it out. You've got a month," said Max.

*

She called Fish in Ottawa the next day.

"What can we do about this?" she asked. "I presume it's punitive."

"Punitive?" He had known who she was as soon as he heard her name. "Oh, I wouldn't go so far as to say that. Merely a routine administrative measure."

"We're still covered by Garuluk's license till next month."

"Please don't put it that way, will you?"

"But there's nothing to prevent us finding another operator with a number, is there?"

"No, but I wish you wouldn't put it quite that way."

"I suppose that the problem with finding another operator is that you'll go after him, too. With another routine administrative measure."

"Well, as you probably realize, there's a great deal of paperwork that doesn't get done in this country." Fish sounded censorious.

"But how do people ever get into this business, Charles? I mean, is it possible?"

"Do you want me to answer that officially?"

Helen laughed. "No, actually I want you to answer it unofficially," she said.

"Either way, the answer is, I don't know," he replied.

"Well, anyway, I just wanted to talk to you. Without actually telling you anything. Or getting any suggestions," she said. She knew he was not supposed to advise her.

There was a momentary silence.

"Have you thought of applying, yourselves?" he asked.

"For a charter license? But surely I couldn't get one of those by next month."

"No." He was cautious. "But then, you see, there would be some indication of your intentions."

"I see," said Helen thoughtfully.

"The Air Transport Committee is a very reasonable body. If you were to have a license application on file—"

"And also have another operator letting us use his number, but only temporarily—"

"I'll send you the format," he said. He seemed to sigh with relief.

"Do you really think we've got a chance?" she asked.

"Of what?"

"Getting started. Legally, I mean."

"Oh, yes. In the fullness of time."

Helen laughed. "Somebody told me it takes ten years to get a license."

"That's only in difficult cases," he said.

"This isn't one of those?"

"Oh no," he replied. "Not a particularly difficult case at all."

After she had hung up Helen reflected that it might, after all, take less than ten years to turn down a license application.

*

The Co-op was still out of commission. Henry had not been able to convince the Co-operative Association that a routine resignation had taken place and after a certain amount of arguing someone at headquarters had decided to call in the police.

They came from Mountain River with Max.

Helen went in to the Co-op to help Henry. He was being characteristically suave with the police. But the records were in a very serious mess. It seemed as though the manager had given up hope several months before he actually decided to leave.

"This ain't larceny," said the police officer, whom Helen now recalled was named Dave. "Fella must have been on dope. Ought to be a drug charge in it."

Henry raised his eyebrows politely as though to say, Dope? And what might that be, pray tell?

Helen spent an arduous afternoon trying to grasp what might have been in the manager's mind from the records that existed, and convey her interpretation as clearly as possible to the police. It was an improvement over allowing them impound the accounts. For the time being the Co-op was closed, but if it remained closed where would Island Crossing buy soap, lamp oil, and skidoo parts? Because he cared about things like this Henry had become the Chief.

It was getting late when Helen turned around and found herself face to face with Max who was lighting a cigarette in the office doorway. She guessed that he had come to pick up the police and take them back to Mountain River. He was wearing all his outdoor gear, looking padded and muffled and icy.

Henry, standing beside Max in a striped shirt and reading glasses, seemed much more a creature of modern technological civilization.

Max was smiling at Helen in pleasure and surprise.

The police looked from one to the other.

"I'll walk you out to the airstrip," said Helen, returning Max's smile. She went to get her parka.

It amused Helen, on their walk through town, to see that the police were inclined to be romantic, even sentimental, about Max and her. They evidently felt they had been in on this from the first. When Max kissed her goodbye at the pilot's side door before getting into the cockpit, she noticed the two men spying on them from within.

The fact was that they were gaining respectability from each other. She had once been too weird a phenomenon to be explicable to a red-blooded policeman. Max, on the other hand, had been living just on the right side of spending the odd evening in a cell. But now that they were together, they were a couple, an attractive young couple.

After she waved goodbye, she went back to the Co-op to help Henry clear up. She could now get on with writing up the charter license application, for the forms had come in the mail.

For a change she got home somewhat later than Max and found him peacefully eating a plate of fried eggs at the table and writing a letter. He got up immediately and began to fry an egg for her.

"What are you doing?" she asked, hanging up her parka and going over to the table to look.

"Writing Christmas letters."

"Christmas? Well, it is nearly Christmas," she said in surprise.

He passed her the letter and she read:

Dear Son,

123

Hope this finds you as well as it does me.
I must close now. Just wanted to drop
you a line.

"They'd probably like to know a bit more than that," she suggested.

"I was going to send a couple of hundred dollars to each of them."

"Well, good, but can't you tell them about the flying and so on?" said Helen.

He sat down with a sigh and took up his pen. He wrote:

P.S. Still keeping a plane in the air.

It occurred to Helen as she ate her egg that she was not writing Christmas letters to anyone. Her sister would probably phone her on Christmas Day. Her mother would be at parties on the cocktail circuit in Florida. Her father never called or wrote to anyone.

She was used to the way her family ignored Christmas. But this was not an ordinary Christmas.

Max was copying his letter onto another sheet of paper; one for each boy, she surmised.

"What are you thinking about?" he asked.

"Nothing," said Helen. She put down her knife and fork. "Just about how happy I am."

He smiled at her and she went around the table to sit on his lap.

"Are you happy?"

"Yes, I am. It's nice, coming home like this, having fried eggs—" As usual, she wasn't able to tell him how she felt. "Happy," "nice," they were as close as she was able to come to it.

Max was conducting an investigation of her clothes. He found her brassiere.

"I was just wearing it in honour of the police," she murmured, lying back in his arms.

"What were you doing at the Co-op?" he asked. "Wasn't expecting to see you."

"Oh, Henry asked me a while ago—" She had her eyes closed. He was removing the brassiere. "He thought it would just be a little writing job." She felt her nipple stiffen against his palm as it slipped through his gentle, stroking fingers.

"The cops said you were a big help."

He was kissing his way down her neck to her bare breasts.

124

"What else did they say?" Helen asked suspiciously.

"Said I was a lucky guy."

She opened her eyes and saw that he was laughing at her.

"And they're going to use our airline," he said. "From now on they're using our airline all the time." He stood up to finish undressing her.

"Well, all right." Helen said. "Our airline. Why not?"

Max wrote another Christmas letter later that night.

"Who's this one to?" asked Helen.

"My foster mother."

She was unable to resist looking over his shoulder to see what he would write.

> Dear Mom,
> Still keeping a plane in the air...

The next day Helen began to work on the charter license application forms. They were driven to it, but she realized that this application had been the solution from the beginning. It was quite complicated, especially the financial section, where she had to produce definite figures about a range of assets they didn't have: buildings, docks, hangars, tools, gas caches, spare parts, contract engineers, offices, and supplies. It was all hypothetical. It was, in fact, all lies.

But she was hoping to finish it by Christmas. It would be some kind of a present for Max, she considered. She really didn't have anything else. Aside from her job on the Co-op accounts, for which she would be paid only if the Co-op ever opened up again, she had no income this winter. So she was keeping the application a secret.

Max was now even busier than before. He was bringing back the trappers and their huge families from the bush. But as the town currently had no store, he was also conveying all of Island Crossing, family by family, to Mountain River to sell fur, eat french fries, buy liquor, candy, cigarettes, canvas, thread, snuff, tea, and rice; and then flying them all back again, riotous and triumphant.

Since it became dark so early in the afternoon, one of her functions was to turn on the airport lights: a string of bulbs laid out on tripods down one side of the airstrip, which she had to plug into the power pole.

It was a freezing day, the temperature at minus forty degrees with a good stiff wind blowing.

A woman had gotten out of the Beaver and was walking away. She was tall and her stride was somehow bold. But Helen had seen from her face that she was a native, not a white woman.

"Who was that?"

"Some Woodcutter," replied Max briefly.

He crawled under the cowling and returned a moment later with a rope in his teeth. He was wrapping the Beaver's engine in its blanket for the night.

"Delilah!" exclaimed Helen.

She turned in time to see Delilah rounding the bend in the road into town. She had not taken the lakeshore path. But she could be going to Sarah's house the long way.

Max was trying to hold the blanket fold down against the wind with his elbow while he tied the rope. Helen went over to help.

"Think that old woman'll get better now?"

"Maybe." She wasn't sure. What was wrong with Sarah was very mysterious.

"I'm cold. Been cold all day," he complained. "Something's the matter with her too." He surveyed the blanket-wrapped nose of the plane. "Don't know what it is."

"Let's go home." She took his arm and they began to walk against the wind together.

They entered the cabin. Max discarded his parka and sat down on the steps of the loft to undo his bootlaces. The dog headed for his place under the stove, circled around three times and lay down, heaving a sigh of relief and contentment.

"Got to get a mechanic."

"How are you going to do that?" His hands were stiff with cold and Helen went over to help with the boots. She knelt in front of him, looking up in concern.

"Not sure. I'll take a look at her myself first. Don't think I can get her to Buffalo Neck the way she is."

He stood up and headed for the bed, plunging face down on it as usual.

"Only ten days till Christmas," said Helen.

He had been flying every available moment of daylight.

"I feel like getting into bed and just staying there till next year."

Helen sat down beside him and started to rub his back. Max groaned, rather like the dog, and she began doing a thorough job of it.

But Delilah was still uppermost in her mind. She had come home for Christmas.

CHAPTER TWENTY-SIX
Hard Rock

MAX WORKED on the plane all the following day. The temperature had sunk even further and the lake was producing fog. At least the wind had stopped. But Max was not able to find out what the trouble was.

Helen recognized how thin a thread their success was hanging by. If their problem was a serious one, they might need a new engine. They couldn't afford an engine. But more to the point, they couldn't get one, or any spare parts, or even a mechanic.

It was not the first time she had come face to face with what a dangerous, chancy business aviation was. So much depended on the nerve and skill of one man. And that was not enough because there were so many other factors: constant bad weather, the vagaries of an old machine, the pressure of seasonal work. Max was inclined to regard these things philosophically as luck or fate, but they worried Helen when she thought about them. What if he had not made it home last night with the plane?

She and the freezing, grumbling dog spent the afternoon holding tools and trying to make themselves useful.

It was almost dark when the Mountain River Air sched came in, empty and late, as usual. The pilot threw out a mail bag and strolled over.

"Got a problem?"

"No," said Helen crossly.

"You bet," said Max. "I thought you quit," he added.

He got up from his crouch on the ground under the nose and let the other man take a look.

"Well, I guess I could give you a hand."

"Need more than that. I don't know what the hell it is."

The Mountain River Air pilot seemed to know what he was doing. Humming to himself, he got a flashlight and a little screwdriver out of some pockets of his flight suit.

"Why are you letting him look?" said Helen privately. "We don't want Brutson to know we have trouble."

"Jake's an engineer."

"I am an engineer," agreed the pilot from inside the engine. "And I quit working for Brutson. I was taking this Cessna off his hands. He doesn't really need it since it's broke all the time anyway. I saw the mailbag in back and thought I'd drop it off."

"You were stealing the plane?" said Helen, startled.

"Yeah, but that's no reason why you shouldn't get your Christmas cards."

"I heard there was a little trouble," sad Max.

"Yeah. A little trouble getting paid." Jake stood up and dusted the snow off his knees.

Helen laughed. Stealing your wages seemed to be the norm in this business.

"Are you intending to sell it?" she asked, indicating the plane. It was rather younger and handsomer than WWW and painted in gay red candy stripes.

"No, ma'am. I'm going to hide it." He peered at her. "Brutson's going to have a stroke. He nearly had one when he got that letter of yours last month. Write it yourself?"

"She did," said Max.

"Nice to meet you ma'am." Jake pulled off his glove, but suddenly funked the handshake. "I had kind of a different idea what you were like." He turned to Max. "Well, let's do it. Then I'll be on my way."

Helen hung around for a while to watch. Jake was another one who travelled heavy. He had a rolling toolbox in the back of the plane. He was also carrying a Diesel heater and a parachute. They covered the Beaver with the chute, which expanded like a circus tent, filled with warm air from the heater inside. Then they pulled in the runway lights and set up housekeeping, with Max holding the tools this time.

After a while she went home. There was a pair of fresh caribou ribcages lying on the doorstep. Abraham Balah had been hunting for Sarah. Ribs were the best part. It was very generous of him to give them to Helen.

She went inside and started to make an extra-large pot of boiled meat.

Nothing happened for some hours. Helen fell asleep. It had been a cold, exhausting day.

At last she heard the dog whining to come in, then the scrunch of footsteps in the dry snow outside. It was after midnight.

"You fixed it!"

She could tell from Max's expression, nonchalant and relieved.

"Yeah, but don't tell anyone I said so." Jake was dour. "I wonder about some of the things I do on this little crap, like your Beaver."

Max was washing his hands, sniffing the cooking meat.

"A Beaver isn't exactly little," Helen remarked with dignity. Brutson's Cessna was considerably smaller than WWW.

"Well, it is, compared to an airplane."

"Why? What kind of airplanes do you usually fix?"

"Fly, ma'am. I only make with the tools when I'm taking a little holiday." Jake looked at the dirty washing-up basin that Max was proffering and put his hands behind him.

"DC-3. I'd like to fly one of those sometime," said Max, drying his hands on a towel. Jake backed away from the basin now. Helen had seen his hands, which were pale and small and delicate like a girl's, but dirty, with a deep, ingrained blackness around the nails.

"Trouble," he said. "Always trouble with the whirlygigs."

"What were you flying?" Helen asked.

"DC-6, Electra, Boeing 737, that kind of stuff. Striped mostly, with stars. Colour like that can help when you're getting in; helps when you're getting out, too."

"Where was this?"

"Trade routes, ma'am. South of the equator. Central America too. Export-import, we call it."

"Do you mean drugs?" she asked.

"Coke, the all-American choice. Not in bottles. The other kind."

Helen raised her eyebrows He had been bragging to impress them, and she didn't believe a word of this.

"Must be a lot of money in that business," Max said wistfully.

"It's a patriotic duty, that's how I see it. Flying for the President of the U.S.A. Doing the dirty work. Plus, as you say, it remunerates well. The only thing is, you can get kind of well known." The engineer's mannerisms with his hands were obsessive. He wrung them together.

"Have some supper." Helen put a steaming plate of ribs on the table.

Max sat down and began dishing out the meat, his sleeves rolled up, being a good host.

"Pay you in cash, I guess," he said, passing the plates.

"Cash or hard rock. I prefer rock, myself. More fun to have around, and it's portable."

Helen looked at Max. She saw that he was being taken in, but he was enjoying himself.

"So you're an American too," she said, picking up a rib and biting into it. Jake was a Texan, going by the accent, and she thought she recognized his type. Canadians were very quick to let any American string them along. They felt naive and backward, and it made them easy to take.

"What's this stuff?" Jake was looking into his plate.

"Caribou ribs."

Laying down his fork, he carefully extracted a caribou hair, a longish white one, from the broth. Then he stared at it, an hallucinatory expression of disgust on his face.

It was always very hard to get all the hairs off ribs. Max would have made the effort, but Helen had ceased being squeamish about things like this long ago.

Jake was looking terrible, his face pallid and twitching. It seemed an excessive reaction to a caribou hair. He stood up.

Helen put down her fork. Max stood up too.

Jake now produced a terrifying, dry, I'm-going-to-be-sick-on-an-empty-stomach belch, and fled out the door.

"My God," said Helen. "I left a hair on it."

"Yeah, but that's not what's the matter with him," said Max. "Tell you later." He went out the door with the engineer's parka.

Helen no longer felt like eating, so she cleared the table. She scraped their plates into the dog's dish.

She put another stick of wood in the stove and opened the draft. Then she sat down on the bed with Section Two of the charter license application. She wanted to proofread but she couldn't keep her mind on it.

The man had been trying to impress them with his stories. But why such an extreme reaction to a hair on the caribou ribs? It could hardly have been a single hair that had made him sick.

All at once she guessed the answer.

Living in safe, isolated Island Crossing, she had become unperceptive about things like this. Jake's behaviour had been more than just odd. Whether he flew the drugs or not, he was probably taking them.

The strange thing about it was that she wasn't frightened.

She shoved Section Two under a pillow and went to re-adjust the stove.

After a while Max returned with Jake, who was back to normal. Max was the one looking a little strained. They must have had a rough time of it out there, but the man had taken what he needed.

"Sorry, ma'am," he said.

"Not at all." Helen continued to sit on the bed, guarding the secret of her papers.

"Let's have tea or something," said Max.

"Good idea."

"I don't drink tea."

"I wish we had some whisky," said Helen.

Max shot her a worried glance. He knew what was wrong with Jake but perhaps he thought she still didn't.

"I don't drink whisky."

No one spoke while Max made the tea; they were all somewhat uncomfortable. Helen felt that Max was wondering about her reaction to the engineer's strange behaviour. She wanted him to know that she was not afraid.

"Why don't you just take the plane back," she said. "You can't really hide an airplane."

"Think it might make you kind of noticeable too," said Max.

"What about my wages?"

"Write the Labour Board," Helen suggested. "I guess Brutson hates letters."

"That's true."

She watched him go through a set of compulsive gestures with his hands.

And stop snorting it, or smoking it, or popping it, or shooting it, she wanted to tell him, but didn't. Getting him to take the plane back was enough, she felt.

"I'll help you go get her warmed up," said Max.

In a little while she heard the Cessna roaring off in the direction of Mountain River. With ironic pleasure she imagined Brutson's relief. It had certainly been a tremendous piece of luck for them. So why not do Brutson a favour, after all?

"Did he really fix the plane?" she asked Max when he came in.

"Think so."

"I wouldn't take his word for it."

131

"Nope. But it works again." He sat down and began taking off his boots. "Boy, that guy sure has daydreams."

"The kind that come out of a pill bottle."

"Yeah." He laughed. "You should have been out there under that parachute this afternoon. Told me a few things."

"Well, don't tell me what they were, all right?"

Max was looking at her acutely. "Scare you?" he asked.

Helen shook her head.

She hadn't been afraid of the mechanic. She was afraid of her husband. He was really the only person she was frightened of. All her fear stemmed from that one fear, and the strange, half-frozen state she had been in before Max entered her life had been entirely due to it. She knew that until she found some way to get rid of the burden of that fear she would never be entirely free.

He began to undress while she did the chores, filling the stove and the kettle, and letting out the dog.

"Trouble with this business is that every way of making money is wrong," he remarked. "I used to think it didn't matter. Would have done something like him if I'd got the chance."

"Running drugs? But that was all lies." She paused. "Don't you think?"

"Yeah," said Max. He sat down thoughtfully on the side of the bed, waiting for Helen to let Bootleg in. She turned to blow out the lamp.

"Some of it was lies," he said.

CHAPTER TWENTY-SEVEN
Christmas

THE SHORT days before Christmas passed quickly. Max was busier than ever before, bringing people back from the bush and taking them to Mountain River with the fur. It was hard work for him in cold weather and darkness, putting the warmed battery into the plane in the morning, feeding it with bottles of warmed oil, pumping the freezing, volatile gas, and taking off in the first rays of light from the distant sun. Back again in the late afternoon to land in twilight with the help of the bulbs strung out along the side of the airstrip, unloading, swaddling the plane in blankets and removing the battery, then trudging heavily home. He ate, slept, woke, ate, and left again.

Meanwhile, Helen perfected the complex web of invention that constituted the charter license application. It was clever fiction, composed of scraps of incidental knowledge, memories of airports, what she had gleaned from seeing Garuluk's place in North Winnipegosis and from cross-examining Max, all strung on a set of figures that she was sure were consistent, even if they had no reference to any external reality.

And like everyone else in Island Crossing, she started a brew pot. But unlike her neighbours, who used a porridge of improbable ingredients including dried beans and crackers, she made homebrew from canned pie filling—mince, this year.

They woke up on Christmas morning to church bells in the air. Max had brought in the priest the night before.

She thought he might still be asleep but when she returned from the porch with an armload of wood, he had risen on one elbow and was looking at her with bright eyes.

"Did you remember it's Christmas?"

Helen nodded, smiling.

He stretched luxuriously, raising his arms above his head. "I'm not going anywhere today."

Helen set out the coffee pot and began measuring coffee into it. Usually Max was up first, making breakfast and warming the house. The small domestic reversal was pleasant. He lay back, his arms now folded behind his head, looking lazily at the ceiling.

"Didn't have Christmas last year," he remarked.

"You were driving a truck?"

"Yeah. So I forgot about it. Somebody reminded me a couple of days later. Took the night off and got drunk. Didn't seem the same, somehow."

She came to sit down on the side of the bed.

"Know what?" His eyes swept over her, his lips were smiling.

"What?"

"Tell you later. Bottle of wine under the bed, though. Glasses too."

Helen saw that he was not prepared to be cynical. It was not just a day off, but the right day off. The glasses were champagne glasses.

"Start with bubbly. We'll have the bean liquor later," said Max, popping the cork.

He wanted her to get back in bed. Looking at him over the rim of her glass, she began to explain how people celebrated Christmas in Island Crossing.

"Visiting."

He groaned and reached for his trousers.

But as it turned out they were up early enough to be outside before the village emerged from the church door.

It was not very cold, a good day for a walk. They went first to look at the airplane.

Max inspected it from the side, walked around it twice, looked up into the clear sky, whistled, and threw a snowball at Helen. He said:

"Like a dog with two tails. What do we do now?"

She laughed.

"You never go anywhere on the ground, do you?"

"I didn't know there was anywhere to go."

"Do you want to see an archaeological site?"

"Sure."

She led him down the trail through the muskeg. It was hard walking, but they had been preceded that morning by two people on snowshoes. Helen thought she knew who they were.

"Somebody's been out here already," he said.

"I know."

"Your old woman?" he asked. "Thought she was sick. But it looks like her track."

Helen was surprised. She would not have known just by the track.

"This one is Henry," said Max. He pointed to a detail in the snow.

"It's the family's camp," she said. "The original place. They came here to fish—for thousands of years, probably."

They arrived at the clearing, hardly a clearing at all any longer, grown head-high in alder and willow.

"Where's the old bones and stuff?" he asked mildly.

Helen was pushing her way through the bush, holding back the branches for him. At last she came out on the bank of the little creek and waited there for him to catch up.

"About here."

He was silent, but not uninterested.

"There's a fish run here in the spring. They made a trap with stones in the creek. There's nothing much to see now."

"Thought there'd be a grave or two."

"Hundreds of them."

They looked down at the little creek between its miniature cliffs, silent now under the burden of the ice. The clearing behind them was full of ghosts. Sarah had once peopled it for Helen, telling of her own birth, the birth of Henry, the death of her mother.

Max jumped down the bank.

"I see how they did it," he said.

He began pointing it out to her, assuming she didn't. The drift of the creek was apparent to him, even under the ice. Helen was again surprised into admiration. He was squatting on his heel, one knee up, picking out the disposition of the stones.

He stood up and they resumed their walk on the icy river, Max in the lead this time.

Helen was wrapped in thought. She had come here before on a winter's day with someone who showed her how the fish trap worked: Paul, her husband. She remembered how impressed she had been, how completely the significance of his work filled and absorbed her.

Henry and Sarah came here for some kind of manna from the place: what that was like she now realized, she could never know. Helen usually came here to recap-

135

ture some of the feeling she had had that day with Paul, and to meditate in bitterness.

" ...didn't have to go to church," Max was saying cheerfully.

"What?"

"I was talking about Christmas."

"Oh, I see. You were probably brought up as a Catholic, were you?"

"Didn't know there was any other religion. Heard about that the same year I saw an airplane. So I decided not to be a priest."

"A wise choice," she remarked. She was still feeling depressed.

Max stopped and turned around suddenly, taking her parka by the pockets.

"Tell me something about you."

"Me?" Helen came up short, breast to breast with him.

"You never talk about yourself," he said.

"What do you want to know?" She was taken aback.

"Got any brothers and sisters? Somebody wake up on Christmas morning and pull your hair?"

Helen thought of her father, the surgeon, her sister, the psychoanalyst, her mother, the neurotic. She had not had a secret life, not a conscious one, anyhow, until she had gone to university. She owed whatever she was now to Paul and Marion. Her family were like wraiths to her.

"My sister," she said, "thinks it is normal to be divorced."

"I want to know about you," he said.

"Well, she says I should get a divorce, finish my degree, and—"

"What degree?"

"My master's degree. The degree I was supposed to be doing when I came here. My husband was doing his doctorate."

He said nothing, looking at her keenly.

"According to my sister I am fleeing reality."

"Heard something like that one time myself. My wife made me go to a counsellor."

"A marriage counsellor?"

"Nope. A job counsellor. He said I was flying in the face of the facts."

Helen laughed. He laughed too, but he was still holding onto her parka.

"So what happened?" he said.

"To me? You know how it turned out," she said. "He left."

Max was silent.

"You want me to tell you about it, don't you?" she said at last.

He nodded. He let go of her parka and began lighting a cigarette. Helen turned away slightly and fixed her eyes on a little willow bush on the overhang of the bank.

She had never told anyone but Sarah.

"We met in graduate school. He was already doing real research, on these people here. I was doing my M.A. out of the library. And, you know, a summer dig in Greece, that kind of thing. What he was doing was big. It was original. He told me about his work. I started to help. I fell in love with him. It was as if I began to exist then," she said.

She could tell Max didn't like this even though she was not looking at him.

"You've never even told me his name," he said.

"Oh. Paul. Paul Ayre. I fell in love, got married, and began to exist all in one year. That was six years ago."

She was not sure he would understand what she was saying. The notion of a woman coming to life and falling in love with a set of ideas was not in the realm of Max's experience. But he wanted to know.

"My sister says I let him dominate me intellectually. I became sort of his child or something. But that's the kind of theory she goes in for. The fact is, he was a brilliant man—a brilliant anthropologist. He wanted a lot from me. I gave it everything I had. But somehow that wasn't enough."

Max moved slightly. She saw it out of the corner of her eye.

"What is it?" she asked.

"Nothing."

"There is something."

"Okay. This is making me jealous," he said reluctantly.

"But you asked."

"Yeah. Go on."

"We didn't begin to quarrel, exactly," she said. "It was just that I wasn't good enough. And he was completely absorbed, self-absorbed, according to my sister. Anyway, she doesn't know anything about it—not this part. He started to criticize my work. Then he began acting as if I was stupid. I was living like a serf as it was, doing joe jobs on his project, bibliography, that kind of thing—everything in my life on his schedule. I'd already given up on my M.A. And then he began to accuse me of sabotaging the project, trying to ruin it."

"He was crazy."

137

"Neurotic, maybe. Not crazy. But I never tried to sabotage his project." She spoke passionately. "And I couldn't take the humiliation. He was telling me off in front of other people, calling me names, constantly saying what a fool I was. Then he began to hurt me. Physically, I mean."

She turned away from Max even more. This was the part she found hardest to tell. She was angry, but that did not mitigate the shame and degradation she felt; the anger made it worse.

"At first it was stuff like pinching and pushing. One time he slapped me and I got a nosebleed. Before we came here it got very bad and I sometimes had to stay home until the bruises went away. I thought things would get better here, and they did for a while. But then it all blew up and we had a fight. I thought that he was going to kill me. He thought so too. I believe that's why he left, finally. He left the next day.

"I spent the night out in the bush. He locked me out. To keep himself from killing me, maybe. I was in pretty rough shape. I'd lost a lot of my hair. Black eyes, cracked nose. Frostbite. I wanted to die. I was trying to die out there. But Sarah found me. She took me in."

She didn't look at him.

"Thought it was something like that," he said.

"Does it show?" she asked in bitterness.

"Yeah, it does. Somebody broke your nose. I thought a lot about you and that old woman too."

He took her arm and they began to walk slowly. She still did not look up.

"You see 'em here. The ones that took it and the ones that are still taking it. I guess she took it herself once. Now she helps out the ones that're still taking it. Is that the way it goes?"

"Yes."

"Maybe that's why she doesn't have much use for men," said Max.

"So now you know." Helen lifted up her chin and stared forward blindly. "So what, right? Work it through. Get therapy. Get better. That's what my sister says. But I'm okay. I'm fine. Why shouldn't I live here? At least here no one pretends."

She could feel his arm pressing against her side, but she was standing up stiffly, resisting comfort.

"I don't blame myself anymore." This was entirely untrue. "It's hard to talk about, that's all."

"Guess I know something about that," he said. "You don't really trust anyone after something like that. It happened to me too. My step-dad. He used to make me stand up on a chair while he belted me. 'Take it like a man,' that's what he said. Couldn't help crying—screaming for help too. Used to pretend I never cried, afterwards. I used to lie there in the barn, crying, pretending I never cried. Pretending it never happened."

Helen had stopped walking. She put her arms around him.

"Well, maybe it wasn't quite the same," he said, holding her. "I knew my step-dad was just beating me for the hell of it, not for anything I did. But the thing about you is, you think it was your fault, that something about you made him do it. Think you ruined his life, don't you?"

"No. Yes." Helen was crying. Crying for the little boy who had lain in the barn, pretending he had never cried.

They stood there hugging one another in their bulky winter clothes.

Finally, she lifted her head and smiled at him. She was feeling curiously light-hearted. It was good to have told him about Paul.

"So," he said. He seemed hesitant. "What I wanted to ask you—"

"Yes?"

"I'm on the map at least?"

"Of course you are."

He kissed her. But she knew he was not satisfied. He wanted a better answer than that. But she couldn't tell him what she knew he wanted to hear.

Max said:

"I got you a Christmas present."

"Really?" Helen had not been expecting one. She was intending to spring the charter license application on him later, when they were in bed.

"Maybe this is a bad time?"

"No, no. It's okay." Helen looked at him attentively, drying her eyes.

He produced a small object from an inside pocket. There was a guilty smile on his lips.

"Been like a cat on hot bricks over this for a week," he said.

He opened his palm. It contained a large heart-shaped piece of jewellery, an enormous ruby surrounded by big diamonds. Flamboyant, old-fashioned, and ostentatious, it was the sort of thing that might have appeared on the front page of the *National Enquirer* in Elizabeth Taylor's cleavage.

"For me?" Helen was horrified.

He was fumbling in his pocket again. "I got some kind of a chain for it. Of course I couldn't find a gold one."

He put the pendant into her hand. Helen stared at it. She belonged to a class of society that didn't own jewellery. An engagement ring, a nice pearl necklace, that was all. They spent their money on houses, books and trips to Europe instead.

In any case, this piece could not be anything but a fake. For if it were real, Max could never have afforded it.

Max threaded the chain through its loop. He was intending to hang it around her neck. She turned obediently, bending her head and lifting up her hair to let him fasten it. A moment later he turned her around again and unzipped her parka slightly to settle the ruby above her breasts.

Helen looked down at it. The brilliants flashed at her, cold and blue.

"Where did you get it?"

"From that Mountain River Air pilot."

"And you gave him some money for it?" She looked up sharply.

"All the money," said Max.

"But Max! You were going to buy an airplane with that money!"

The guilty look returned to his face.

"Thought you'd say that."

"He told us a bunch of lies that night."

"Yeah, but they weren't all lies. Remember how he said he got paid in hard rock? Told me this is worth a lot more than what I gave him. But I guess he wanted the cash."

"He wanted the cash to buy drugs! Oh, don't you see—?"

But Helen suddenly caught herself. She sounded like her mother. From his point of view, it was a present. A stupendous present. One did not argue about a gift like that.

"Oh Max!" She began to laugh. "You wonderful man!" She kissed him. "No wonder your wife sent you to a job counsellor!"

"Never gave her one of these."

"She wasn't trying to get you to buy an airplane, either. This is the nicest present anyone ever gave me."

"Really?" He was looking happier.

"Really." She looked down at it, trying to find some adjectives in her vocabulary that would describe it. Even had it been real, she would not have known what to say. But she was trying to act out her pleasure so he wouldn't be disappointed.

"I like it almost as much as an airplane!"

He caught her in his arms and began to kiss her, the kind of sexual kiss a man gives a woman who is naked except for an enormous jewel. Helen realized that for him the necklace was a symbol of their secret life together, a celebration of sex. Like the plumage of birds, the dance of the mayfly, the baboon's bottom, it was inherently a sexual thing. She suddenly understood the fatal allure of jewels.

"Let's go somewhere."

"Where?" Helen looked around at the snowy trees. "Not here."

"Let's go home and lock the door."

"Okay."

Laughing, she let him pull her along, retracing their steps on the river. He was walking very fast.

But there was someone standing in the clearing by the fish trap, apparently waiting for them. A tall woman, who at first appeared almost of supernatural height because of her stance up on the riverbank. Helen thought it was Sarah. But it was not.

CHAPTER TWENTY-EIGHT
A Wedding

IT WAS Delilah.

"Hi," said Helen. She stopped, panting, and zipped up her parka, then pushed her hair out of her eyes. It was not a dignified moment.

"Hi," said Delilah.

"We were just looking at the fish trap." Helen couldn't help laughing at the absurdity of this explanation. If Delilah had been standing on the riverbank for more than a moment, she would know what they had been doing.

"You're—Dallas, aren't you?" she said.

"Yeah."

"I'm Helen. I know your mother. I'm a friend of hers. This is Max," continued Helen quickly, seeing a look of reserve cross Dallas' face.

She continued to regard them in silence, interested and a little wary.

Dallas was as tall as Sarah, tall for an Indian woman. She looked like Sarah too, confirming Helen's view that Sarah had once been beautiful.

"We were just going to go home and have a drink," Helen went on, laughing a little once again.

Dallas smiled at her.

"Won't you come with us?"

"Okay."

They began to walk home and she fell into step behind them.

"Henry said you were in a film."

"That's why I grew my hair like this." Dallas picked up the end of a long braid.

"He told me you were pretty damn nice-looking," remarked Helen.

"Oh yeah." Dallas laughed. "He's my uncle. I had to remind him of that a few times."

"What is the film about?"

"Incest," said Dallas. "It's over now. So I came home."

"Welcome back," said Max.

"You brought me," she reminded him. "Nice we've got a plane here now. Everyone is talking about it."

"Come in." They had arrived at the doorstep.

Dallas took off her snowshoes with difficulty and stretched out her legs one after the other. "I've lost the hang of it," she said.

They were Sarah's snowshoes. Did this mean Sarah had let her daughter come home? Helen didn't know how to ask this question.

"Abe let me have them," Dallas went on. "He always helped me."

It was still a mystery what Abe was doing with all Sarah's things.

"Time for the hooch," said Max.

"It's homebrew," warned Helen. Dallas was a more sophisticated visitor than the ones she had been expecting.

Dallas was looking around the cabin with a smile.

"Nice cabin," she remarked. "I'm going to have one like this myself someday."

She was wearing moccasins and the kind of leggings the older women wore. Like the braids they suited her tall, calm beauty.

Helen was rather excited. She had often wondered about this woman; because of her own relationship to Sarah, she had sometimes thought of Dallas as a kind of sister.

Helen was still mourning the loss of her friendship with Sarah. Sarah had felt that she had to put Helen out of her life because of Dallas' return. There was something that she thought Helen would not be able to understand. Perhaps it was something she believed no one could help her with.

Sarah had killed a man. But what did that have to do with Dallas?

"Are you staying here for a while?" she asked.

"Maybe for good," said Dallas.

The door now opened and a number of people, some of them already very drunk, entered the cabin.

Helen sprang to take possession of the brew pot. Some of these people showed signs of having started early on something more potent. She began pouring small doses for everyone, and Max passed out the mugs. Quite suddenly, there was a party going on.

"Here!" Henry spoke to Max. He was taking off his watch. "Christmas present for you."

"No, no. Got one of those already." Max was laughing.

"You think you got a better one?" Henry looked at the arm Max held out for inspection. "Give you my belt instead."

"Holy Smokes!" Max protested. It was a beadwork belt, a very elaborate one. Probably his wife had just finished making it for him.

Helen saw that Max had never been in on one of these potlatch sessions, where the men of the village gave away all their Christmas presents, usually to some worm-eaten whiteman like the Co-op manager.

Now he was getting a pair of embroidered slippers, a bead-fringed vest, a pair of beaver mitts. Max was bewildered, attempting to refuse.

Of course, he didn't understand the shame he was supposed to feel, the meanness of being a whiteman before the gratuitous generosity of the free people of the woods. But he ought to understand in a way, she thought, since he was, after all, a man who had that very afternoon given her a $4,000 necklace.

"I'm going to give all this back tomorrow!"

Women never did this kind of thing. But they made no protest as their art was displayed, their handiwork given away for nothing.

Helen found herself suffering a little from injured pride. What was Max to them? He had been here only a few months. She had lived over two years in this village and usually got five pounds of sugar or a little dry meat at Christmas, both from Sarah.

"Cut it out! I didn't give you guys anything!"

She glanced at Dallas. Dallas was watching serenely, still firmly in control of her mug of homebrew. But a man was sitting on the bed beside her. It was Eli Balah, the man who had given the girl named Rosaleen a white rug and two bad black eyes.

Without looking at him, Dallas passed her cup and he took a drink, then passed it back. Of course she would know him; they were probably cousins. But the gesture seemed so intimate, as though they were a couple of long-standing, that Helen was momentarily shocked.

"Now!" shouted Henry. "The wedding! Dearly beloved, this man and this woman been livin' in sin before our eyes three months now and it's time for them to get married."

"What?" Helen found herself being pressed forward into the limelight. "But we're married already! I mean, I'm married and Max is married."

"Just do what I tell you," ordered Henry. "I'm the Chief in this place and I'm goin' to see to it that you guys are legal."

They had stood her up beside Max, who was laughing silently.

"But you can't get married when you're married already!"

"You don't say," remarked Henry coolly. "Where's your dress?"

Somebody helpfully pulled the sheet off the bed, and Helen, still protesting and laughing, draped it around herself like a sari.

"Didn't bring my book. Get a book."

"Book got to be black."

"Helen got books."

"Hey, Henry! You can't be priest. You been married twenty years! Got five kids!"

"Nothing is impossible."

"She don't have a ring."

"Hey, look at that necklace, though."

Max prevented them from removing her necklace to pass it around. Then, on an inspiration of her own, Helen got the Air Carrier Act in its black binder from the second step of the loft stairs.

A man slumped by the wall, nearly comatose with liquor, began to sing a drum dance song slowly and haltingly, like a march rather than a dance.

"Shut up, Norman. The wedding goin' to start now. Stand there like that and I'll read you about what you got to do." Henry opened the Air Carrier Act, stared disgustedly at the page for a moment, then closed it again with a snap.

"Read it yourself," he suggested. "Thing is, I'm just here to pronounce you man and wife."

"The kiss, that comes next!"

"Hey! Call that a kiss?"

Max gave her a more interesting and thorough kiss. He was highly amused. His eyes were sparkling with pleasure.

"Have a dance now!"

"Can't have a dance. The drummers is all drinkin'!"

"Have a drink, then."

"I'm going to kiss the bride," announced Henry. He gave Helen a kiss of indecent length, then stepped back, grinning impudently at Max.

"Got to make sure there isn't any more sin around here," he said.

He seized a passing mug and pressed it into Max's hand.

Helen was trying to explain the necklace to a couple of people.

"Max gave it to me for Christmas," she said.

In the lamplight it looked less like a Woolworth toy.

"If my old man gave me a Christmas present like that—!"

"Jeez, I'd marry him too!"

"But we didn't really get married."

"Yep. I guess we married you all right."

"It's real pretty." Dallas was having a look.

"Pretty," agreed Helen. "But—"

Henry put his arm around Dallas' shoulders.

"You met my niece?" he said.

"Out by the fish trap this afternoon." Dallas disengaged herself calmly.

"You went out there?" Henry was surprised. He gave Dallas a shrewd look; he was not as drunk as he was pretending to be.

Dallas merely smiled.

Helen wondered whether Dallas knew that Henry had also paid his dues to the place that morning. But she had gone to sit down on the bed again beside Eli Balah.

The party went on. At last the brew ran out and they managed to escort the stragglers out the door. They had been trying to serve tea for the last half hour.

Max stretched, then yawned.

"Not even drunk, myself," he remarked.

"We didn't get much of a chance." Helen was tidying up. She put the sheet back on the bed.

"I had a nice time, though." He lit a cigarette and sat down, smoking peacefully.

Helen continued to clear up, reflecting on the party. It had been fun; they had received the blessing of Island Crossing.

Max was getting undressed.

"Got more Christmas presents today than I ever got before in my life," he said, looking down at the pile of gaudy clothes.

"You can't return them, you know."

"Made me feel kind of small." He got into bed. "I didn't even give anyone a bottle."

Helen hesitated. Then she said, "I have a present for you."

She went to get the charter license application. She gave it to him, then did the last chores and began to get undressed.

Max was very quiet.

Helen turned down the lamp, ready to blow it out. Then she looked over at the bed.

He had only got as far as the title page. He laid the application down on the quilt and looked at the ceiling.

"It's all right, Max," she said.

"I screwed this up, didn't I?" He stared upwards. "This was going to be a really great Christmas present, only I screwed it up."

"Well, it's all just a tissue of lies, anyway."

She was sorry she had shown it to him now. But they were going to be in a terrible predicament next month unless they sent the application in and got another operator's number in a hurry.

"Yeah, but I spent all the money. And you don't even think that thing I gave you is real."

"That's not true! I—"

He suddenly began to get out of bed, throwing back the quilt with energy. "Diamonds scratch glass, don't they?"

He was trying to unfasten the chain from around her neck.

"Don't." Helen put her hand over the pendant. "You gave it to me. I like it."

"I want to make sure it's real."

"Don't do it, Max," she pleaded. This was leading to disaster.

"I don't know why I didn't think of that before."

"You gave it to me. That's good enough, isn't it? I think it's beautiful."

"That's what I thought when I gave that guy the money. But now I'm not so sure."

He was insistently trying to take it out of her hand. Helen kept curling her fingers back over it. Finally she gave up. He took it.

Her heart sinking, she watched him go to the window overlooking the lake. He stood there with his back to her for some time, scraping the frost off the pane.

Helen felt like crying. She had screwed this up, not Max. How would he recover his pride; how could she ever make it up to him?

Max turned around, but Helen was now afraid to look at him. She got into bed miserably and slid down under the covers.

He blew out the lamp.

Then he sat down on the edge of the bed.

After a moment her eyes adjusted to the snowlight from the window and she saw that he was reaching for her. She put up her arms, but he began to refasten the necklace around her neck, bending down over her on the pillow. The pendant slid coldly into place against her sternum.

"There's no way of telling about the ruby."

"But the others—?"

"The diamonds are pretty big, though, so it's probably real too."

She wanted to tell him she was sorry, for being ungrateful, for doubting—there was something she was sorry for. But he was kissing her, seducing her, removing her from the realm of all sorrow.

It was the fatal allure of jewels again. The ruby was really sex itself, compressed into a tiny, brilliant package.

*

Max had to get up early the next morning to take the priest back to Buffalo Neck. When Helen awoke to the usual delicious smells of coffee and breakfast, he was sitting on the foot of the bed, already fully dressed for the weather outdoors. He was stowing her charter application back in its folder, then in its envelope.

"I finished reading this," he said.

"Was it all right?"

"It was like reading a novel," he replied.

They exchanged a smile.

He looked for a moment at the pendant hanging between her breasts.

"Anyway, I'm going to mail it."

"You really have to, I'm afraid."

"Well, I guess it'll take years for those flapjacks to get around to doing something about this. Maybe I'll make some money."

"No you won't. You never will!" She laughed, putting her hand over the pendant. It was already a familiar gesture, just making sure it was there.

"Maybe I will. By spring." He considered her for a moment. "It's beginning to make sense."

He kissed her briefly, looked again at the necklace, and went out the door with the envelope.

And from her position in bed, Helen now saw, sparkling in the light of the rising sun, a large heart drawn among the frost flowers on her picture window. Inside the heart she read the inscription:

M.M.
loves
H.A.

148

CHAPTER TWENTY-NINE
Making Friends With Dallas

HELEN MET Dallas several times in the next week, at the store and on the village road.

She had been curious about Dallas and she still was. Everything about her was a mystery: her background, but also her relationship with Eli Balah.

Helen was not sure what terms Dallas was on with her mother. She was shy of asking anything about their relationship, remembering the look of reserve that had crossed Dallas' face when she told Dallas that she was Sarah's friend. There was no way of revealing the secret connection she felt they had through Sarah.

Then Dallas invited Helen for a cup of tea at her house, and Helen went, looking forward to it, and glad just to get away from her small, stuffy house during the dark days.

It turned out that Dallas was living with Eli in his old father's shanty down at the church end of the lakefront.

There was no sign of Eli. The father was in the only bedroom behind a blue calico curtain. He was smoking, coughing incessantly. Maybe Dallas had given him money for cigarettes. Helen didn't think he usually got much of his pension cheque. Eli spent most of it at the bar in Mountain River or on bootleg hooch.

"When you're young, you pick someone, I guess," Dallas was explaining. "Eli and me picked ourselves a long time ago."

"But Dallas," said Helen. "Are you sure—?" She could understand that they might have picked one another at sixteen. But she felt Dallas knew nothing of what Eli was now.

"Nothing's sure," said Dallas. "But I knew I could stay here. I need a place to live until I have my baby."

"You're pregnant?"

"Going to have her in May." Dallas put her hand on her stomach lovingly. "She doesn't show much yet, does she?"

"But how do you know that it's going to be a girl?" Helen was laughing. Dallas wanted her baby to be a girl, that was clear.

"Oh, the doctor told me. She said I should have amnio. That's when they stick a needle in there to see if the baby's okay. And you are okay," she added to the baby. "You're already a girl."

"So that was the reason you came back!" Helen exclaimed.

"I'm a Woodcutter," said Dallas. "This is where I come from."

Helen could only understand this intellectually, since she had never had such a feeling—the strong pull of the place where you come from. But Dallas was part of a tiny, isolated linguistic group, even smaller than a tribe, which nevertheless had clung secretly, tenaciously, to a sense of its own tradition. It was what they cared about most of all, this spirit of place. It was why Dallas had visited the fish trap on snowshoes borrowed, by way of Abe Balah, from her mother.

"I always kind of wondered whether that was what was wrong with me, where it all started, that I wasn't born here. And I didn't want her to suffer the same way."

"You weren't born here?"

"I was born in Winnipeg. Mother kind of went crazy after her first family died. So she lived out there for a while and had me. Then she came back and married Ephraim Balah. He was my step-dad."

Helen remembered Sarah saying in her harsh, dry voice: I think she's been a whore. Maybe Sarah had been something like that herself; life for an Indian woman on the streets of Winnipeg probably had not changed very much in thirty years. But then, how could she be angry at Dallas?

"The baby's dad is a whiteman," Dallas was going on, dreamily. "The guy who produced that film I was in. He wanted me to marry him."

"But you didn't want to?"

"No. For one thing, he could never understand this."

This. Helen had been looking around at the house while Dallas talked. It represented a type of poverty and degradation that a clever, thirty-something Toronto filmmaker could never understand. The floor was made of bare boards save for a small square of torn linoleum. Several windows were broken, and one leg of the table had been damaged. There was no furniture to speak of: a cot mattress lay on the floor against the wall, and there were a couple of mismatched chrome chairs.

But the room also showed signs of Dallas' presence. For one thing, it was clean. The cracked windows had been mended with cardboard and tape. The table stood squarely on the floor, its leg lashed to a block of wood. A kettle simmered on the stove and there was a faint, appetizing odour of meat soup under the cigarette smoke.

Dallas got up restlessly and went to the door. She looked out. It was a nice day, with the cold, clear light of morning fading to a little pink in the west. The time was 2:00 in the afternoon.

"Let's go fishing," Dallas said. "Do you like to go fishing?"

"On the ice, you mean?"

"Yeah. I've got a couple of good holes. You like trout?"

"Of course."

They put on their winter clothes and trudged down to the lake with Dallas' gear: a hand axe, a couple of lines, and two bags of rags for kneeling on.

"I'm crazy about fishing," Dallas was saying. "Besides, I don't like to stay home all day with that old man listening."

Helen nodded. It was women's fishing again.

"That guy I was telling you about. The baby's father. He writes me letters. Wants to see her after she's born. Wants me to come stay with him in Toronto."

The idea of Dallas living with Eli and receiving such letters struck Helen as a little bizarre. Dallas was completely unfazed, however. Part of her charm was her honesty.

"Maybe I will," she said.

"Do you want to be an actress?"

"Maybe that too." Dallas laughed. "It was fun," she said.

"It would be a career for you, Dallas."

"Never had one of those before. Weren't you some kind of anthropologist when you came here?"

"Yes," said Helen. "But it was my husband who was the anthropologist."

They had left the village and were now striking out over the ice. After they got around the point, Helen recognized that Dallas was taking her to a familiar place, the riffle where Sarah had caught the pike.

"You had a husband, huh?"

They were going single file, Dallas walking ahead.

Helen reflected. She felt she could talk to this woman, calm, tender to her unborn child, and so independent, like Sarah.

"It was a bad marriage from beginning to end," she said. "He beat me."

Dallas nodded. "Some guys are like that," she said.

151

Some men are like that; it was the way they were, apparently. Was this true of Paul? It was so hard to explain that he was not a lout with a club, or a drunk, or some kind of psychopath.

"I screwed him up," said Helen.

"That's what you think," Dallas told her.

They had reached the riffle. The hole had filled in with ice, but Dallas at once jumped down fearlessly and began to chop it out again. Then she climbed up, panting slightly. Helen had already arranged the ragbags and the lines, and they now knelt on either side of the hole with the lines in their mittened hands, waiting under the pink and blue sky.

"Go on, tell me," said Dallas.

"I still thought he was wonderful, even when he was doing all those things: saying cruel things to me in public, making me do his typing and pointing out what a lousy typist I was, and, oh, pinching and shoving, that kind of stuff. The crazy thing is, I thought he was wonderful. I think I was always just trying to get his attention."

Dallas nodded, frowning at her line. She was jigging it a bit, impatiently.

"He knew that the way he could really get to me was by denying sex. And he did that. He did it a lot. So I had an affair. It was really just a one afternoon thing, with another student. It was nice. And it made me feel so guilty I went home and confessed."

Helen looked down at her line, which was jigging too. Her hands were trembling.

"Well, he was impotent after that. And he began to beat me up."

"Why didn't you just kick him out? You didn't have any kids or anything."

"But I was kind of spellbound. It's hard to explain."

"That's what they say," Dallas agreed. "I was in a centre doing therapy. Kicking my habit," she responded to Helen's look of inquiry. "I heard a lot of stories. Been beat up myself too, but I never stuck around with the guy."

"The horrible thing was that I had a secret weapon. We were torturing each other. He was so bright, so smart, he could lay out his arguments, utterly devastating arguments, but there was something he was ashamed of. Something I could get him with."

Dallas smiled at her. "You're pretty smart yourself, I think."

"So I went on doing it," said Helen. "Having affairs and telling him about them. Here too."

"Here?" Dallas was startled.

"With Henry."

"Oh, Henry!" She laughed. "I was thinking it might have been Eli. It's funny that could make me jealous."

She stood up and stretched.

"We're not getting anything here. Let's go to another place."

"Hang on." Helen had gotten a bite. A moment later, she pulled up a little trout, too small to keep. Dallas immediately took it from her and removed the hook.

"Want it?"

"No. But maybe we should stay here."

Dallas released the fish and crouched again on her ragbag.

"Go on," she commanded, dropping in her line.

"Well, after I told him about Henry a few times, he couldn't take it any more. So he really tried to kill me. That scared him so much that he left."

"And you stayed on."

"Your mother," said Helen. "She helped me. Maybe you don't know about her She's helped lots of women like me. She's saved some lives, I think."

Dallas said nothing. But she was looking kindly at Helen.

"So this guy you're with now—?"

"He's not like that at all." Helen spoke quickly. "But this isn't that kind of thing."

"You didn't get over the other one yet, huh?"

"No."

It was true. Even though she was living with Max almost as though they were a married couple, and even though he had openly declared that he loved her in the heart on the window, she felt a reservation that would not go away. There was something that was not settled, that could never be settled, between her and Paul.

Dallas seemed to be turning something over in her mind too.

"Eli," she said at last. "I think he's that way. Like your husband."

Helen knew he was. As far as she was concerned, Eli was a lout with a club. It was even more mysterious how Dallas could care for him if she understood what he was like.

"I don't want to marry him. But I don't want to marry a whiteman, either. It's not that I don't want a man." Dallas looked perplexed. "But I want to be free too."

"You're very brave, Dallas."

"No, I'm not."

"But you're trying to make your own way."

"Yeah. I don't want it to be like that, but it seems to be the only way I can do it."

The water in the hole, which had been gently icing over in the cold of the afternoon, was suddenly boiling with fish. Dallas pulled one in, and Helen got one right after her. Then Dallas dropped in her hook and got another. Helen knotted a new leader with her freezing fingers, then dropped the spoon on the ice with a clatter. Dallas, the daughter of her mother, reached over and firmly pressed her line into Helen's hand, then picked up the leader and spoon while Helen caught a fourth fish.

They walked home somewhat later in the sunset light with five fish. They were cold and tired, but they were friends. As they parted, Dallas said:

"Let's go fishing again, okay?"

CHAPTER THIRTY
What It's All About

GARULUK PHONED them up in January. He got Helen. Max was flying, as usual.

"They're drivin' me out of business," he said hoarsely.

"Yes, but we're not going to bring back the plane," she told him. "We'll get another number somehow."

"So I did what I had to. It was the only way. Too much trouble around here."

"Financial trouble? Or was it legal trouble?" asked Helen delicately.

"Religious trouble." He breathed heavily into the receiver.

His wife, Helen recalled.

"Too much sin," she said. "Is that it? Whisky, adultery, things like that?"

"The church is getting into the business," he told her. "They've got my Cub already."

"Do you mean—" The light was dawning on Helen slowly. "But do they have a charter license?"

"First they were just flyin' preachers around. But now—"

"They realized there was money in sin," said Helen thoughtfully.

"So we worked out the lease. They're givin' me 10 per cent."

She explained the situation to Max that night.

"At least we have a number again," she concluded. "Garuluk has turned all his affairs over to the church, apparently."

"Oh boy! The Holy-bolies." He rolled over. They were in bed as usual.

"But it doesn't make any difference to us, does it? They're going to give Garuluk 10 per cent for the lease."

"Thought that was all the church was supposed to get," he said. "But anyway, these 10 per cent deals aren't legal. There's some damn thing called a dry lease—"

"What a terminology there is in this business! Haywire, chisel-charter, dry lease..."

"Lot of dirty words as far as I'm concerned." He smiled at her. "Still enjoying yourself?"

"Really, I am. What's the name of this church anyway?"

"Holy Rocker Congregation. They don't dance."

"I should hope not. Dance? Mrs. Garuluk?" Helen was diverted.

"The rocking is some kind of trance the preacher goes into. Agaric was telling me about it one time."

"I'd like to see that." Helen had once taken a course on the practices of obscure Protestant sects.

"There's probably a lot of money in it," said Max dreamily. "Wish I'd thought of it myself."

"Money," she said. She didn't care much about money. But it mattered to Max. "Is that what it's all about?"

"What?" He raised himself on his elbow, interested.

"Well, life. Why you're doing this. Flying."

"It's why I'm doing this, yeah." He considered. "But it's not what it's all about."

"What is it all about then?" She really wondered how he would answer this question.

"Some guy asked me something like that once. I was flying helicopter fuel to a forest fire. Forestry took me. Couldn't say no, even though I was doing something else. And they make you go till you drop in your boots. Loading forty-five-gallon barrels, no one to help, and the dock was covered with six-inch spikes all set to rip open the floats. Anyway, there was this flapjack from a newspaper hanging around."

"A reporter?"

"Yeah. The guy kept asking questions like, 'You like flying? What is it you like about flying?' I'd been going forty-eight hours by then. Told him I hated it. I really did, too. Finally he said, 'Thought flying'd be the thing you really enjoy doing. So what do you like to do? What do you like to do most in the world?'"

"And you answered—?"

Max was laughing, his guilty laugh. He turned over on his back.

"Told him, screwing a woman," he said. "Screwing a woman. That's what I like doing most in the world."

Helen thought of the fifty women Max had slept with, not counting her. She rolled her eyes.

"That got rid of him. Don't know whether he even bothered to write it down. I guess he thought I was going to say fishing or mowing the lawn."

But from another point of view, it was true. Max did like it, she was sure, more than anything else in the world. He liked sex more than any man she had ever known.

"Being here like this," he went on, "it's what it's all about."

She rolled over on top of him and he clasped her upper arms in his hands, a firm, warm clasp. They were lapped around in peace: the slight crackling of the fire, the yellow light of the lamp, the snoring of the dog on the rug. She was soothed by the way they lay together, by their idle, playful conversation. This peace and intimacy was a kind of trough created by their lovemaking. They had already made love; they were going to again, probably quite soon.

"I just can't figure it out," he said. "That guy you were married to."

He knew there was more to it. But she couldn't tell him what she had told Dallas.

There was something so bad about what she had done to Paul, she felt that it would harm Max too.

"You had a wife yourself," she parried.

"I told you. I was sleeping with other women. Not sleeping with her. She got kind of a rotten deal. Married her before they invented sex."

"When was that?"

"The year I was twenty-five," he replied promptly.

"Was that how old you were when you got married?"

"No. I was twenty-two."

Helen laughed.

"Must be living life backwards or something," he continued. "Found out about sex after I had a wife and two kids. Didn't meet you till I was forty."

"Me?"

"You." He looked into her eyes.

But Helen couldn't come to terms with this idea, either. She had not been able to digest her marriage into something funny and bitter the way he had. She felt in her heart that she would never marry again; she could never have children. The love of all innocent things would never be hers.

She put her face down on his shoulder. He stroked her hair.

"So now I'm working for the Holy-bolies," he said. "Well, I knew you'd think of something."

CHAPTER THIRTY-ONE
Freddy and Mickey

Dark February passed and it was March. Almost spring, with two more winter months to go.

One night Max came home from Mountain River with Mickey. Mickey became extremely sulky when he saw Helen. She was waiting for Max, as usual, by the power pole at the end of the airstrip.

They walked home, Max explaining cheerfully, while Mickey said nothing.

"Thing is, if you're going to drop out of school, go stay with somebody who's going to make you go back sometime. Happened to me too. And I went back."

Helen wondered whether Max did not see, or was merely ignoring for reasons of his own, the marks of a fight on Mickey.

He had hitchhiked to Mountain River, it seemed; no easy thing, as Mountain River was connected to the outside world very tenuously by a marginal road built every winter that lasted only through the cold months.

He refused to call his mother, even when Helen suggested it, and Max seemed willing to let him have his way about this too.

They had a rather silent meal. Mickey was sullen. Helen felt invaded, although she tried not to show it. Max seemed preoccupied. Afterwards he laid out a sleeping bag for Mickey in the loft.

"At least he picked me to come to," he told Helen later when they were in bed.

Unfortunately, with dark February gone, Max was busy again. So it was Helen who got Mickey, even though he had not picked her, nor had she picked him.

At first, he sulked. He didn't like her being there. But then he got used to Helen and became critical of everything else. There were no teenage amenities in Island Crossing. Helen had no TV, no stereo, no VCR, and she never listened to the radio.

Mickey would have nothing to do with the children in the village, and it was true there were very few of his age. He was extremely bored.

He lay around all day reading comic books, turning the radio on and off, and complaining.

Max made him do things. He made him take a bath, chop wood, remove his boots before coming inside. But Max was not much at home. And Helen did not want to be this one's mother. The situation might have been better with Freddy.

But one thing was clear: Mickey had come because of trouble with Christopherson.

Dinner with Mickey. It was muskrat. He wouldn't touch it. He wanted pizza, or spaghetti, or burgers and fries.

"Well, eat the potatoes, anyway," said Max. "Then your teeth won't drop out."

Lunch with Mickey. He ate whole jars of olives, or peanut butter in globs on a spoon.

Breakfast with Mickey. He didn't get up for breakfast. Sometimes Max hassled him and he came downstairs just as his father was going out the door.

Mickey destroyed Helen's privacy. She was used to being alone. Now she was never alone. And he was destroying her love life. They made love furtively, late at night, but only when Max was not too tired to stay awake.

But when she wished that Freddy had come instead, she had had no idea how soon that wish would be granted.

Freddy showed up less than ten days later, coming in with Max on a late afternoon trip from Mountain River. He had hitchhiked, like Mickey.

She heard the two boys talking.

"Fucking Chris," said Mickey. "What'd he do to you?"

"Nothing," said Freddy.

"Asshole. Bumsucker."

"Shut up!"

"So why'd you take off?"

"Mom."

"Was he fucking around with her again? I'll fucking kill him next time—"

"Why do you have to be so fucking stupid? She cried for about three days after your stupid showdown. I figured I had to go after you."

"How'd you know where I went?"

"You stole the address off me. I'm not as dumb as you are, see?"

If Freddy had turned up first, she might have been able to get the whole story out of him. But he had come out of solidarity with Mickey, and their solidarity put her on the outside. Looking at their blank faces, she realized how hard it would be to be their mother; but under the circumstances it was even harder to be herself.

Max was beginning to get a blank look himself.

"What are you going to do about them, Max?" she asked him one night under cover of darkness. "There's no school for them to go to here."

"Yeah, I know."

"And there's nothing for them to do. They can't really stay with you."

"Yeah."

She felt he was being defensive.

"I don't want to complain."

He gave a faint snore.

Helen met Dallas in the store. She was beginning to look pregnant now.

"Want to go fishing again soon?"

"Let's go for a walk right now." Helen wanted to pour out her irritation to someone who would sympathize.

They walked along the lakeshore.

"Make 'em do stuff," Dallas suggested.

"I do. I tell them to get wood and things. They do it. Then they go upstairs and fall down flump! on their sleeping bags. They're like robots; they only respond to direct commands."

"You know it's spring. There's a lot going on in the bush. I want to go out, but Eli—" Dallas broke off, turning her face away.

"Is Eli drinking?" Helen asked bluntly. Dallas was really not looking very well.

"Yeah."

"Can't you stay somewhere else, Dallas? Can't you stay with Sarah?"

Dallas shook her head. She said nothing.

But Helen had decided she had to talk to Dallas about Sarah.

"Sarah was my friend," Helen said. "She was really my only friend in the world. After—after what I told you about, she was the one who took me in. But she got mad at me when she was sick before Christmas. And then she shut me out. And it's still that way. Is it that way with you too?" She looked inquiringly at Dallas.

Dallas nodded.

"It was really because of you that she got mad at me, I think," Helen went on. "She was calling herself bad, and saying she wanted to die. Then she began to talk

160

about how she thanked God when you were born; how it even gave her back her faith to have a baby again after the others died. When I told her she should answer your letters and let you come home because she still needed you, she got very fierce with me."

They stood side by side looking out over the ice-bound lake with its waves of snow.

Helen said:

"I'll always love her. I'm very worried about her too. I can't understand what Abe Balah is doing there all the time."

"Why him, you mean?" asked Dallas. "He's my step-dad's brother."

"He is?" Helen knew that family relationships were always significant here. But Helen had been wondering what his involvement was and whether it was part of what was the matter with Sarah.

Dallas was looking at her now.

"Do you know she shot my step-dad?"

It was a shock to be told, even though Helen had heard part of the story before.

"That's why I left," Dallas continued steadily. "Took me a long time to understand some things. Why she did that. I think I do now. But she still won't let me see her."

"But what is Abe Balah doing to Sarah? Is he hurting her? Is he keeping you away?" Was it revenge?

"Abe?" said Dallas in surprise. "He wouldn't hurt her. He's helping out, that's all. You said she was sick."

"Really?" Helen was incredulous. "But why would he do that? Didn't you tell me he was the brother of your stepfather?"

"I think it's because they picked each other way back," Dallas replied. "But something got in the way. In those days, it was up to your parents who you married."

Helen was amazed. It was something she could never have guessed.

Abe was in love with Sarah. And was Sarah in love with him? Helen realized that she was resisting this idea partly out of jealousy. Dallas said they had picked each other and that must mean that Sarah had secretly loved Abe all these years.

It explained why Abe had shown up when Sarah got sick and why he had all her things now. There was nothing sinister about it; it was even a little romantic.

Helen had never thought romance was a motive anyone in Island Crossing had for doing anything. Apparently she was wrong, as she so often was.

161

Dallas touched Helen's arm and they turned around and began to walk back to Eli's house. "Better come have tea," she said.

The house was no longer so tranquil and orderly, so Helen guessed Eli was drinking at home too. It was hard for Dallas, a mistake to have gone to him, but she had no other place to go.

Helen was not looking forward to going home herself.

"Maybe I can get Eli to do something with those kids of yours," said Dallas.

*

It seemed wrong that the boys had not told anyone what had happened at home. Max was doing nothing to find out; Helen had the feeling he didn't want to know.

She decided to work on Freddy. Freddy was the only one who would tell her anything, she was sure.

"Stop a minute."

Mickey had already gone upstairs and dropped on his bedroll with a clatter of boot heels and elbows. She apprehended Freddy before he could go up.

"Freddy, what are you going to do? Can't you go back?"

He looked at her in terror, paralysed like a rabbit.

"What happened?"

He swallowed.

"Look, just tell me, did Mickey have a fight with—?"

He nodded.

"And your mother? Was it because Christopherson was hurting her?"

He was pale and sweating. He didn't want her to know. Why was it always the lot of victims to be ashamed, she wondered.

"Does she have any idea where you are?"

"With Dad."

Helen was horrified. They had run away. But what was happening to Missy?

Suddenly he was going upstairs on all fours like a monkey, and she realized that she'd let up on the pressure too soon and he'd escaped.

Perhaps this was what it was like to be the parent of troubled adolescents. Her sister had been a troubled adolescent but in a different way, sexually rebellious and violently articulate, to the shock of their reserved, upper-middle-class parents. These children did nothing but sleep and lie around restlessly. They were rude to her, but only by omission. She felt that she was not a source of grievance to them, merely an inconvenience like no TV and an outdoor toilet.

And Max was now never home.

They had gotten a small contract with the government through the game warden to haul fuel out to caches within a few hundred miles of Mountain River. The Beaver was the right size for the job; the caches were small and far-flung, and Max was spending his time in Mountain River, nights as well as days. He came into Island Crossing when he picked up a trip. There he changed his clothes and looked exhaustedly at his dissatisfied children and his annoyed mistress.

CHAPTER THIRTY-TWO

Nunc aut Nunquam

Dear Helen,

Nunc aut nunquam, I'm afraid. (That means now or never, Helen. I don't suppose you learned Latin in school.) Anyway, nunc.

But keep your hair on, dear. This is business strictly, with tents, winter camping gear, and also very carefully measured quantities of food.

And me. I am coming too. I am looking forward to seeing you.

Keep well and don't worry, okay?

Marion

P.S. It will be soon. Expect us by April 1st.

CHAPTER THIRTY-THREE

Now

S HE WENT home, desperate to be alone, but the boys were there.

Helen had a sleepless night. The boys were still there in the morning. They went out after lunch and, to her surprise, they were gone for quite some time.

When they came back they were behaving very strangely. Helen had been out herself chopping wood and shovelling snow in an effort to dispell the dense fog of despair that surrounded her. They seemed to be having some kind of feast when she came in, with peanut butter and oranges and large quantities of sliced bread. Later, while she sat unseeing on her bed, they went upstairs and stamped around, arguing in whispers, but she wasn't listening.

So Paul was coming back. She ought to have prepared, to have written, gotten a lawyer, concentrated her powers somehow.

The boys came downstairs quietly and put on their winter clothes. Then they went out together.

It was such a relief to be alone that she did not consider for a few minutes where they could have been going. But then she realized that they had been carrying their bedrolls.

Following the spoor upstairs, she found the loft in an appalling state. The worst part was the stink of dirty clothes, which were dumped around in heaps, apparently just as they had been shucked off: two pools of socks with concentric underpants and jeans, the shirts as a kind of shrubbery to one side.

Going back down to the kitchen, she found that they had eaten or taken all the bread and all the peanut butter, leaving the jar behind, its top screwed on crookedly.

She put on her boots and parka and tracked them into town. Henry overtook her as she lost the trail by the old freezer shack behind the Catholic mission.

"Got rid of 'em for a couple of days, eh?" he said in good humour.

"Really? They didn't bother to tell me."

"Oh, they went off with Eli. Strong young bull moose like that: do 'em good to get out in the bush."

"What? Where did they go?"

"Out on his dad's place, I guess." He indicated a mountain about sixty miles off with an airy wave.

"My God, Henry! They went to the bush with Eli? Will they be all right?"

"Why not?" He shrugged.

"Well, but—Eli!"

"Hey, Eli's all right. He was born out there, know that? He's a pretty useful guy when it comes to cold weather and living rough."

Helen was surprised to hear any good of Eli, even from Henry, whose political instincts didn't always permit him to speak the truth. She looked down the skidoo tracks leading out of town. It was too late to stop them. But if something happened, how could she ever explain to their mother?

"So your old man's coming back here," Henry went on briskly, turning her away from the skidoo trail and walking back with her towards town.

"Yes," she said. He would know, of course. Paul had probably called him.

"Coming back to stay with you?"

"No!"

"But it's the same deal, I guess," said Henry. "Writing a book, he said. He'll have to stay somewhere."

"Not with me."

"How much could you make out of a book like that? A book on us."

Henry was convinced that anthropologists must live very high on the hog thanks to information they had got from him. What perplexed him was how to take advantage of this scam himself, how to cut out the middleman. Helen had stopped trying to argue with him when she realized that a tenured job at a university, a house, two cars, a summer cottage, and a yearly trip to Europe or some even more interesting part of the world was riches by any standard. And all of this could be based on information Henry gave someone like Paul.

He seemed to notice her abstraction.

"Going to have some trouble with him over your other old man, I guess," he remarked with a grin.

This was, in fact, what she was thinking about.

"Well, I'm your friend. As long as I'm running the Co-op, you're welcome to come see me in my office anytime," he said.

"Very funny."

Helen went home and looked despairingly around her disorderly house.

She was still worried about the boys. But she was angry at them as well. They should have told her they were going with Eli. She was even angrier at Max. The boys were just boys, after all, but she was not their mother. Max was never home any more; he was not their mother either. In fact, he had been letting them drive him away from her, she realized with grim humour. She had now joined his family—or it had joined her—and Max was taking his usual initiative, running away.

What did she see in him in any case? She wondered what it was she had ever seen in him. Had they met in some larger place, a city, she would never have dreamed of living with him; she would probably never have slept with him. The only thing he had going for him was that they had met in Island Crossing.

No one should base a relationship on geographical accident. No one should have to do as much explaining as she was going to have to do shortly when Paul and Marion arrived.

Suddenly, she came up short again, foundered on this fact.

She was going to have to fight, possibly for her life.

Paul wanted his notes. She couldn't give them to him. He was going to demand his diaries. He could never have his diaries again. The house was only a minor issue compared to those notes, those diaries. His whole life was invested in them, and she could not let him have them.

For they were what invaded her most of all. Paul was only mortal, but he knew and she knew that he intended those notes and diaries to live forever. He wanted to give her iniquity eternal life.

She had to be strong. She had to fight.

She began by packing Max's suitcase.

*

But it was not until the next evening that she heard the sound of the Beaver. She had been sitting dully at the table for some time, so she continued sitting there.

When Max came in it was a far cry from the way he had come home in the winter.

He did not bother taking off his coat and boots, but just came straight in, poured himself a cup of coffee from the leftovers on the stove and sat down at the table opposite her. He cleared a small area and began to write up his log book, not seeming to notice the orange peels and other debris lying there.

He looked up at her briefly, making a sound of greeting, and then went on with his calculations, his lips moving as he added up the columns.

Helen felt bitter tears spring to her eyes. In the winter, their cozy house, Max's joy at arriving home, the smell of rabbit stew, the way he used to fling himself on their bed: it was all gone—as if it had never been. Their love affair was really over. She had to face it if he could not.

This was the person who had been Missy's husband.

"Max," she said at last. "Did you know the boys were going to the bush?"

"No." He went on adding. He didn't look up.

"They didn't tell me, either."

He made no reply. She had not captured his attention.

"You haven't been home for days."

"It's this gas haul."

"Well, maybe that's true."

"Maybe?" He paused, looking up at her in surprise. "*Maybe* it's true?"

"Well, all right. It's true. But I think you should be looking after your kids a little better."

"But they're here." He seemed not to have grasped that she was really angry at him.

Was she? Was she really angry at him?

Helen now began to speak vehemently.

"They're here. But I wish somebody else cared a damn what they do while they're here. They can't communicate with me apparently."

"Kids—" he began.

"Yes, but they're your kids, not mine. They leave their junk all over the house. You should see the upstairs. And this—" Helen indicated the table, strewn with stale food. "They never pick up anything, even their own pop cans. And they don't help with anything—they won't even move unless I give them a direct order."

Max looked at her, then around the messy room.

"But it's not just that. It's you too. You're gone all the time. The contract, yes, but I think you're avoiding the whole problem. Whenever you're here you're asleep."

"I've been pretty busy."

"You aren't even worried about them, are you?"

"Where'd they go?"

168

"To Mount Denys—with Eli, for God's sake."

"Didn't they say anything before they left? Didn't you talk to them?"

"They never say anything! They took their sleeping bags. I noticed that after they went out. What if they get lost? What if they get hurt? It'll be my fault!"

"Helen—" He waved his arm helplessly. Once she had found this gesture amusing and charming. Now it seemed to express not ironic submission to fate, but his own inability to cope.

"Did *I* talk to them? How can you ask *me* that? Do you ever talk to them? Or to me any more?"

Max was now running his hand through his hair and she found herself hating this mannerism as well.

"But that's not all," she went on. "This is my place. It's the only place I've got. You moved in. That was all right. We had a nice time. But now we're not having a nice time. We're having a dreadful time. We're not even having a time, you and I. It's all over between us."

"All over?"

"Well, when were you last at home? When did we last sleep together? When did we last talk to each other? Not in weeks. Not since they arrived. That was weeks ago, Max."

"But they won't be here forever."

"How do I know that?"

"They're just—"

"On the lam. Something terrible happened. You never asked them what it was. You never even called Missy to tell her they're here."

"Okay, I'll call her! I'll talk to them, too."

"You can't do that now, though," she said coldly. "Neither of us knows exactly where they are."

"But it isn't over between us."

He got up and approached her persuasively. He had a three days' growth of beard. And he smelled a little, of the bush and of sweat.

She put out her hand to prevent him touching her. She was quivering with tension.

"I think it is."

"Sure, my life is a mess. I wish I hadn't got you into all that. I never tried to get you into it."

"Well, maybe that's the whole point, Max. You just let things like this happen."

"Yeah, but lately I've been trying—"

"Lately!" She snorted.

"I didn't know they were going to come," he protested. "And I've been working."

"Okay." Helen took a step back as he took a step forward. She realized that so far all she had managed to express was her frustration about his kids. She didn't want him to think that she was bringing their relationship to an end because she didn't want to look after his kids. She had to tell him about Paul.

"I'm going to do something—" he was saying.

"No. Don't do anything. You can't do anything, anyway. There's something else. Look, Max, my life is a mess too. I asked you to stay here and that was all right for a while. But I've got my own problems and I've got to work them out alone."

There was a pause.

"What are you talking about?" he asked.

She saw that she had not explained anything.

"I got a letter from Marion today. Oh, you don't even know who Marion is! Marion Karnagowski-Weagle is a very well-known anthropologist. She's my husband's academic advisor. Anyway, they're coming here. He's coming here and so is she. This month. To work on his project. To finish it."

"Is he moving in here?" asked Max. He spoke quietly.

"No. He's not moving in here. I'm staying here. Right here in this house. It's mine. And I'm going to fight for it."

"You think you hate him. But maybe you don't. Maybe you still love him."

"I don't! You don't understand. I did something awful to him. But what he did to me—I'll never forgive him for that. It's not even a question of forgiveness. It's a question of revenge. But it's going to be clear. Just so he knows that it is revenge. No mess. No complications."

"Me, I'm a complication?"

"You are. If he's going to come here, I need to be able to fight. I don't want to make it easy for him. There aren't going to be any reasons but the real ones."

"Like me being in love with you? Or maybe you being in love with me?"

"I'm not in love with you," she said. Seeing his face as she said this, she felt a wrench. "Look Max," she continued. "I'm sorry. We had a nice time. But it's really over. You have to face that. Perhaps I wasn't ready to have a man—somebody who had problems of his own. Maybe I'll never be ready."

"You think this is pretty simple," he said.

"No, I don't. I'm just trying to make it as simple as I can."

"Yeah, but you're not facing things either. You said *reality*, you said *life*. There's no way you can make life simple. You can't just tell me to get out like that. Like, I'm sorry, it was fun, but now, get out!"

She had made him angry at last.

"You liked me as long as things were going pretty well, but as soon as they got tough, you decided to get rid of me."

She suddenly couldn't speak. She had never been able to fight back effectively, using words, or any other way.

"You're ashamed of me," he went on. "You're not saying that, but it's true. Me in my dirty clothes with my kids in trouble, meeting your educated friends. You don't even want your husband to know I exist."

He was right. Max in his dirty clothes with his kids in trouble, was just the right sort of handle for Paul. She wanted to offer him nothing, no personal detail of any kind, that he could turn against her.

"And what's all this about revenge? I don't know what you're doing to him. Because it seems as though you're taking it all out on me."

"No! I'm not trying to hurt you!"

She was trying not to cry. His being angry seemed to help.

"Well, you are hurting me! What you said about the kids was true. I see what a—a flapjack I was about that. But this. I don't get this at all. I was giving it everything I had, this thing I've got with you, Helen. You started me off. You wanted it to be a success, that's the only reason I was working this hard, and now you tell me you're going to kick me out and that'll make it simple?"

"Maybe it won't. But I can't handle everything, not all at once."

"Well, I can't either. I came home to do up three days' worth of log book entries and get a few hours sleep. Now you kick me out. Where can I get a bed?"

"You could go to the Co-op," she suggested. "Henry would let you use the manager's apartment."

"You thought of that, did you?" He folded his arms.

"Please don't be mad, Max. I packed your suitcase."

"You had it all planned out, did you? Have to get rid of me fast, because—when's he get here?"

"Soon. Tomorrow, maybe."

She felt miserable, even ashamed. But she had no time for these emotions

"And that's all there is to it. Like a one night stand? We had a good time. Now it's over. Goodbye."

171

"Yes."

"Well, maybe it is over then."

He took up the log book, stuffing it into the front of his vest. Helen realized that she had never seen him angry before. When he tripped over his suitcase in the porch and exclaimed, "Holy Smokes!" she nearly ran after him, but he went out the door, taking the suitcase with him, and she remained in her house alone.

After a moment she went over to the table, put her head down and began to cry.

There was a sound of aircraft noise over the lake. Max had taken off and was heading for Mountain River.

When she finally finished crying, she sat at the table trying to prepare herself for the contest with Paul.

But her house, for the first time since she had lived there alone, was sending her a contrary signal. Where is Max? it was asking.

CHAPTER THIRTY-FOUR

Never

HELEN STAYED home for the next two days. She was afraid to go out. Paul would be in Island Crossing and she had to be ready, she had to be in possession, waiting for him. It was the only high ground she had.

The afternoon of the second day she heard the Beaver come in and then take off again. Max must have brought someone in, probably Paul and Marion. But she did not go out to see. She stayed home, tensely marshalling her resources. They would have to set up camp first.

Paul came in the morning. He was alone, as she expected.

Paul couldn't afford to have Marion see what it was like between them. He would probably have put this in conventional terms to Marion: something about needing to talk, something about privacy. Marion always went along with conventional explanations. They aroused her curiosity since she lived almost outside of convention herself. She liked seeing how things like that worked.

He didn't bother to knock, but she had heard his footsteps and merely continued to sit at the table.

There was something different about him. He was still a good-looking man, tall and slim, with blond hair and aquiline features. Now there was something else about him, something less suited to his austerity, his authoritarian personality. Perhaps it was the way he was dressed: hiking boots, rugby pants, preppy, colour-blocked parka.

He was standing on the threshold, looking around the house. But he was keeping his distance. After a moment, she guessed that he was frightened of her; or rather, not of her, but of what he might do to her.

She had not realized so clearly until now that he shared her terror. But she had taken her revenge. She expected him to get his.

"You finished it," he was saying. "Quite a good job, really."

"It's mine," said Helen. "I live here. You're trespassing."

"I know."

She was surprised. Was he being conciliatory?

He came over and sat down opposite her. He took off his toque and ruffled his short hair with his fingers.

"I just want the degree," he said finally.

"I don't care."

"That letter I wrote you was a mistake. I know that. I should never have sent it."

"You shouldn't have," she agreed.

"I was frustrated. I didn't understand you then. It seemed to me that you were playing some petty game of revenge. But I understand things better now."

"You think you do."

"I know you've been living here, brooding about it. I understand you. I even understand myself. I've had therapy. I put in time, Helen."

"So what?"

"So you say. But you haven't sat in a circle with a bunch of thugs and murderers and said: I beat my wife. I'm sick. I did that. Do you know what that's like? No, you don't." He was vehement.

Helen was startled. He had been in therapy, and evidently he saw that as penance. It was a surprise that he had humbled himself enough to ask for that kind of help. But she didn't believe it could really have made a difference.

"You aren't going to apologize," she said in sarcasm.

"I wasn't going to, no. Do you want me to?"

"Yes! I want you to go down on your knees, Paul."

"You're still angry, aren't you?"

"Yes."

"You need help, I think," he said.

He was exactly the same. Underneath it all, he was as arrogant as ever. He understood himself and he understood her in exactly the same way he had before. Under some description everything he did was right, everything she did was wrong. With him it was prevarication, with her it was lying; with her it was murder, with him, self-defence. He had put in time; she was seeking petty revenge, she was brooding, she still needed help.

He was now telling her something in the jargon of the headdoctors, as Dallas called them. It was strange to hear the drivelling terminology of her sister issuing from his mouth.

"Don't tell me that stuff."

"Maybe I'm trying to help you, Helen."

"No, you're not. I know why you're here. I know what you want."

He paused.

"I want my notes and my diaries," he said.

"But you are never going to get them."

He looked at her, startled. Helen suddenly felt exhilarated.

"You'll never get them. Do you know why?"

"Is it because of the diaries? Helen, I swear—"

"Go ahead and swear. You won't get them."

"Let's get this out in the open. There's a reason why you're scared to give me the diaries, I see that. But I'm not writing a popular novel about you, Helen. You screwed the Chief. Christ! You even screwed my friends. But how am I going to use it against you. And those diaries are my life. My whole life!"

She shook her head.

"As for the notes, look at it this way. What is it to you? I just want my Ph.-fucking-D., that's all. How does that affect you?"

He was becoming agitated. But she was amazed at how well he contained himself. He remained sitting down, glaring at her, but still seated.

"Do you know why?" she repeated. "You don't know why."

"All right, I'll crawl. I beat up on you, Helen. That's true. I did that. But Jesus! It happened once. And there was a lot of provocation."

"It wasn't once."

"All right, it wasn't once."

The eye contact between them flickered. Then he looked down at his fingernails, spreading out his hands on the table. It was astonishing how well he was keeping his gestures under control.

"That's not why, though," she said. "You can't have them, and that's not why."

"Then why?" he demanded.

"I burned them."

"What?" He leapt to his feet.

"I burned everything."

"You didn't."

"I did."

"You can't have!"

"I did!" She stood up to face him, turning her head to look up at him. He was a tall man.

"I don't—believe you." He was speaking through his teeth.

"Right here in this stove."

He was going to hit her now. She saw him raise his hand, and although she didn't want to, she shut her eyes and ducked—a reflex.

When she looked again, he was just standing there. Perhaps he had put his hand down quickly. It was at his side. Or perhaps she had merely imagined him raising it.

He shook his head. "No," he said.

"I really did."

"I really don't believe you."

He sat down again.

Helen became aware that someone else in the room had an opinion about this conversation. It was Bootleg. He was standing right beside her, gazing intently at Paul, his neck ruff slightly elevated. She was not the only one who had seen or imagined Paul's raised hand.

She sat down too.

"With your background—" Paul was saying.

"You don't know what I can do!" she cried. "You thought you transformed me into an intellectual. And then you spent years telling me I was a half-wit. Now you're pretending my background wouldn't permit me to burn your papers?"

"When did you do it?"

"After you left. You left them behind, after all."

"I was out of my mind," he muttered. "Why did I leave them behind?"

"Because you thought you were never coming back. Why did you come back?" But this was not going quite as she had imagined it. Slightly stunned, Helen put her hand up to her forehead.

"You've rehearsed this," he said suddenly, acutely.

"What?"

"This is basically a trap, isn't it? You don't want me to get better. You can't imagine that I tried!"

Helen watched him struggling for self-possession. But he was not going to hit her. It was strange. He was not going to kill her, either. The ultimate catharsis had not occurred. He was merely trying not to cry. Helen felt rather like crying herself.

The dog lay down.

"All right. But I don't believe you burned them. You've hidden them somewhere. I understand that this is your revenge. You hate me, et cetera. But you couldn't have burned them."

"You can look around if you like. But they aren't here."

To her surprise he did look around. He even went up to the loft. He looked in the kitchen cupboards, under the mattress.

"This place is a mess," he said. "Who are you sleeping with?"

She had not touched anything in the house since Max left. Helen realized that the house betrayed her.

"I've often wondered whether it was just for my benefit or whether your whorish behaviour would continue after I left."

"Whorish behaviour—"

"Well, your promiscuity then. Your nymphomania. I know you don't like the words. But it was what destroyed our marriage, after all. You slept with my friends. You slept with everyone. Who are you sleeping with now?"

Helen was mute. He was still smarter than she was. She had forgotten that for a while. Nothing escaped him.

"That pilot who brought us in," he said. "He must be the one."

He was looking at her closely.

"But you don't really know what you're doing with him, do you?" His voice was cold. "Maybe you think you're just fooling around. But that kind of guy's a complete cynic about women, believe me. He'd have made the rounds in a place like this before he got to you. And he probably doesn't much care what he leaves behind him, either: kids, syphilis—"

"That's not true."

"No? So I'm right? Well, I think I ought to warn you then."

"Shut up, Paul. This is none of your—"

"Maybe it is, though. Maybe it is my business. You're still my wife. I think you need to know the facts of life. That guy is probably married too. Did he tell you that?"

"You don't know anything about my life!"

"He's probably married and he's slept with everything female in the village. Doesn't that bother you?"

"Stop it."

"You know, what you're doing isn't just sick, it's kind of dirty. Now I'll tell you what," he continued. "I'm going to stay here. I'm going to work here. And you'll have to see me every day and put up with it. You could eliminate the problem by giving me back my things. But you won't. Maybe you will after you've had to put up with it for a while. You're going to find this pretty unbearable, living in my house, seeing me every day—"

"It's not your house!"

"It is, of course. I built it. Even your friend, the Chief—you should hear his opinion. It might surprise you."

It didn't surprise her. Henry would bide his time, waiting to see who was going to win. He was on Paul's side when he had to talk to him on the phone.

"And now, goodbye. But it's not goodbye, Helen. I'll be here."

He went out.

He did not even slam the door, to her annoyance.

This was the worst nightmare. He had not believed her. He intended to torture her for things she did not possess.

She had rather expected to be dead by now. Or at least very badly hurt.

But he had simply refused to believe her.

Then she remembered Marion. She still had to see Marion. Perhaps that was what had gone wrong, that Marion had come with him.

She sat at the table, waiting for Marion. Presently she began to feel hungry. She couldn't remember when she had eaten last. But living with Max had made her a creature of regular meals.

Max himself missed nearly every meal, but the fact was, he expected meals. Before he came, she had lived like Sarah and the rest of her neighbours, eating dry meat, cooking when she pleased, at any hour of the day. Now she was on Max's imaginary schedule.

She spread the last of the strawberry jam from the boys' sandwich-making operations on a pilot biscuit.

CHAPTER THIRTY-FIVE
Marion

"LUNCH? At 4:00 in the afternoon? Give me some. I'm starving." Marion sat down opposite Helen and began nibbling on a biscuit.

"You and Paul must have brought food." Helen was surprised at how glad she was to see Marion. Marion was someone you could never forget once you had been under her spell.

"He *doles* it out." Marion rolled her eyes. "Using *scales*," she added.

That was typical of Paul. He had probably spent hours before they came computing what they would need. Helen's fish and rabbit days had only started after he left.

She suddenly remembered Paul's vacuuming schedule. He had posted it on the back of the front door of their last apartment. He vacuumed Tuesday, Thursday, and Saturday from 9:00 to 10:00 p.m. She vacuumed Monday, Wednesday, and Friday from 5:00 to 6:00 p.m. Sunday was a general tidying day. No one vacuumed.

"Speak," Marion directed.

Helen laughed. She couldn't imagine a vacuuming schedule designed around Marion. Could she really be sleeping with him?

"I burned them," she said.

"He doesn't believe you."

"I know."

"He says you wouldn't have been able to do that."

Helen had been a meticulous bibliographer. As a graduate student, her assistantships had all been based on bibliography. Later she had almost become Paul's personal property, a bibliographer who made no mistakes.

"What do you think?"

"I wonder," said Marion. "But is this all you have to eat?"

Helen produced a can of Spam.

"Oh well," said Marion. She got up and began looking through the cupboards herself. After a moment she came upon Max's champagne glasses and stood back, raising her eyebrows.

"I have nothing to do with this—whatever it is—siege." She began to make tea.

"As his dissertation supervisor, I thought I'd come along and find out something about the subject matter of the dissertation." She poured water from the kettle. "But I'd forgotten how cold it is here in April."

Marion had started her career in the Pacific. But she had done many other things since, most of them in the North. She was a brilliant linguist among her other talents.

"You know, you're quite different," Marion remarked, giving Helen her cup and sitting down. "Whether you burnt his stuff or not, you've got a lot of guts telling him you did."

"Well, thanks."

"You can see why he thinks it would be out of character, can't you?"

Helen saw herself in the past. A book, a pamphlet, the reprint of an article, even a scrap of paper with some writing on it: her life revolved around the preservation of texts, sacred as potsherds.

"Really," said Marion, "I could almost wish I were you. There's so much I'd like to burn!"

"What, for example?" Helen was rivetted.

"My first book," said Marion. "And my memoirs." She laughed. "Except I'll never write memoirs."

Helen laughed too. Marion's memoirs would be a rich plum pudding of academic scandal. There were her four marriages, and her six children; there were also the lovers from the four corners of the earth, from New Guinea to the Arctic.

Marion was not a beautiful woman. She was shorter than Helen and had a broad-bottomed figure, the product of childbearing and middle age. But her intelligence shone through her body: her physical movements, which were clever and exact, the mobility of her face, and the expressiveness of her keen, grey eyes. She was magnetic, a person with power; she had a very clear sense of what she wanted and how to get it.

"Why are you doing this, Marion? For Paul?"

"Yes."

"Why?" She knew why.

"You know why. But I'll tell you how it happened. First of all, I'm between divorces."

Helen laughed.

"I'm just trying to give you a complete picture. Paul was driving a cab and he came to see me in my office and tried to sell me on the anthropology of taxi-driving."

"Driving a taxi?" Helen was horrified. "Paul was driving a taxi?"

"Why not? He had to support himself." Marion shrugged.

Helen looked at her with love and admiration. Marion was never a snob. In fact, a criticism of her character might be that she was too much the reverse.

"Oh yes, well it was hardly dissertation material. Maybe a popular book. But really, he's an academic type. So I encouraged him to go for the real thing again. He had a lot of trouble getting started. He went off to a witch doctor."

Witch doctor, popular book, academic type, anthropology of everything. It was a forgotten language. Helen was drinking it in. Marion was like that. You could listen to her speaking this recondite lingo, and hardly know her as a formidable academic producer, editor and associate editor of two journals, well-known author of standard texts in two or three different areas, a pioneer in Northern Canadian studies. She was a very famous woman.

"But now that I'm here I can see why he was gnashing his teeth," said Marion. "You're blooming."

"I'm happy here," said Helen. She reviewed this statement for truth. It was true. Then she remembered Max. It was not true any longer.

"I thought you were pulling the wool over your eyes."

"What do you mean?"

"Oh—depriving yourself. Confusing denial with power. I don't just mean sex," she added. "But obviously I was wrong." She extended an arm to bring the room into the conversation.

Helen looked at her house through Marion's eyes. Max had furnished it gradually over the winter: cooking pots, chairs and a new table to replace the one from the dump; a rug, not just the petroleum sheepskin by the bed; even pictures, most of them of airplanes. Over this was the patina of use: the pleasant, homely existence of their winter together, and then the detritus left by the boys—a comic book in a corner, orange peelings now in the wastebasket, cushions piled up carelessly, a half-done crossword puzzle. It looked as though a small family lived here, a very untidy family with two adolescent sons.

"It looks as though you've made your recovery," said Marion. "But he hasn't."

181

"You think you know what's wrong with him?" Helen was suddenly furious.

"The first orgasm is like a truth serum, you know. It all comes pouring out. The other side of the story seems so much more intriguing after that."

"But you knew at the time. All of you knew. You just stood by while it was happening. That time he slapped me, that was nearly in public! I went downstairs and had a nosebleed—I thought my nose was broken. But no one said anything. No one even asked me about it."

"I wonder why. A kind of prudery, do you think?"

"Whatever it is, I don't care about that. Admit that you knew, Marion. You knew at the time."

"Yes," said Marion. "I admit it." She looked at Helen thoughtfully, leaning her chin on her hand.

She did not bother to apologize. Marion had an intellectual understanding of what had happened to Helen, but she had no empathy. It was typical of her that she would not pretend to that.

Whatever her relationship with her husbands and lovers, no one could ever have systematically humiliated Marion. It was simply unthinkable that this could ever have happened to her.

Helen realized that this was where the idea that it was her fault came from. She had believed that it was something about her, something that she had done. She couldn't help thinking that even now, when she saw that there were some people to whom it could never have happened.

"Perhaps it was harder to interfere because you are both so smart."

"Oh come. I was nothing but an academic slave."

"We all wondered why you gave up on your M.A. But I wasn't your supervisor."

"Paul didn't want me to have you as my supervisor. You were his."

"Yes." Marion was still thoughtful. "So have you given it all up?"

"The anthropology of taxi-driving, you mean?" Helen spoke scornfully.

Marion chuckled.

"Let me tell you something else," she said, putting her fingertips together. "I'm going to Columbia."

"You wrote me that. That's certainly a coup, Marion. But are you sure the Ivy League is really right for you?"

"What? Oh, I see. It must have been my spelling. Not Columbia. They'd never give me a chair, not unless three or four people were to die quite accidentally by taking poison all at the same time. No, no, I mean the country. Colombia."

"Really, Marion. Your spelling!"

"I'm excited about it. My sabbatical. A hot climate. Back in the jungle."

"Murderers. Drugs."

"Indeed. Very thrilling. But the secret, you see, is this. I'm not taking Paul."

"Oh."

"So you understand what I mean about nunc aut nunquam. Paul has to finish his dissertation this spring. If he doesn't get it done—" She drew her finger across her neck with a grimace.

For Marion it was as simple as that. To collaborate with her was to be seduced by her, intellectually, and often physically as well. When she got bored with the project, she would put an end to the sex, and vice versa. This was the statute of limitations on Paul's Ph.D. In Marion promiscuity and ruthlessness were combined with an outrageous honesty about her own motives.

"Too bad," said Helen. She stood up stiffly.

Marion also stood up. "This is just for your information," she said. "If you don't want to give him the notes, so be it. But I wouldn't like this trip to be an utter waste of time. How do you feel about doing something with me yourself, maybe even a little paper."

"No." Helen shook her head.

Marion smiled at her. Still smiling, she looked around the room again.

Helen suddenly noticed a Cheesies bag under her foot and threw it in the wastebasket on top of the orange peels.

"Someone else is staying here," said Marion. "The pilot who brought us in?"

"Why do you say that?"

"He seemed to know who we were. I love bush pilots," she added.

Helen was silent. The champagne glasses, the messy room. Paul had noticed. Of course Marion could tell. The calendar with the picture of a DC-3 was staring her right in the eye.

"Anyway, I do hope so," Marion stretched. "You look happy. I want you to be happy."

She turned to pick up her parka, then came over to where Helen stood and kissed her briefly, formally, on the lips.

"See you tomorrow," she said, going out.

CHAPTER THIRTY-SIX
Replying to an Intervention

IT WAS still the afternoon of the same day.

Helen went to sit down on the bottom step of the stairs in the sun. She was completely numb. She really didn't have any feelings one way or another about what had just occurred.

Her eye fell on the Air Carrier Act. Lying neatly beside it on the stairs was the license application and the intervention of Mountain River Air.

She had not even thought of all that since she had got it a few days before, together with Marion's last letter. But now, numb as she was, she felt a faint flicker of interest in what the intervention said. Looking at it under the circumstances would not be different from going to the library to track down two or three entries under "gymnophagy" after a quarrel with Paul.

She could write a reply to it. Perhaps she wouldn't be here any longer. But Max could still get a charter license.

It was quiet in the house except for the tapping of her typewriter. In the distance, she heard the roar of the Beaver landing or taking off. She had lost track of Max's movements.

It was already three days since she had packed his suitcase and told him to go. She shut her mind to this calculation and went to look up the litres to gallons conversion for gasoline.

Helen found the intervention very interesting. Brutson's lawyer argued that Max could never make a go of it in Island Crossing and that the application should therefore be denied. But he also argued that Max was so successful in Island Crossing that he was ruining Mountain River Air. He used the fine lawyerly expression, *in the alternative*, to assert this contradiction.

Helen supposed that this was the way capitalists were accustomed to think. The competition was making a cheap, shoddy product that no one needed, and at the same time was driving them into the poorhouse.

And this was obviously just what the Air Transport Committee was expecting to hear.

The porch door opened quietly and when Helen raised her eyes from the page Max was in the room.

She stood up, scattering papers.

"Is that guy here?" he demanded.

"Who?"

"That guy you're married to."

"No." Helen collected her wits. "Why do you think he's here?"

"You kicked me out because of him coming back." Max was looking fiercely around the room. "I just came here to see—"

Helen now saw with love and concern that he was looking thin and wild. His old hawk-like look of smoothness was gone.

"—if you were all right," he said.

"Oh Max, I told you. He isn't staying here."

"Have you seen him?"

"I talked to him," she said.

Max sat down in a chair. He looked bristly and dirty and his shoulders were slumped.

"I finished the gas haul," he said. "Been flying three days straight. Forty-five-gallon drums. Load 'em up. Fly fifteen or twenty minutes. Unload 'em. Jump in and fly back. Load 'em up.... The worst thing was that you kicked me out. I couldn't stop thinking about you seeing him. I'm damn jealous," he said.

"But you don't have to be."

"Don't even want him to know about me, do you?"

"It isn't that."

"Did you tell him about me, then?"

"No, but—oh Max, it wasn't that!"

Helen covered her face with her hands. But he was right. It was that.

"I didn't really explain," she said.

"Didn't explain? You didn't tell me anything!"

"No. It's very hard to tell."

"Maybe you'd better."

"Yes. I will." Helen put her face back down in her hands for a moment. It was going to be very hard to explain what she had done.

"The physical violence I told you about—between Paul and me—"

"He beat you up," said Max, frowning.

"I told you how it started. With him humiliating me. Being sarcastic and so on. But then we stopped sleeping together. So I had an affair. With another student. A friend of his. But he was a friend of mine too. And I told Paul. That was when the real violence began."

Max nodded. He sat watching her.

"So I knew I could hurt him that way. I did it to hurt him. With a lot of people."

"With a few people," said Max. He lit a cigarette.

"But you don't understand, Max," she said. "I told him all about it every time. And he kept a diary—"

"Wrote it all down, eh?" he said.

"Yes. Everything. Here too," she continued.

"Here?"

"I slept with Henry here." She began to cry. Max moved, but she put out her hand to stop him coming closer, trying to control herself. "I was playing anthropologist—for Paul. Besides, it's what everyone wants to know, isn't it? How others do it?" She looked at him in defiance. "I was curious myself."

"I was all over the North last summer," he said. "Maybe I did some stuff like that too."

"But you didn't go home and tell your wife. To torture her."

"Whatever I told my wife, at least she never wrote it down."

"Well, anyway, that was why he beat me up here," she said. "Why he broke my nose."

"Because you screwed Henry?"

"And told him all about it. Yes." She hunched up her shoulders. "Now I'm telling you."

"I already knew anyway," he said.

"How?"

"When I asked Henry about you the first time I met him."

"He told you?"

"He just kind of made it clear. Said you needed a whiteman."

"So you thought—?"

"I thought he was giving me a piece of advice."

186

"Okay, Max. But I had Henry—" she was fierce "—on the Co-op manager's desk, and other places. Here in this bed too. And then I tortured my husband with it."

"Well, so what?" said Max. "He beat you, didn't he? Broke your nose. That wasn't right."

"No, but it was why I couldn't get you into it," she said. "The whole business was too dirty. You don't have anything to do with all that."

"That was why you kicked me out?" He sounded bewildered. "It was too dirty?"

"Because of what he would say. About you and me. I couldn't fight."

"You thought you were going to have to fight?"

"I was afraid," she said bitterly. "I even thought he might kill me this time."

"Why? Because of you and me?"

"No. Because of his diaries and his notes. He left them behind, you see. I could never give them back. I told him I burned them."

"You thought he might kill you because you burned his diary?"

She saw that he didn't have the faintest idea what she was talking about. The written record of a life, the research notes, they would not be significant to him the way they were to Paul. He could not be expected to understand that to burn someone's book was an appalling crime, perhaps the highest crime.

"It was my revenge," she said.

Max got up and put his cigarette butt in the stove. Then he stood looking at her.

"Let me just see if I get this," he said. "He beat you up because you were screwing around with other men. And so you figure that it was your fault."

"I did that to hurt him."

"Yeah. But he beat you up. You think it's your fault. But it isn't your fault."

That was what he had said at Christmas. And another softer voice in her mind said: "Those psychologists were always talking about fault."

"As for revenge," he went on, "you'll never get that. No matter what you do to him. I used to dream about killing my step-dad. But I figure I'd still be dreaming about it even if I'd done it."

Helen considered this answer. But it was not subtle enough. Killing him would not be enough, that was true. What she wanted from Paul was lifelong frustration and remorse. She had even been willing to trade in her own death for that.

"And me," he said. "You kicked me out. That was to keep him from throwing dirt at me?"

"I had to fight," she said.

"Without me getting any mud coming my way?" He laughed. "Maybe I wouldn't have minded a little mud. For you."

This was not quite right either. She had not been trying to protect him.

But she saw that she had trivialized her relationship with Max by treating it as though it were a complicating detail. She had insulted him. Maybe she could let him get this wrong now.

And looking at Max, she realized that she had been wrong too. What was between them was not in the least like the affairs she had used to torture Paul.

It was strange to realize that she had the power, without really doing anything, just being herself, to make someone love her. Or that she could care about another person this much again. She had been a fool to think that she could cut this out of her life. Pride and snobbery, the idea of absolute self-control, dislike of his weakness and fear of his messy attachments; they were all beside the point.

He had gone back to sit down and she approached him cautiously. He moved his head back to look up at her standing in front of him.

They stared at one another for a moment and slowly Max's lips curled up into a smile. He was reading her mind. Helen burst into tears.

Max stood up to embrace her, turning her head around persuasively with his hand.

"You're all screwed up."

"I am," said Helen, sobbing.

He wanted her to look into his face

"But you're in love with me."

She was mute.

"I love you. And you love me. Say it."

"I love you."

"You love me." He spoke firmly. "Look what you were doing when I came in."

Helen had dropped a sheet of paper on the floor just in front of him. She looked down at it sideways and read:

" Mountain River Air is implying, in a series of threats and innuendos ..."

Max was laughing.

She smiled, still reading:

"Island Crossing Air submits that all of these allegations are false, and in particular ..."

"So now you're going to tell him about me. Let him throw some dirt." Max pulled her down on his knees.

She put her arms around his neck and rested her head on his shoulder.

"He guessed already." She remembered this with a surge of bitter anger.

"About me? Well—" Max drew breath. "Okay!"

"You don't know the kinds of things he was saying."

"Oh, yeah. Sure I do. I just hope he thinks I'm good."

"It bothers him." Helen laughed suddenly. It had not occurred to her that Max would feel himself a sexual competitor of Paul's.

"Sure hope it does!"

He began to kiss her, at the same time unbuttoning her blouse. Then he stopped suddenly, looking upwards.

"Where are the kids?"

He had apparently just remembered them.

"Still off with Eli," she said.

"That's good." He sighed. "About them—" He had stopped trying to undress her and now he looked anxiously into her face. "I've got to do something about them."

"You do," she agreed.

"I stuck you with the kids. Didn't think about it, really."

"Well, you were busy."

"I thought about what you said. It was all true."

"They are terribly messy."

"Yeah. Kids that age. Sleep eighteen hours a day. Then they think they know everything. Except they can't do whatever it is and they can't talk about it, either. And you're so nice-looking you're driving them crazy. I remember what it was like myself." He smiled at her.

"You think that was the problem?" Helen laughed, incredulous.

"I'm going to have a talk with them when they come back."

"About what? Cleaning up and chores and so on?"

"No. I think they should go home. See, I kind of liked having them come to me. Thought maybe it meant they trusted me."

"They do trust you, Max."

"Yeah, maybe. But I ran out on them a long time ago. I think she's the one they want."

"Well, they should call her, anyway," said Helen. She was worried about Missy.

Max gave a sigh of exhaustion.

"You're still wearing all your things," Helen remarked, surprised.

"Haven't had anything off in a week. Think I smell."

"You could have a bath." She was unzipping his parka. "I'll make some coffee. When did you last eat?"

He was trying to help her with his huge Arctic boots.

"Look! It's almost night. You don't have to do anything else today. You could just get into bed and go straight to sleep."

"No," he said.

"Well, what then?" She finished peeling off his down overalls and stepped back to lug them away.

"What you said a little while ago—" Max sat down on the edge of the bed. Helen followed and began undoing his shirt. "Was it really true?"

"What I said? What do you mean?"

"Not very many people have ever said that to me. Missy did, but that was sure a long time ago. And before that, there was my foster mother, she used to say it. But you—" He was teasing her gently, she perceived. "You never did. That was the first time."

She was strangely reluctant still. There was a frightening magic in certain words.

"You said—" He was prompting her.

"I said I love you."

"That's what I mean. I just wanted to hear you say it again."

He really didn't smell, merely of sweat and fresh air. And even though things were once again extremely complicated, Helen realized as she went over backwards in his arms that some of the things she thought very difficult were unexpectedly easy.

CHAPTER THIRTY-SEVEN
Tristes Arctiques

SHE AWOKE blissfully to familiar smells. Bacon. Coffee. Soap. Max was evidently having one of their sketchy winter baths, for she heard him splashing in the porch. There was silence after a while, then the clink of the bucket handle and the sound of the door opening and closing as he took the slop water outside.

She sat up and looked around her with pleasure. It was daylight already; the cabin was flooded with spring sunshine. It seemed like home again now that Max was back.

There was a cup of coffee beside the bed, steaming a little, waiting for her. She drank from it, and then began putting on her nightgown, noticing happily that she felt stiff.

Max came in and started to read her reply to the Mountain River Air intervention. He leaned, shirtless, against the edge of the table and read a page, his lips curling into a smile.

" 'Baseless accusations.' "

"Well, they are," she said indignantly. "We answered every one of those complaints."

"So you did."

"Do you see this? He called me 'deceitful.'" She came to lean over his arm.

"Called me a damn liar the other day. Those weren't his exact words, either."

"Do you think it's good enough?" she asked.

"Oh, it's great. I bet Brutson has to use his dictionary. If he has a dictionary," Max added.

"Yes, but it doesn't matter about him. It's what Ottawa thinks that counts."

"You want to know what Ottawa thinks?" Max put his arm around Helen and set the reply down on the table. "I bet Ottawa wonders what you look like every night before it goes to sleep."

It was almost like the winter. The same domesticity, the same playfulness, the wonderful sex, the feeling that they were alone in the world and totally on each other's side.

Someone was knocking at the door.

Max was not going to let her spring away from him.

Marion stuck in her head.

"Helen? Oh!" she said merrily, seeing Max.

"Marion," said Helen.

Max let go of her reluctantly. He lit a cigarette and folded his arms, still leaning back on the table.

"You're the pilot who brought us in, aren't you?"

"Of course he is," Helen felt cross and a little anxious. "Max, this is Marion."

Marion was giving Max a frank and admiring inspection. Looking at his smooth muscular chest and the small hard brown nipples, Helen remembered some of her pleasure of the night before. She felt that Max's body was hers; she didn't like Marion seeing it.

"The last time I flew in a Beaver was in New Guinea," Marion was saying.

"Beavers all over," he replied. "Sahara. All over Africa."

"Oh? Were you in Africa?"

"No. I just saw them coming back. Some of them were still in the barrel. A few years ago you could get a thirty-year-old Beaver that was like new."

"Not this one you're flying, though."

"No," Max agreed. "Not this one."

He offered Marion a cigarette and she took it unself-consciously. She didn't smoke.

"Want something to eat?" he was asking.

He liked Marion. It was slightly annoying.

"Anything but trail mix." Marion gave a histrionic groan.

"Bacon and eggs. Toast, too."

"Toast!"

Marion had spent years crouching over smoky fires in the rain forest with the natives of New Guinea. She cared about toast as much as she liked cigarettes. But she

192

was just a very good dancer. She had selected Max as a partner and she was letting him lead.

"What's this?" Marion had noticed the pile of typed sheets on the table. She picked them up, looking inquiringly at Helen.

"We've got a thing going here," Max told her. He was turning toast on the stovetop, his cigarette clenched between his lips.

"We're starting an airline," Helen said.

"You didn't tell me about this yesterday." Marion was reading, her eyes flicking down the page.

"Helen and me are partners."

"So I see." Marion had a very mobile face. Her eyebrows moved up and down as she read. She put the last sheet down and laughed heartily.

All at once Helen relaxed. With Marion it would have been all right if Max were cooking human head on the stovetop; she would just have been pleased to be along, making notes.

"What's this thing you're wearing?" said Marion suddenly.

Helen looked down. Marion was pointing her finger, the astute, short-nailed, slightly freckled finger of a middle-aged academic, at the jewel on her bosom.

"Got it off a guy who claimed he was hauling drugs down in C.A.," said Max happily. He put the hot plates on the table and came over to look as well. "I gave it to Helen."

"And is it real?"

"Sure." He pointed out the heart on the window.

"Helen, my dear child, you never cease to surprise me." Marion now sat down at the table and began to crunch her toast with relish. "I really am beginning to enjoy myself, although I must say, I was wondering last night."

"What did you do last night?"

"Huddled in my tent eating trail mix." Marion put a forkful of fried egg in her mouth. "Paul was writing up his notes," she added.

"Notes?"

"Well may you ask." Her eyebrows went up expressively.

In the usual Island Crossing manner, Dallas appeared in the doorway, not bothering to knock.

"Want to go fishing, Helen?" she said.

Marion had finished eating. She went over and got into the bed at the foot end, pulling the quilt well up over her knees.

"Who is this?" she asked Helen.

Dallas was smiling at Max.

"Your kids went out with Eli," she said shyly.

"Helen told me." Max was also shy with Dallas. Flirtation was his usual way with women, Helen guessed. But Dallas and Marion were people he had to take seriously. He saw that, apparently.

"This is Dallas," Helen said. "She is an actress. And Marion here is an anthropologist." One had to warn people, after all.

"An anthropologist?" Dallas looked at Marion with interest.

"An actress? But didn't you just invite Helen to go fishing?" Marion was looking at Dallas with equal interest.

The mutual interest was, again, slightly annoying.

"I wanted to go fishing with her because I wanted to talk to her. I think Eli'll be back today," Dallas said to Max.

He nodded and put a plate of breakfast in front of her.

"Give Junior something to eat," he suggested.

"Junior? Oh. Okay."

"Dallas is going to have a girl," Helen said to him.

Marion was very interested. "A girl," she said. "But how do you know?"

"Amniocentesis," said Dallas.

There was a very loud knock at the door. It opened at once and Paul came straight in, not bothering about his boots.

"Marion! Are you here?"

Helen froze.

Then Max seemed to fly over from the stove, because he was there, right beside her. And the four of them were all staring at Paul.

"I see it," said Paul, "as the ideal vehicle to explode that sixty-year-old methodology we were talking about. I mean—" He was speaking only to Marion. "—what kind of framework was she using? In light, among other things, of modern linguistics—"

"And genetic dating," agreed Marion. She yawned. "But there's a whole world out there," she went on. "Why do you care about her mistakes?"

"I agree," said Helen.

"You agree?" Paul turned around to glare at her. "What do you agree with?"

"I agree with Marion."

"Oh, I see. You agree with Marion." He dismissed her impatiently. "As I was saying—"

"For God's sake Paul, eat some breakfast or something." Marion raised her knees under the coverlet, then raised her shoulders and her eyebrows in turn.

Max had been holding a fold of Helen's nightgown bunched in his hand. He let go of it suddenly.

"Bacon and eggs?" he asked.

Paul was startled.

"Oh yes, the pilot," he said.

But he fell silent as Max made his way over to the kitchen. Max was still not wearing his shirt. Paul had apparently noticed this for the first time.

"Warm enough in that tent?" Max asked Paul.

"Yes," said Paul shortly.

"No," said Marion.

"You had both the good sleeping bags."

"Two eggs?"

Paul took his plate from Max in silence. But he did not seem explosive to Helen any longer. It was strange. He ate slowly, saying nothing, looking at Max occasionally with a small frown.

Marion was talking to Dallas about fishing. But she was watching them all out of the corner of her eye. The story was going to turn up in her memoirs. Because she would have memoirs, in spite of what she said.

If Marion had both the good sleeping bags, she and Paul must not be sleeping together any more. Helen was annoyed to find herself making this deduction.

Max was looking for his dirty shirt under the bed. Paul watched this closely. Max found it eventually, between the pillow and the wall. Then he came over to Helen, putting it on.

"Got to go soon," he told her. "Got to do one of Brutson's scheds for him."

"Well, give him my love if you see him. Or maybe you could just give him this." She held up the reply to the intervention.

"Better mail it. He's running out of names to call me."

Paul's mouth, closed in a munch, now opened for speech. But the door flew open and in on a rush of fresh cold air came Max's kids.

"Hi, Helen!"

"Hey, did we ever have a good time—!"

"We made a spruce lodge!"

"Sure was cold!"

"Eli got an elk."

"Not an elk, you jerk! A moose."

"He's goin' to send you the liver."

"Oh yeah. But we're not eatin' any."

"Hey," said Helen. "You went off without telling me."

"Thought you'd say no."

"Dallas said we could."

"Didn't anyone tell you?"

"Henry told me. Still, you ought to have told me yourselves. But you had a good time? No frostbite or anything?"

"Almost."

"When we took the skidoo through that overflow."

They were warming their hands at the stove. Mickey's cheeks were ruddy. Even Freddy was looking happy and excited, without the shadow of his usual anxiety. It was such a pleasure to look at them that Helen promptly forgave them for everything.

"His kids?" Marion was amused.

"Yes," said Helen.

It struck her that the boys had been speaking almost exclusively to her. They were used to a universe ordered as a matriarchy.

She glanced at Max. He was also smiling at the boys. But he was getting dressed rapidly. He had buttoned his shirt and was assuming his oil-stained overalls and vest, his parka, his boots, and his double mittens.

Dallas had taken over the cooking.

"Make toast," she said to Mickey.

"Boy, this is good!"

"Hey, you know what Eli ate, Dallas?"

"He ate moose nose!"

"Nose is the best part," said Dallas.

"You ever ate that?"

"I'm Indian, see. You forget?"

"Oh yeah."

Max was standing by the door, all ready to go. He could never come to terms with the matriarchal universe. This morning Helen was merely amused by that.

"After breakfast," she said to the boys. She spoke serenely. "Go upstairs and clean up. That place is a pigsty."

"We left in kind of a hurry," agreed Freddy.

"There's washing your clothes too. It's about time."

Max cleared his throat. "Got to go," he said. "Do what she tells you, right?"

"Right."

"Back in the good old days we'd have fumigated that loft," said Helen, warming to her theme. "We'd have burned sulphur. It would have got rid of the smell, at least."

"Oh yeah. Socks."

"It's a nice day," said Dallas. She went to the door. "You should make them do that wash outside. Light a fire under the washtub. I could make you a good fire."

"All right."

"Bye, Dad."

Max was making his escape.

Helen hesitated. Then she went after him, hastily pulling on her boots over her bare feet.

She caught up with him beside the woodpile. Dallas was chopping kindling, her back turned tactfully their way.

"I guess you could tell him all about last night, but I don't know that he'd believe you," Max murmured in her ear.

"Don't make fun of me, Max." She laughed.

He gave her a shorter, slightly less explicit kiss and pushed her towards the door. "You're freezing."

"I just wanted to—"

"Yeah, but I'll be home tonight."

He propelled her more insistently in the direction of the door.

Paul was standing there, watching them. He disappeared instantly.

Max ran rather heavily in his big boots down the lakeside path. He was going to be late doing Brutson's sched.

Reluctantly, Helen went back into her house, clasping the folds of her thick nightgown around her.

Paul was ignoring her. He had started to talk to Marion again.

"So, as I see it, the first two chapters could be methodological," he was saying, "arguing that she is not only out of date, but also—"

"Go ahead. Think about it." Marion was still in bed. She lifted the coverlet and swung her legs to the floor. "But I don't give two sticks for method. You've got to get some data. That's what it's really all about, Paul."

She looked out the door, watching Dallas and the boys making the washtub fire.

"Well, I'm going back to the tent," he told her.

"I'm going to stick around here and invite myself on a fishing trip," said Marion. She put on her boots and went out. A moment later, they could hear her talking to Dallas and the boys in her distinctive drawling voice.

Helen prepared herself for some onslaught from Paul. At the very least he was going to call her a liar. But she felt curiously little fear of what he might say for she had the higher ground. She was the one with friends, children, and a lover.

"You heard her," said Paul dryly. "I need the data."

"I don't have any data, Paul."

"I don't believe you." He was putting on his parka. "From what I just saw there's no reason why I should believe anything you say."

"Just leave me alone, Paul. I don't care what you think."

"Exactly. So just give me—" he spoke through his teeth, pulling on his mitts. "—my things, and I'll keep my opinion to myself."

"No," she said.

"No? Then I'll be seeing you."

Helen spent the afternoon helping the boys boil their wash. It was fun for them and they found it as strange as eating moose nose.

And in the meantime her friends went fishing. Her actress friend and her anthropologist friend.

CHAPTER THIRTY-EIGHT
Feminine Company

IT WAS a nice day. April had brought the spring sun with it. The boys were off somewhere with Eli probably and Helen was left alone to ponder. It was strange, but the turn events had taken left her cheerful and even inclined to laugh when she thought about the last few days.

There was a clatter of boots on the porch and Helen left off her humble household chore, cleaning the lamp chimney, to see who was coming. It was Marion and Dallas. They were collaborating on a project that involved going fishing every day.

Marion plunked down a garbage bag on the table and Helen saw that it contained two large lake trout.

"Fish dinner," Marion explained. "We're doing filleting today."

"She wants to know everything about fish," said Dallas, smiling.

"Everything about everything," Helen told her.

"Got a good sharp knife, Helen?"

Helen got out a knife. Then she put a few sticks on the fire and sat down placidly on her bed to watch. She always enjoyed watching a real expert fillet a fish.

"My God, how did you do that?" exclaimed Marion. Dallas had ripped the skin off one side of the fish with a swift movement.

"Wait. I'm going to make a note. Can you do that slowly?"

"Can't do it slowly."

Dallas turned the big fish over and began making incisions on the other side. Then she seized it at the tail and ripped, with one violent twist of her wrist. Again the skin came off all in one piece.

"Got any flour, Helen?"

Helen produced flour, lard, and the frying pan.

Then she watched as Marion began to work on the other fish. Helen had learned this skill herself from the same person who had taught Dallas. But it had taken her a lot longer. Marion was, by anybody's standards, a fast learner.

"Where are the kids?" Dallas asked Helen. She was beginning the frying, laying chunks of fish in flour, then in the hot fat.

"Somewhere with Eli, I think."

Dallas nodded. Helen was surprised that she hadn't known.

"But this is not the way you cook fish here," said Marion, looking into the frying pan.

"On the fire is best," said Helen.

"Or boil 'em for soup. I learned how to fry fish when I was working in a construction camp. I always think of that cook. He was a little old drunk Italian, but he taught me a couple of things."

Helen thought of her diet before Max. Basically, she had been living at the beginning of the Iron Age. The frying pan, the pancake turner, the corkscrew, all of these were post-Max.

Marion passed her a plate of hot fish, and sat down on the other end of the bed. Dallas continued to cook and a mountain of crisp chunks rose on the plates at the table.

"I thought your boys'd be here to eat some of this."

Helen was having a good time. Feminine company, disorderly eating habits; she thought of the summer to come, the long light days when, unconfined by their houses, the people in the village ate and slept as they pleased.

"Marion made a spear," said Dallas. "Took a knife and a broomstick and put 'em together. There was a bunch of little kids standing around. She showed 'em how to use it too. I don't know whether I ever saw anyone use a spear here. You ever see that, Helen?"

Helen shook her head. "Your mother would know," she said.

"I could ask Abe," said Dallas doubtfully.

"They must have used spears at the fish trap."

Dallas' eyes became introspective. She nodded.

"By the way, why did your mother call you Dallas?" asked Marion. "This village doesn't have TV."

Dallas smiled, coming back from the fish trap.

"My mother called me Delilah. Named myself Dallas later."

Helen's detective organ informed her that Marion knew nothing about Sarah. Or the fish trap and what it meant to Dallas.

200

"So will you help with this little thing we're doing, Helen?" Marion took another piece of fish in her fingers and hopped back into bed with it. "It's more or less linguistic. And you're just the person to do the charts."

"Doesn't Paul think you're trespassing?"

"Why? He's not doing any field work at all. Just sitting in the tent writing up a tiny diary." Marion shrugged and licked her fingers.

The boys burst in the door and there was a moment of hectic activity.

"Fried fish!"

Dallas started to cook again. They were telling her where they had been with Eli.

When they finished eating, Mickey stuffed a last juicy, crunchy morsel into his mouth and put his boots on.

"Goin' out," he announced, looking past Helen's ear.

Freddy took a paperback up the loft stairs and flopped down on his bedroll with a groan.

"Kids!" said Dallas. Marion was chuckling and rolling her eyes.

Helen smiled, too. She had now moved the boys from the mental category Awful to Normal. They were very annoying, it was true. But that seemed to be just what everyone expected.

Dallas put on her jacket, not bothering with a social explanation. No one ever did in Island Crossing.

"Bye," she said, going out.

Of course, Eli might be home by now.

What would it mean, to have picked someone? Helen didn't know. Island Crossing was such a small group of people, such a little place. There were only a few people you could pick. And were you then stuck forever with the one you chose? Helen hated to think that Dallas was stuck with Eli.

Marion reached out for a pillow and Helen passed her one from her end of the bed. Marion settled herself comfortably under the quilt.

"Since you ask me about Paul, I'll tell you," she said. "He's chasing a wild hare. I keep telling him, 'Look, there's a perfectly good piece of field anthro here. You've already done it, so write it up, and we'll give you a gold star. Then you can get a post-Doc and start something new.' But he just goes on about methods: hers, how wrong they were; his, how right they are. Who cares? She was a pioneer in the area."

"Paul is a perfectionist."

"He's a vivisectionist, if you ask me. Do you suppose they'll be carving me up like that in sixty years?" asked Marion dreamily.

201

"Better than being forgotten, Marion."

"Is it?" Marion sat up energetically. "You know, I hate Ph.D. students. What I like is to work with a person who has something interesting to say. Somehow, everyone I get hold of turns into a Ph.D. student." She sank back on the bed.

"Or a husband," Helen remarked.

"Or both." Marion chuckled. "It's like the gift of Midas, isn't it? How they turn out—when I touch their perfect bodies with my mind."

"At least Dallas won't turn into a Ph.D. student."

"No, I suppose not," said Marion. She sounded regretful, however. "But we are doing this little thing on fishing. Women's fishing. 'A Little Vocabulary of Women's Fishing Among the Boreal... .' or 'Some Elements of a Vocabulary of Women's Fishing Among... .' Something like that. And you are going to help, right?"

"As long as I don't have to be a Ph.D. student either."

Marion laughed.

Max came in and began taking off his winter gear quickly, smiling at the way they were sitting tucked up, one at either end of the bed.

"Where'd you get the fish?"

"Marion went fishing with Dallas." Helen sat up. "Oh, dear. The boys must have eaten it all."

"That's okay. I had a lot of fish today. Went around the camps. Trump Lake, Otter Lake, Round Lake, Jackfish Lake, Trout Lake. Sick baby at Loon Lake. Had to take 'em into Mountain River."

"The people are going out on the land, are they?" asked Marion.

"Spring hunt. Beaver, this time of year. Fish runs," said Max.

"They're taking their families now that they have the plane," said Helen.

"Gave me fish everywhere I went," he continued. "Fish guts done over the fire at Round Lake."

"Interesting," murmured Marion. She was groping for her notebook.

"Have to take that baby back," Max was telling Helen. "Then I'll do a sched last thing tomorrow. Brutson's still down for repairs."

Marion got up and put on her parka. She was as direct as an Island Crossing person, Helen noticed. She never offered social explanations either.

"Stay for supper?" asked Max.

Helen remained calmly in bed. Marion wasn't going to stay. She was tying her bootlaces. In a moment she would be gone.

And they would be alone together. Or almost alone. Helen felt that Max was looking forward to this too.

CHAPTER THIRTY-NINE
An Unexpected Visitor

THE DAYS were drawing out. Max was flying to the bush every day.
Helen was helping him again. He seemed to have a different crazy load every time: gas in leaking ten-gallon drums, children, teams of dogs. Max lifted a grandmother into the plane, and then Helen passed up the hand-crank sewing machine. When he returned, the plane was full to the window sills with frozen fish.

He was exhausted to the point of speechlessness every night, the way he had been in the fall before the ice came. In the North the changes of the year were the hardest times. The weather was bad, or at best unpredictable, and everyone was in a hurry to get into the bush or out of it.

It was almost time to take the plane off skis. Very little snow was left. But the lakes were still frozen. And dangerous. They were covered with icy slush, slush that covered the breaks and leads and the overflow at the river mouths.

Helen had been keeping track of Max's timetable all the past week. She went out to wait for him at the airstrip at the end of the day.

She was sitting on the gas cans beside the power pole one evening, when Paul stepped out of the bush and began walking purposefully towards her.

"What are you doing here?" she demanded.

"What do you mean? I happen to have a camp in that clearing." He indicated a swamp off the road behind them. It was presently frozen, but Helen knew it to be muskeg, good for blueberries, but inundated in the spring.

"Why on earth did you choose that spot?"

"The pilot suggested it." He spoke of Max with a certain venom.

The drone of the Beaver could now be heard in the distance, but Helen was too annoyed to pay much attention.

"Keeping busy?" she asked.

"Working over my notes."

"What notes?"

"Some that you don't have." He looked at her furiously.

"I burned them."

"I refuse to believe that."

"But don't you think I've done you a favour?" Helen liked having the upper hand. "Are you sure you're cut out to be an anthropologist at all? You really don't like other people. You look down on us all from such a height."

Max was now landing. But Helen was enjoying herself too much to stop quarrelling. It was interesting to watch Paul control his body. Despite the violent clarity of his utterances, he kept himself stiffly at attention, arms straight down at his sides.

"Anyway, you can always start over somewhere else. Like the Trobriand Islands!"

She felt he might even do the impossible and implode, or simply go up in smoke.

Paul was replying vehemently, but she couldn't hear a thing he was saying over the cough and roar of the Beaver's engine. She watched with pleasure as his mouth opened and closed, infantile and unreadable, the only part of him that moved.

Max shut off the engine and got out of the airplane with unaccustomed haste. He walked hurriedly over to Helen.

It had at last occurred to her that the confrontation she was having with Paul had the makings of a first-class scene once it included Max. But Max did not even seem to have noticed that Paul was there.

Someone was getting out of the plane on the other side. Helen could see her legs, her feet in city shoes groping for the step on the strut.

"I didn't get a chance to call you," Max was saying.

The legs were followed by a tight skirt with a kick pleat and the bottom of a thin jacket.

"I mean," said Max, taking her by the shoulders, and still unaware of Paul, "I didn't know that this was going to happen."

"What are you talking about?" There was something wrong. Helen was alarmed. "What is it, Max?"

"Jesus," he said. He put his forehead down on her forehead. "First the kids, now this!"

"Well, well." It was a familiar voice. "We meet again. I'm so sorry but I forget your name."

Helen disengaged herself from Max and gazed at Missy, mouth open.

Missy was an unusual sight in Island Crossing. Red fingernails. Eye make-up. Lipstick. Permed hair. Leather coat. Shoes.

But on closer inspection she didn't look so sophisticated. Her hair was ruffled. Her ungloved hands were blue with cold. And her mascara showed signs of recent tears.

Helen saw that Missy was close to hysteria.

*

They were at home and Missy was having a cup of coffee. She had stopped shivering finally, and her feet were clad in a pair of Max's socks. She wore Helen's parka over her shoulders, her own jacket on her knees.

The boys sat in front of her on the bed, Mickey surly and uncommunicative, Freddy's glance flitting from one adult to another.

"You could've called me, at least," Missy was accusing Max.

"Yeah. Should have."

"You should have," Helen agreed glumly.

"Aren't you even sorry? I was worried about you." Missy had turned on the boys.

Freddy cleared his throat. "Chris—" he began.

"I'm not goin' back if he's there," announced Mickey.

Missy looked down at her hands, locked together in her lap.

"I'm not going back either," she said.

"But then—" Helen was tentative. "Where are you going to go?"

"I don't know!" Missy began to cry, and Helen felt a tightness in her own chest and throat. She knew that Missy hated crying in front of her and Max and the children; Missy was afraid of being weak.

But the boys were beside her instantly.

"Hey, Mom, it's okay."

"We're goin' with you."

"Don't worry, Momma."

They were hugging her. She was hugging them and weeping. Helen turned away in relief.

"We were scared that Chris'd be the one to answer the phone."

"Your dad should have—"

"Yeah, but then you'd have been mad at him."

Helen stole a glance at Max. He was looking at the scene of reunion before him a little sadly. But his sadness was not due to a sense of inadequacy, or the things that he might have done or undone, she thought. He was sad because he knew that Missy was the one they wanted.

To her horror, she now caught sight of Paul standing beside Max, wearing the same slightly sad expression. How had he got there? With difficulty she recalled her encounter with him as Max was landing the plane. It all seemed as though it had happened years ago.

Missy was coming to herself again. She had noticed Paul too.

"Who's that?" she asked abruptly.

"Oh, sorry." Helen was trying, absurdly, to be casual. "This is my ex-husband, Paul Ayre."

"Does that make him some kind of brother-in-law of mine?" snarled Missy. "This is old home week, I must say."

But Helen felt she could rely on Missy not to lose her control. She was just being a little mean because she was ashamed of crying in front of strangers. Helen was much more worried about what Paul would do.

Max had also noticed Paul and was giving him a cup of coffee.

Paul was tall and beautiful as an angel. He was one of the Scandinavian Scots, with a high-bridged nose, piercing blue eyes, lips that suggested sex only by its absence from the thinness and purity of their line.

Max was a more North American type, she thought. But she could no longer look at Max impartially. In fact, she was burning with anxious jealousy. Missy had once upon a time told Max that she loved him.

"He kept on buggin' me, Mom. He just couldn't leave me alone."

"He was always talkin' about killing guys."

"Yeah, but he didn't bug around with you the way he did with me."

"Called me a little twerp."

"Well, I'm through with Chris. He did a few things before, but no one gets to slap me around. No one gets to do that twice, anyway."

Helen shot a glance at Paul and was amazed to see that he was watching Missy with sympathy and attention. Perhaps it was true that he had learned something in therapy. But she could still scarcely credit it. How could Paul have brought himself to sit down with louts like Christopherson and talk about his problem?

"Have you been staying here?" Missy was looking around the small, crowded room.

"Oh yeah. Upstairs. Helen let us stay there. You could sleep up there too. She could, right, Helen?"

Helen nodded. Missy would have to stay there. But she was seeing her house through Missy's eyes. No electricity. No running water. No plumbing. One room, essentially. How could she have ever thought it was so civilized?

"We did our laundry."

"Boiled it."

"Shot a moose."

Well, not us, exactly. Eli did. But we were along."

"Slept in a spruce lodge."

"You ever eat rabbit stew, Mom?"

"Rabbits are first cousins to rats. That's what my mother used to say."

Paul put his empty coffee cup down on the table.

"I guess I'll be off," he remarked to Helen. "It's been interesting."

"Has it?"

"Yes. A contribution to understanding—maybe." He smiled politely at Missy, and Helen suddenly imagined him later, hunched over his diary in the tent, writing by the light of a pocket torch.

There was something unreal about him. Helen watched with unhappy eyes as he put on his boots. He existed, but in the midst of Max's flesh and blood family he passed unnoticed, almost like a ghost. It was not his profession, or his social class, or his temperament, but some inward struggle he was having, some conflict she knew was there, but had never understood.

He had taken therapy; he was trying to change. He wanted to overcome that part of himself, whatever it was, with which he had to struggle. She saw clearly now that he had come back to Island Crossing neither to torture her nor to try to make amends, but simply to pick up the pieces of his life. Helen knew she could never forgive him. But at least he seemed to know what it was she could not forgive him for.

She was standing looking at him, touched, still fearful, curious—about herself as much as about him.

Max said:

"Want to stay for supper? It's rabbit stew."

Pressing food on people was Max's way of expressing territoriality. He had his arm around her waist too, she noticed.

Paul shook his head and stepped into the porch.

"Rabbits are first cousins to rats," he said. "My mother would have said that too. But I've got plenty of jerky and trail mix. Enough to last until you change your mind, Helen."

CHAPTER FORTY

25 Percent of an Airplane

HELEN CALLED Fish in Ottawa the next day.
He seemed pleased to hear from her.

"Did you enjoy reading my letter?" she demanded.

He laughed.

"I really don't know what I would do without you, Charles. Hardly anybody enjoys reading replies to interventions the way you do. Is the application being processed now?"

"I wrote a précis of it for the committee."

"Really? Have they seen it then?"

"Not yet. These things take time."

"Do you think they'll look at it soon?"

"Oh, I wouldn't be surprised."

"I believe we have to have an airplane."

"25 percent of one is all the law requires."

"We may have the money for that."

There was a long pause. She waited. He was going to tell her something.

She had the idea he was looking around to make sure no one at his end was listening.

"Have you given any thought to the definition of 'dry lease'?" he asked.

Max had told her something about dry leases. She couldn't remember what.

"Well, you might look it up," said Fish.

"Okay."

"I'd just like you to be fully in the picture."

"Right."

" I think you'll find there are a lot of women in aviation these days."

"There are?"

"Not that we get to talk to them much." He sounded rather melancholy.

Helen was taken aback. But nothing Fish said lacked a full measure of significance.

"So you are not—er—married to this pilot? This isn't a personal question," he added.

"It isn't a personal question? As a matter of fact I'm not."

"Then you can solve your problem," he said.

After Helen hung up, she spent some time pondering this mysterious conversation. How did marriage enter the picture at all? Fish liked talking to her, but he was certainly not in love with her despite what Max had said. She was merely an intelligent listener out in the sticks.

She determined to look up dry leases right away.

Chapter Forty-one

You Ever Want Your Mother?

THEY HAD Finally succeeded in hiring a new Co-op manager. The next day Helen was coming back from the meeting carrying a package of celery. Under Henry's management onions were the only vegetable the Co-op usually had in stock.

She was standing in the dingy April snow outside her house listening to Max and Missy have a quarrel. Missy was berating Max. But Helen had also heard him shouting at her.

She put her bag of celery down on the doorstep. It would freeze if she left it there. But she felt an extreme disinclination to go in, even though they would probably stop arguing if she did.

Max called Missy a bitch. Helen put her hands over her ears. She wished she didn't have to think about this too. She was in an impossible position.

Missy had burst into tears and was raving at Max incoherently. Max was swearing a little. But Helen was arrested: he never swore.

Helen waited, irresolute.

There was silence inside.

She leaned against the porch wall, pressing her hands together until the blood went out of her fingers.

Max said something she couldn't hear.

It must have been something conciliatory because Missy answered him a moment later.

Helen listened a little longer to reassure herself. But there was only a murmur of voices from within. Then she walked away dismally, clasping the celery and wondering where she should go.

Light shone from Sarah's windows. But Helen was still barred from Sarah. She never saw her and she sometimes wondered if she was even still alive. Somehow everything had changed: Max, Dallas' coming back, even Sarah's relationship with Abe stood between them now.

Helen was walking down the main street of town, having left the lakeshore, and she decided to visit Dallas. She didn't usually go there without invitation because she was afraid of Eli, but she felt driven from her home that night. It was a desolate feeling.

She arrived at the shack in time to hear another fight going on inside.

A woman was screaming, but the voice didn't sound like Dallas. She was shouting abuse; no one was getting hurt. Not yet.

Helen stood for a moment clasping her celery, and wondered what she should do. She thought the fight might become violent. But her friendship with Dallas hung in the balance. It was a delicate question, how much one could know.

She heard furniture scraping the floor, and then a crash and the ringing noise of breaking dishes.

Helen prepared to go in. She had to make sure that Dallas was not going to get hurt. There was the unborn baby to consider too.

But now Eli came flying out, weeping and swearing. He gave Helen a black look, then ran off down the road, pulling on his jacket with a violent sob.

Dallas stood in the doorway looking after him.

"Dallas!"

She was all right. She was crying like Eli, but she had not been harmed. Whatever had happened, whoever had been screaming, whoever had pushed or gotten pushed, Dallas was not hurt.

"You'd better come in," said Dallas. She drew Helen inside, then sat down on a chair and cried for several moments.

The room was a mess and there was a strong smell of liquor. Helen had already guessed that Eli was drinking. After a minute her eyes adjusted to the dimness and she became aware that someone else was there. It was Rosaleen, the girl who had gone fishing with Sarah in early October. She was lying on the cot mattress on the floor and she was quite pregnant.

She was the one who had been shrieking.

There was no sign of her older child but the little one, now a toddler, was playing with some pieces of kindling over by the stove.

Helen put down her celery. After a moment she busied herself with righting the table, which lay on its side on the floor. She was trying, strangely enough, to do what she thought Dallas would have done in the same circumstances. Dallas always seemd so sure of herself, kind and friendly, never making judgements.

There was a smashed bottle of rye whisky, which partly accounted for the smell. Helen found a broom.

"Could I have a cup of water?" said the girl on the mattress.

Helen found a cup and got water from the butt.

"Oh yeah, I remember you," said the girl. "You and that old woman. Well, I decided to come back anyway."

With a subtle gesture she indicated her belly. It was obvious why she had decided to come back.

"Where were you all winter?"

"I went to stay with my folks in Buffalo Neck. Now I come back and *she's* here."

Dallas had stopped crying.

"Make tea," she ordered. Her voice was dry and hoarse like Sarah's.

Silently, Helen started to make tea.

Everyone here knew what had happened. No explanations were needed. None could help anyway.

But the situation was too squalid for Dallas, Helen thought. This shouldn't have happened to her.

Like the situation at her own house. Helen gritted her teeth, laughing a little. It wasn't very amusing.

"I came here because I couldn't go into my house," she said, giving Dallas a tea-cup. "Max and his wife are having an argument."

"His wife?" Dallas looked up, surprised.

"Yes. His wife arrived last night."

"Oh. To get the kids?"

"Yes. And to get away from her boyfriend, I think. Now she and Max are having a fight about money. I couldn't bear to stay there and listen."

"I'm not going to stay here any longer," said Dallas. She gave Rosaleen a cold, penetrating look. "You shouldn't either," she said.

Rosaleen continued to lie on the mattress. Helen had a chilling sense of the girl's helplessness, her inability to protect herself.

"Where are you going to go, Dallas? I'd ask you to stay with me, but—" It was obvious that no one could stay with her.

Dallas shook her head.

She was crying again, silently, big tears falling out of her eyes.

No one had told her about Rosaleen and Eli. Helen had not told her either. It was the rule they all lived by: to talk, to interfere, was something people did only if they were drunk or trying to make trouble.

But how much did Eli matter to Dallas anyway? She wanted her mother. That was the person she had wanted all along.

Dallas began tying up her mukluks.

"Come with me," she said.

Helen put her parka back on. She looked anxiously at Rosaleen. Still lying down, Rosaleen rested her warm teacup on her rounded belly.

"See you," she said to Helen.

They were going to Sarah's house. Helen divined this from the short cut they took, a path she now never used. Dallas was deeply preoccupied, walking fast in the gathering dusk.

She said:

"I want to have this baby. And I'm not going to give her up."

She stopped in her tracks. "Maybe this is the only way," she said. "Now I've got nothing. Do you think she'll see me now?"

"Yes," said Helen. She looked at her friend with sympathy and pity.

The Dallas of Christmastime, self-confident, healed, living with a man—perhaps that was the daughter Sarah wouldn't see. But Dallas now, homeless and desperate to keep her baby—Helen was sure that Sarah could not refuse her.

"I'm scared of her," said Dallas. "She hasn't been letting me come near. Your place was the closest I could get."

Helen felt surprised and strangely fearful. It was true that she herself had been avoiding this path.

"You know that she has the power?" Dallas put her hand on Helen's arm.

"Yes," said Helen. They had started to walk again very slowly.

"I guess she's the last. The last one in my family. Maybe she's the last in the world. I'd forgotten all about that till I came back here."

Helen was shivering. It was now really dark and she was cold. The idea of a circle of power around Sarah's house was oddly compelling there on the lakeshore.

"I'm not sure she'll let me come in either," she ventured. "She rejected me."

"But she loves you," said Dallas fiercely. "She loves me too. See?"

They were at Sarah's door.

They stood there, side by side, and after a moment the door opened and Sarah, tall and gaunt, appeared in the lighted aperture. She looked down at them and after a moment she beckoned them to come in.

Helen was in tears. Her estrangement from Sarah had seemed absolute. The most deeply wounding part of it was that she still loved Sarah and could never repay her for the years of her support and friendship. But perhaps, somehow, she had done something like that now.

She glanced at Dallas and saw that she was crying too.

Sarah drew her daughter in the door.

Helen paused. She knew that she had to leave them alone together.

"Sarah," she said. "Will I see you again?"

Sarah nodded.

"Then I'll go now."

She stepped off the doorstep and the door closed behind her. The tears were ice on her lashes and her cheeks. Inside the house, she heard the sound of sobbing in two strong female voices, the fierce, wild tones of Dallas and the harsh, sad note of her mother.

She went home.

She met Freddy and Mickey lingering apprehensively outside by the woodpile.

"Let's go in," she said.

She lifted the latch and led the way. But no one was yelling any more. There was a good smell of dinner cooking.

CHAPTER FORTY-TWO
Dry Lease

THE NEXT evening Helen was typing up the charts for Marion's "Dialect of Women's Fishing" paper. It was the sort of drudgery she used to do for Paul and she wondered why she was doing it now. Marion was not a native shaman but she could wring blood from a turnip. It was going to be a nice little paper, Helen could see that.

She was sitting on the floor by the loft steps with her typewriter, as usual.

Missy seemed to have taken over the housekeeping altogether. They had had spaghetti for supper: Missy wouldn't cook the rabbits that Abe left on the doorstep.

There was a lot of cheerful talk, however, and Helen gathered that Missy and the boys were intending to leave, possibly even quite soon. They were discussing school now. Freddy thought he might still be able to finish part of Grade 12. Mickey was not so optimistic about his chances. Missy was talking about various repairs that needed to be done at home. She must have gotten quite a lot of money from Max the other day as a consequence of their dispute.

Max came in and the cheerful talk instantly ceased. His haggard appearance put everyone on edge again.

"Supper's cold," said Missy.

Max looked at Helen. She took her hands off the typewriter and looked back at him disconsolately. He had not even come home the night before. Helen thought he must have slept in the plane.

"I better go chop wood," said Max.

"Mickey already did."

"I'm going to do some more. Not hungry, anyway." He went out.

A bleak silence descended. Missy began to do the dishes.

Helen couldn't concentrate on anthropology any longer.

Something in the Air Carrier Act was bothering her: the regulations about leasing. There was an insurmountable obstacle. She really had to talk to Max. But he was in full flight from his family again. If he was going to chop wood outside, this might be her chance.

Max was looking at the wood Mickey had cut. He was holding the axe, his shoulders slumped. Helen knew how humiliated he felt, bested in the quarrel with Missy, unable to sleep at home. Missy's arrival had invaded Max's life even more than her own.

"Max—" She spoke tentatively and he looked at her in apprehension. She knew that if she told him it was over now, it really would be over.

But she was not going to tell him that.

"It's just about—" Helen tried to reassure him with her prosaic tone. "About what the Air Carrier Act says. About leasing."

"Oh."

"About dry leases," she continued.

Max rested his hands on the axe handle, looking down.

"You see, the regulations say that in order to get a charter license you have to own 25 per cent of an airplane."

"I've got enough money, I think," he said. "Stole it from the Holy-bolies."

"Yes, but some people might call it wages."

"Some people might."

"Well, anyway, if you think we can get Agaric to agree to sell 25 per cent—"

"He'll sign anything if you send him enough money."

"—then that condition would be fulfilled. You would own 25 per cent. But there's another twist."

Max looked at her patiently.

"There are two kinds of leases. There are wet leases and dry leases, but all you can get is a dry lease."

"If you say so."

"No, no. First of all, Charles Fish said so, and then I looked it up and it's in the regulations."

He smiled at her and, encouraged, she went closer and put her hand on his arm.

"So you will own 25 percent of the plane, and you and Agaric will have to lease it to the Holy-bolies until the license comes through. And you'll have a dry lease."

"No problem then?" He was looking into her face and she saw with dawning hope that there was a faint sparkle in his eyes. Could it be sex? This conversation would once have been sex itself. Talking about the Air Carrier Act was what they did before, after, and sometimes even during.

He began to embrace her and she slid her arms around his neck. It was really very cold and dark out there, away from the lamplit windows. But this was something, at least, in a cold world. They exchanged a long, cold, passionate kiss.

"There *is* a problem," said Helen, as soon as she could speak. "A problem with the lease."

"A problem with the lease?" He put the axe down to free his other hand.

"You see—under the terms of a dry lease—you can't—" He was kissing her again. But where could they go? There was nothing but a snowbank on the other side of the woodpile.

The outside door of the porch now swung open and Missy emerged, carrying a canvas woodsling.

"Talking?" she inquired. She began to fill the sling from Mickey's neat pile.

Max and Helen had sprung apart.

"You must be cold," Missy went on.

Max started to disappear into the dark yard.

Helen pulled herself together.

"Please," she said to him. "I have to tell you."

"Well, *please*," said Missy. She held the door open. "Come in then."

They preceded her, single file.

Max went over to the kitchen ledge and stood there, folding his arms. But the kitchen was no longer his preserve. Missy set down the woodsling and instantly displaced him to rinse out the coffee pot in the dishpan.

Max and Helen stood staring at one another in the middle of the floor. A pool of water was forming around Helen's boots.

"With a dry lease, you can't supply the air crew," said Helen desperately. "You can't supply the air crew directly or indirectly, that's what it says."

"Oh, *that* was what you had to tell him."

"Directly or indirectly?" Max sounded bewildered.

"You see, if you owned the plane together with Agaric, and you leased it to the Holy-bolies, and then you worked under their license, you would be supplying the aircrew."

"Supplying the aircrew?"

"She means you'd be flying it, dumb-bell" said Missy. She joined the conversation, putting her hands on her hips. "Let me get this. You can't own it and fly it? That's a pretty strange law."

"It is."

"I mean, I thought the whole idea was to get hold of an airplane and fly it."

"The problem only arises if you have to have a dry lease." Helen was now talking to Missy, who seemed to have a remarkably quick grasp of the essentials. "But it has to be a dry lease. And Max can't stop flying the plane."

"So it can't be done," said Max. He sounded resigned.

"I just can't understand it. It almost seems as though the law exists to make it impossible to get a license. I've been thinking about this problem for days."

"What if somebody else owned the 25 per cent?" said Missy. It struck Helen, not for the first time, that Missy was an intelligent woman.

"Then Max couldn't apply for the license. In order to get a license, you have to own 25 per cent of an airplane."

"Yeah, but he doesn't have to get a license. There's you. Why don't you get it? You're doing it, anyway. All the paperwork."

"Me?" Helen laughed. "But I'm not a pilot."

"Sure," said Max, thinking about it. "If you were the one who owned the 25 per cent—"

"—you wouldn't be flying the plane," Missy finished, impatiently.

"Yeah." Max was still thinking it through slowly. "And we're not related or anything. We're not even married. So you wouldn't be—"

"Indirectly supplying the air crew." Helen pondered. "Are you sure—?"

"Well, it doesn't mean anything anyway, does it? 'Indirectly supplying.' Do they care if you screw? Is that what it's all about?" said Missy.

Helen suddenly recalled Fish telling her; "I think you'll find there are a lot of women in aviation these days." The pilot's girlfriend had to own the plane. That was the solution. She understood him now.

"So how much does 25 per cent of an airplane cost, anyway?" said Missy. "Not that I'm interested."

Max made a sudden, despairing gesture with his hand. Helen had guessed that money was at the heart of his quarrel with Missy the other day. She decided to be forthright.

"About $10,000 for this plane. We don't have that much, but we have the lien from paying Agaric's gas bill..."

Missy sat down at the table. Her lips twisted. She put her hand on her forehead. "Oh, shit," she said, after a moment. "So what?"

Helen sighed. She also sat down. Perhaps they were going to begin arguing again. But her mind was turning slowly over something else.

"Well, it would make a difference to me if you became a millionaire," Missy said to Max. "I suppose that's something to look forward to."

"Oh, come on. This isn't a million dollar deal."

"Anyway, it wouldn't be you, would it? I wonder if she'll make regular support payments." Missy looked at Helen coolly, but there was no hostility in her glance. "Well, go ahead," she said. "I'm not stopping you."

Helen did not reply. There was a long pause.

"Okay, Helen?" said Max. She knew he was wishing they were in bed for this discussion.

She understood what he was asking. Owning 25 per cent of the plane would be like getting married. But it would be worse than getting married. It wasn't a partnership. She would have to own everything. And if she gave everything back, it would be useless to him.

He was asking too much of her.

"Okay," she said.

Max let out his breath in relief.

"Maybe I should have told you to say no," said Missy dryly. "But it's a waste of time trying to give advice. As my mother said when I got pregnant."

Max was still looking at Helen. He knew that the commitment was terrifying her.

"Trust me?" he said. His voice was gentle.

She nodded.

Missy contemplated them for a moment, her hands on her hips. Then she turned to the dishpan.

Helen went back to her typewriter. She pushed Marion's charts to one side and began to draft the 25 per cent ownership agreement for Agaric to sign.

CHAPTER FORTY-THREE
Record of a Life

THEY PATCHED up a deal with Garuluk over the next few days using telegrams as the means of getting his attention. Finally he called.

When Helen read him the short contract, there was a stunned pause.

"So – this'd be you and me?" he asked.

"Yes."

"What've you got on Freddy?"

"What do you mean by that?"

"Is this *your* money?"

The prospect of trying to explain dry leases to Garuluk dawned on Helen like cold misery.

"How'd you get him to go along with it? What've you got on him, that's what I'd like to know!"

It was a very Canadian situation. The legal system and the civil service existed to write letters to each other. Meanwhile people like Garuluk and Max were out there swapping DC-3 engines and owning each other's skis, completely ignorant of the great edifice of legal conditions and paperwork that hung above them, irrelevant, but menacing.

"Say," Garuluk went on. "Maybe when you come down here this spring you and I could get together. Get together and we could fire Freddy, to start with." He chuckled.

Helen sent the money from the post office in the Co-op. She got $6,000 in postal orders. After a moment she passed them through the wicket to Mrs. Henry Woodcutter, who was the post mistress.

"I just wanted to hold them in my hand for a little while," she explained. "You can send them off now."

Mrs. Henry Woodcutter nodded. Helen supposed she felt the same way about having $6,000 in her drawer. That had probably never happened before in Island Crossing.

She walked meditatively through town in the long afternoon light. There was nothing to dread, nothing to fear. A decision had been taken; now it was done. And Missy had been very nice to her all day, cooking lunch and bringing her cups of tea.

When Paul showed up suddenly on the path ahead of her she was not alarmed.

"Hi," she said.

"Fancy meeting you here."

"I was coming to wait for Max."

"Oh yes, I suppose he's due to show up soon."

"Maybe he got held up at one of the bush camps. He's been doing the rounds, hauling gas."

"You're keeping Flight Watch for him, are you?"

"Yes." Helen found herself smiling at him.

"Marion's writing a paper," he said abruptly.

"I know." Helen wondered whether he knew she was doing the charts. She could see how annoying it must be.

"I'm thinking of throwing it in."

"What do you mean?"

"Going bloody well home," he said bitterly. "She came along to do her own thing And no one here wants to talk to me. I'm just hanging around making tea and listening to the jays."

Marion was no longer staying in the camp with him. Dallas was living in Sarah's smokehouse teepee down by the lakeshore, and she had invited Marion to stay there with her while they collaborated on the paper. Helen wondered whether it was going to come out under both their names. But she thought Marion had at last found a person with something interesting to say who was not going to turn into a Ph.D student.

"So you really believe now that I did burn your things?" Helen asked.

"Jesus and Maria, if you hadn't, surely you'd have given them back by now. We'd be rid of each other!"

"You've finally realized how mean I can be?"

"Well, I guess it was because of the diaries. For Christ's sake, though," he went on, "did you think I was going to publish those? Maybe I'd have burned them myself if I'd got hold of them."

"But I mean," said Helen, "You really think I'm such a bitch?"

"Sure you are. But I thought you had more sense, that's all. For one thing, you were also sort of—"

"Sort of an academic? Almost an intellectual, you mean?"

He did not reply, merely turning his head away, and she pondered.

"I wanted my revenge."

"Sure," he muttered.

"You broke my nose, but that was only the last thing you did. The whole relationship—"

"I told you. I was in therapy." He was still talking with averted head.

"Anyway—" Helen's heart was suddenly light. "You can have them back. Even the diaries."

"What?"

"I'll give them back to you. I didn't burn them."

She would never have been able to give them back if she hadn't met him at this moment in time, she felt. It was the power of the adventitious. If she had never met Max. If she had not been waiting here, a little anxious, in the long dusk. If she had not just started to feel her way cautiously towards the future.

He was angry. No wonder, she thought.

"Are you just doing this to get rid of me? So you can really get it on with Mr. Right?"

"Maybe," said Helen. She was undisturbed.

"Because you're making a big mistake there!" he snarled. "You're in a mess. His wife, his kids—what kind of a menage is that, anyway?"

"A mess," she agreed. "Sarah has the notes. I'll get them for you. Sarah would never give them to you."

"No one in this godforsaken place will give me the time of day! Did you put a spell on them or something?"

Helen was startled. Then she laughed. "Well, I just hope the notes are all you need, then," she said. "Happy Ph.D."

It was strange how just one moment of impulse could have overturned her resolution never to give his papers back. She even found herself walking rather fast to get the job done.

She had thrown away her power. Or was she more powerful now that she had shown him what she was capable of? She had been able to ruin him.

She began to run. Now she was going to get rid of him. She didn't hate him any longer. It was quite simple. The marriage was over.

But it was not so simple, she reflected, as she arrived at Sarah's door. There was something quite awful about what she had done. It wasn't good to be strong and powerful and unforgiving. Sarah's life showed that. Decision, restraint, inflexible will —all of these things could be turned to terrible purposes. She had let go just in time.

Sarah and Abe Balah were playing cards. They had a lamp lit and there was a delicious smell of fish soup. It was a cosy scene.

Abe pulled out a chair and Helen sat down, out of breath.

"Fish for supper?" she said, when she could speak again.

He nodded. He was no longer pretending not to understand.

Sarah folded up the cards and, putting on her glasses, picked up a piece of beadwork. Helen was astounded. She had never seen Sarah sew beads before.

"I want Paul's papers," she said. Somehow the beadwork, Abe, the fish soup—they all made it easier to say this to Sarah. Sarah, who had kept her grief and rage locked away inside herself for so many years.

"I'm giving them back. Paul will go if I give them back."

"That will make him go," Sarah agreed.

The alarm clock ticked, the fire crackled, the smell of soup filled the air. The domesticity of the scene made Helen a little jealous. Sarah must have felt the same way about her in the fall after Max moved in.

Sarah made an authoritative gesture, and Abe rose and got the box of manuscripts out from under the bed. They had been in there, sharing space with Dallas' letters and all the other secrets Sarah kept for other people. It amused and surprised Helen to see Abe get up to do Sarah's bidding as if he had been herself or Dallas.

Sarah was as taciturn as ever. But she was looking well, even happy. Her beauty had come back after her illness and she reminded Helen of Dallas. She watched calmly while Helen picked up the box of papers.

Abe poked the fire and put on another stick. He was looking happy too. He must have waited a long time for Sarah. This was what it meant to have picked someone, apparently.

It was now clear what these two were to each other, and Helen rejoiced for them.

She went out the door, then turned in astonishment to look at the front of Sarah's office. The birch tree, the tree that grew out of the wall, was gone. Someone had cut it down. Abe or Sarah herself. What was left was just a plain little shack made of weathered boards—but neat and cozy, with the yellow lamplight shining in the windows.

What had happened to Sarah was like what had happened to Helen this past year. She had let Max in and that had changed everything in her life. Bit by bit it had happened. She had let go of her bitterness.

But she could not be glad that Sarah's tree was gone. Of course, it was a birch tree and they often sprouted up again from the stump. Could that tree really be gone forever?

Helen suddenly remembered her errand and began to run again. She arrived, panting, in the clearing at the end of the airstrip. Paul had made a fire and was sitting moodily beside it. He wore duck boots, Helen noticed; the swamp was thawing. The muck around the fireplace was almost over the tops of his rubbers.

"Here." She handed him the box.

"They're all here?"

"Yes. Why not?" she said. "I don't care any longer, Paul."

He checked. Then he began to go through the papers, systematically, obsessively. Helen watched. She had always hated his scrimshaw way with notes, the way he made them in tiny handwriting, the way he read and reread them, making more notes, notes upon notes.

Then, abruptly, he picked up the diaries in a double handful and held them out over the fire, turning his head to look at her. Perhaps he had dreamed of destroying them himself, just as she had dreamed of it.

"Don't do it," she said. "It's your life, your whole life, remember?"

After a moment he pulled the diaries back from the flames.

"No," he said. "I can't do it."

And then an awful thought struck Helen.

The fire. It was dark. And where was Max?

CHAPTER FORTY-FOUR
Missing

B Y THE time she got home Helen had decided not to panic. Max was probably safe at a bush camp, overtaken by darkness and spending the night.

She would merely go to Mrs. Henry Woodcutter's house and see whether she had heard any news from the bush on her radio. She would go later on. After supper, perhaps.

When she went into her house, Mickey and Freddy were eating canned fruit at the table. Missy was doing dishes, as usual.

She hung around miserably for a short while, unable to eat. No one commented on Max's absence and she supposed it just seemed normal to them. She was the only one who knew what his plans were.

He was undoubtedly at a bush camp, spending the night.

She went out without explanation and walked over to Mrs. Henry's house. She knocked briefly, then went in. There was the roaring, static-filled sound of the radio, with many voices talking at once in several different Athapaskan languages.

The bush radio was not on aviation frequencies. The people out on the land used it for emergencies or to pass on the news. Right now, with so many people in the bush, Mrs. Henry Woodcutter was listening to it most of the time.

She was sitting on the clean bare floor beside the radio. The middle boy, Danny, was playing with a baby, probably the child of Mrs. Henry's oldest daughter. Helen sat down cross-legged and waited while Mrs. Henry turned down the volume.

"Have you heard anything about Max?" she asked.

"They're lookin' for him," said Mrs. Henry.

"They're looking for him?" Helen spoke carefully. But her heart sank. That meant he was not at a bush camp, not one with a radio, in any case.

"Where's Henry?" she asked.

Mrs. Henry raised her hand and turned up the volume. Helen made out Henry's voice in the midst of the static. He was making a speech, or giving directions, for a moment later a number of other voices tuned in with short assenting utterances.

Mrs. Henry turned down the volume again and looked at Helen in silence.

"Henry knows where Max was supposed to go?"

Mrs. Henry went into the kitchen and returned with a map. It was an old map, a game warden's map, cobbled together with tape and covered with notations: Eph Balah's camp, James Woodcutter's camp at Trump Lake, and so on.

Helen indicated the lakes. Mrs. Henry, wearing reading glasses, peered over her shoulder.

"Radio's here," she said. "This is where they're lookin'."

"Have they been looking long?"

"Since dark. Henry called in then."

"Oh." Helen suddenly felt like crying. It was true then. Other people—Henry, the men in the camps, Mrs. Henry—all confirmed that Max was missing. "But they can't look in the dark," she said.

Mrs. Henry put her hand lightly on Helen's shoulder.

"They'll find him tomorrow," she said.

Helen went home. The air, she noticed, was fresh and warm, almost wet. It might even rain. She remembered Max in the fall, wet to the thighs, barely getting the plane out of the ice piled up on shore. The changes of the year were the most dangerous seasons.

She thought of the searchers out on skidoos, trying to get through the overflow on lakes and rivers, fighting the sticky snow.

There had to be a more efficient way to look for a missing plane.

No one at home had yet noticed anything amiss.

Helen hesitated, then went to the phone and called the number of Mountain River Air Service.

Brutson answered, and she told him quite bluntly what had happened. There was no time to play games or even to pretend that they were on good terms. But she needed someone's help; someone who would know what to do.

While she was talking she kept her eyes on Missy. Missy was listening; after a moment she came closer. Then she sat down and covered her mouth with her hand. The boys were also watching Helen with scared faces.

"You've got to call Search and Rescue in Winnipeg," Brutson said.

"I didn't know."

"Yeah. Well, I'll do it then. They'll do one of their electronic searches tonight or tomorrow, not that that'll tell them anything. I guess he had an ELT?"

"What's an ELT?"

"You sure can write a letter for somebody who doesn't know nothing. Emergency Locator Transmitter. They never work anyway. Tomorrow or probably the next day the Air Force'll send up a Hercules with a guy hanging out its rear end and begin looking at the ground."

There was a slight clunk on the line. He had set the receiver down momentarily and Helen heard a woman's voice, a rather relentless voice, speaking in the background. Could this be Brutson's wife? Did he have a wife?

There was a long pause.

Brutson came on the line again. "Okay, I'm comin' over tomorrow."

"Oh—good!"

"I'll be over first thing."

"Thank you. Thank you very much!"

"Don't thank me," he said ponderously and rang off.

Helen put down the phone. Missy burst into tears. Mickey also began to cry, while Freddy looked at her with sad, frightened eyes.

"They're searching for him already," Helen said. "The people out in the bush are looking."

"Oh shit!" said Missy. "If only he hadn't had this bug in his head about flying."

"Did he crash the plane?"

"No one knows, you jerk-off! Maybe he made a landing on a lake or something and just—"

"Yeah, but why was he landing on a lake where there weren't any people? Tell me that, snotface?"

The boys continued to argue, going over the possibilities that had been running through Helen's head all evening.

She made a last late visit to Mrs. Henry Woodcutter's house. But the radio was off; everyone in the bush had gone to bed, preparing for tomorrow.

"It's so warm," said Helen. "Aren't they worried they won't be able to go anywhere by skidoo?"

"Walk if they have to," said Mrs. Henry. "I walk all over those lakes when I was a girl."

Missy was in a state. She was already engaged in a long, recriminatory monologue with herself when Helen got back, and she went on with it after the boys had gone to bed. She was grieving. Helen didn't blame her. It was hard to listen to, though.

"So when he went to work for Garuluk, I just put my foot down. I said: You can't stay here any longer and freeload on me. I'm throwing you out if you don't go and get a job that pays money! Oh, why did I say that? Maybe if I hadn't . . ."

Helen had not had time to explore her own feelings. But she was missing Max. She was scared of what might have happened to him.

And later on, when Missy finally went to bed in the loft and Helen lay down, her body began missing him acutely, even as her mind took her on a tour of the different ways of dying in an airplane crash: being decapitated or crushed to death, being burned to death or suffocated, being blown to bits or cruelly injured and thrown free to die of blood loss and exposure in the snow.

Helen got up and went out early. First she went to the airport and looked for the Beaver, but it was not there. Then she went to Mrs. Henry Woodcutter's house and waited patiently on the doorstep for someone to get up.

It was a very poor day, warm and foggy. It still felt like rain: rain that would be a disaster for any kind of search. Rain that would cover the trails with slush and coat the planes with a heavy, dangerous load of ice.

She heard the roaring noise as the radio was turned on inside.

Danny came out on the doorstep, chewing on a hunk of dry meat. He sat down beside Helen.

"My Dad's at Loon Lake now. They're lookin'," he said. He offered Helen a piece of his meat and she nibbled it, remembering that she was probably hungry.

There was the sound of an airplane and Helen got up and ran the airport. So did Danny, and Mrs. Henry, and several dozen other people. In the crowd she saw Paul and Marion, Dallas, Abe Balah, and Eli's father.

But it was not Max. It was Brutson.

He jumped out of his plane and, after surveying the crowd impatiently, came over to Helen.

"You're the one, eh?" he said.

He was a big fat man with a red face. She had seen him occasionally, bringing in the sched; in fact, he had brought her in with Paul three years before, but there was no reason for him to remember that.

"He ain't answering the radio. I was callin' him on the way over."

"What does it mean?"

"Well, he's not in the air no longer, that's for sure. And he ain't usin' his radio. So, what do you think? Maybe he went to Winnipeg?"

She nodded, hunching her shoulders and pressing her lips together.

Brutson looked at her acutely.

"Didn't get any sleep, eh?" he said. "Can't think too good today, I guess. You been listening on the bush radio?" he continued.

"There's no word."

"Who's the Chief in this little no-horse place?" He snapped his fingers.

"Henry Woodcutter." Helen had the idea that Brutson knew Henry's name very well. "He's out looking. They've got a search going on the ground."

"Well, he's down there somewhere, that's for sure. What the hell did he think he was doin' still on straight skis at this time of year, anyway?"

"It's when the people go out."

"Yeah, I know. Always go on the last day. They got no sense of time, and besides, so what if a whiteman wrecks his plane—he's got plenty more of 'em. Plenty more whitemen too. That's the way they see it."

Helen shrugged helplessly.

"Yeah. Take a guy like that man of yours—been flyin' one, maybe two seasons up North. Probably thinks he knows what he's doing. Put him in a place like this and what've you got? Boom! An aircraft accident."

He suddenly stopped and looked at Helen again.

"Hey! Forget I said all that. Just stop crying, okay?"

They went to her house. Missy and the boys were sitting at the table. There was some indication that they had eaten or not eaten breakfast. Now they had a pack of cards out and were playing or trying to play Go Fish.

Helen took off her parka and pointed out a hook for Brutson.

She was going to introduce them all, but he was galvanized by the ruby surrounded by its glimmering circlet of diamonds on the bosom of her T-shirt.

He stared at it, his eyes bulging.

"Oh yes, your pilot-engineer," said Helen.

"Frigging screwball tried to sell me that thing. That was before he stole my frigging plane!"

"You should be glad we got him to return it," said Helen.

"That was you?" He shifted his lead-coloured eyeballs to her face. "Wanted me to give him $8,000 for that thing. A frigging fake if I ever saw one."

"I don't think so," said Helen. She pointed out the heart on the window.

Brutson went over to examine it carefully. Then he turned around with a discontented look on his face.

Helen hastily introduced them. "Mr. Brutson. Max's kids. And his wife."

"Wife?" Brutson looked at Helen. "Thought you were the wife."

"Make that ex-wife," said Missy, with a hint of her customary snarl. Then she sniffed and drew the back of her hand over her mouth.

Brutson spread out an aviation map and they went over it together, Helen trying to tell him everything she remembered hearing from Max and pointing out the camps as they appeared on Mrs. Henry Woodcutter's map. But he knew what he was looking at anyway. He had been doing the flying here before Max came. Or refusing to do it, Helen thought, recalling a few things she had heard.

"Okay," he said finally. "You kids want to come along? Got to have spotters. We'll go around and take a look."

They departed, and Helen went over to Mrs. Henry's again to listen to the bush radio.

About an hour later Brutson returned.

"Got freezing rain up there. Can't see nothing anyway," he said. "There's rain and snow all over the place. Maybe we'll get a chance later."

Missy had prepared canned soup for lunch. Brutson wolfed it down, then lit a cigar.

"Know how to play poker?" he said to Mickey and Freddy. "I can teach anybody who's got a five dollar bill how to play poker."

After Brutson had won Helen's twenty dollars, he announced he was going to go to the airport. It was still a nasty day. The fog rolled over the lake ice, and drops of slush were in the air.

Brutson was putting on his jacket.

"Goin' to go sit in my plane," he said. "I know this place, see. Like to keep the air in my frigging tires. There's not a guy here includin' women who doesn't owe me a couple hundred bucks. Yeah, well, it was real nice takin' your money," he said, and went out.

The boys looked at each other and went after him.

Helen was going to see Mrs. Henry Woodcutter again.

Missy put a hand on her arm.

"Wait, Helen," she said.

Helen turned around, startled that Missy had called her by name.

"What are you going to do if—if—" She couldn't say it.

"I don't know," said Helen.

"I mean, the kids and I will be all right. We were going to go home anyway. But you. You haven't got anything. What are you going to do?"

Helen looked at her. Missy's eyes were bright. She was on the verge of tears again.

"You could come with us. And stay for a while. There's nothing for you here. If he's dead, you haven't got anything."

*

Helen was in bed and it was still very dark, but she was not asleep. She had been crying, but she was not crying any longer. She was thinking about Max, or rather, not thinking about him so much as trying to throw her mental process out in a long lasso so that it would capture him and bring him back alive.

At the same time she knew some things about herself that she had not known before. She knew that she loved him, but not in the way that she had loved Paul. She felt that it was possible for her to be an independent being, strong and even critical. Her strength counted for something with Max; he actually needed her for it. Her independence, her intelligence, these were qualities that made their relationship better. She would never again love someone the way a young child loves a parent, or the way a believer worships a god.

But it seemed as though she had reached this understanding only in time to lose Max.

Missy was right. There was nothing for her in Island Crossing if Max was dead. She would have to go somewhere else and start again.

She knew she could live without him. But she wanted him.

She threw her longing out into the darkness of spruce trees and muskeg lakes and rivers coiling on to nowhere.

And now she imagined him, and strangely enough, it was a vivid image, very simple and direct, as though the lasso of her mind had really caught something. She saw only his face, illuminated by a fire: his long hawksbeak nose, his dark eyes, his mouth smiling, although he looked sad.

231

Then she remembered the time he had told her about his mother, about his Indian blood. He had been lighting a cigarette from the stove with a spill.

Helen began crying again in bitter disappointment. It was only a memory, after all.

But there was suddenly someone in the room.

CHAPTER FORTY-FIVE
Out on the Land

HE WAS stamping the snow off his boots on the rug. But he knew her cabin. He came right over to her bed at once.

And even though he was in his heavy winter clothes, she recognized Eli Balah.

"What is it?"

"He wants you to come."

She sat up.

"He?" she said. "Who?"

"Henry. We found your old man."

"He's alive? He's not hurt?" she demanded.

"He's fine."

"Where is he?"

"Ptarmigan Lake. Henry sent me in to tell you. The radio's all screwed up because of the weather."

"Oh!" She threw back the covers. "I'm coming. How far is it? Are you going back right away?"

"Yeah, it's not all that far. Thirty miles."

Helen was getting dressed rapidly.

"The plane," she said. "Did he crash it?"

"Or some damn thing."

"Wait. I've got to tell everyone." She was already wearing her parka.

"Let 'em sleep. There's people here that know now. We'll get the radio goin' again tomorrow."

Helen snatched up her big mitts, her sweater, an extra pair of socks, a balaclava, and rolled them all in the down quilt from her bed.

"We've got all that kind of stuff," he protested. "Henry and me were just out of cigarettes."

"I haven't got any."

"That's okay. Got some while I was getting gas. That new Co-op manager's all right."

Helen got on the back of his skidoo and they roared off. A moment later they stopped in front of Sarah's house.

"I'm takin' my uncle," explained Eli. "He knows all the trails. There's a lot of overflow."

Abe Balah came out of the house, pulling on his mitts. Helen caught a glimpse of Sarah in a nightgown, her hair in a skimpy grey braid. She waved briefly and then shut the door. The little house stood there, snug and blank without the birch tree.

They had a long trip through the bush. It was a wet, dangerous time of year for people on the ground. They should have been safe in their camps now, running their fish nets and waiting for the ducks to come.

Helen took turns riding behind the two men. It was not the usual bone-shattering experience of skidoo-riding in town. They were very cautious, and the thick, deep, sticky snow made the going hard. There were long detours, impassable trails.

The men were laughing. Helen didn't see why. Then she looked behind her and saw Bootleg running along smoothly after the skidoos. He was old and slow, but he had a determined look. After all, he had ancestors too.

Helen began to see that Eli was a good man in the bush, just as Henry and Dallas had claimed. He didn't know the trails the way Abe did, yet he had come in by himself to fetch her. And he was doing most of the work: when they had to walk, when they had to push or carry, it was Eli who did the most.

She was wet and cold, sometimes to the point of misery, but her heart was singing. He's alive, it sang. Max is alive.

They had a tea break soon after daylight had really begun. It was still snowing but colder at last.

"Have your cup," said Abe.

He gave her her cup.

Helen laughed. He spoke English.

Abe laughed too.

He sang all the time. She was puzzled, riding pillion behind him. It didn't sound like the chanting of the drum dance. At last she realized that it was country and western. Droned in Abe's monotone, and over the wind and engine noise, it could have been Chinese opera.

Helen had never been so cold. At first she had taken pleasure in the clammy air, hugging her relief, glad of her freedom from the endless waiting, the crying, the card-playing of yesterday.

But it was still a dim day, and it grew colder and more threatening. There was more snow in the air. The trails were now icy and the skidoos sometimes broke through into water. Her mukluks were soaking on the outside, damp on the inside.

After the third tea break, they let her ride in the toboggan, holding Bootleg. But it was not always possible to ride; when the skidoo got stuck, she had to help Eli. Humming to himself, Abe heaved from the other side.

Abe was a bizarre person. But Helen was beginning to like him. His sense of humour had been with him through fourteen years of silence; it had kept Sarah out of jail. Not speaking English came in handy when there was something you didn't want to talk about. When you were protecting someone.

Her companions now began to crane forward, as though they were expecting something to show up. They were on an eminence overlooking a lake. Helen peered ahead, too. But she saw no sign of people or a plane. Some islands.

They began to proceed down the hill, going faster than usual.

There must be something ahead, around those islands.

Then Helen saw the unmistakable track of airplane skis on the snowy surface of the lake. Tracks that were frozen to a crust. But there was no airplane in sight. Her heart sank.

All at once they were surrounded by people: men with heavy clothes, frozen moustaches, long-ashed cigarettes clenched in their lips, women laughing and exclaiming, and many children with snotty noses and red cheeks.

Eli and Abe had got off their skidoos and were having their backs slapped. Helen was helped out of the toboggan with great tenderness by an elderly woman and given a bannock to eat by a small child.

She was in some sort of camp, she noticed. But where was Max?

Eli had said that Max wanted her to come. But what if that was not it? It might be that Max was dead and they had wanted her to see. To come out and see for herself.

"Where's your old man?" said Eli. He offered her one of his cigarettes, then took it himself and put it between his lips.

A moment later they saw Max.

He was trudging around the point of the big island, a small dark figure with a springy walk, even in the deep snow. He was trailed by a slow skidoo dragging a sled.

Helen strained her eyes to see, overcome with relief. She began to nibble on her bannock. It was odd how, even at a distance and swaddled in winter clothes, he was at once apparent to her. She had been looking for someone with just such a walk.

"They were out gettin' the gas," Eli told her.

"What gas?"

"He screwed up, I guess." Eli shrugged. To him, this was something that had happened. People made mistakes all the time. Whatever this one was, it had happened.

A few moments later, Max came up the bank. His eyes lit up at once when he saw Helen. But he was surprised.

"You?" he said.

"You!" she said. She was cold and exhausted, but also excited, and she wanted to cry.

He embraced her gently. Eli was offering him a cigarette.

Henry suddenly arrived in the camp on a skidoo. He jumped off and came over to Eli at once.

"Give me one of those," he said, taking a cigarette.

He drew on it luxuriously, then turned to Max, blowing smoke out through his nostrils.

"This is Ptarmigan Lake," he said. "What are you doing here?"

"Made a mistake," said Max.

"This is the wrong lake."

"Yeah, I know. I thought it was the one they told me, but it wasn't. So I came back to get the gas I dropped off. Shouldn't have. Shouldn't have been here in the first place. I knew there was overflow. But it was the last chance. They'd never have got in to pick it up till after break-up."

Henry frowned.

"They'd have got in. They got here to find you, after all," he said. He extended his arm to indicate the number of people present. He was still frowning, but Helen knew that he liked Max, and none the less for taking a risk and coming back for the gas.

"What happened to the plane?" she asked.

"I ground-looped her," said Max glumly. "Flipped her over on her wing."

"How'd you do that?" Henry was interested.

"I was taxiing and I hit something, a rock or a push-up or something. Maybe it was one of my own ski tracks from before. Then she went around and over."

"But you didn't get hurt!"

Max and Henry regarded her patiently.

"He's fine," said Henry.

"Bandaid, anyway," said Max.

Helen did not admire this sort of masculine bravura. But she was too happy to care. The fact was, whatever they said, he wasn't hurt.

"You're goin' to have trouble getting her out of here if it rains," said Henry.

Max nodded.

"You've probably only got about ten days before she starts to sink."

"Yeah." He seemed a little abstracted. Helen could feel how tired he was from the way his arm lay against her back.

"You'll have to get somebody in here to patch her up, I guess." Henry was being a little insistent. Of course, the people of Island Crossing still needed the plane.

Someone had made a dug-out fire right in front of them, and Helen looked out over the flames at the long twilight on the lake, and rejoiced. Whatever was going to happen, all was well.

Now someone pressed a hot caribou rib into her hand. It was crunchy and gritty from the flames, juicy within. After a week of canned ravioli and Irish stew from the Co-op, it tasted like manna to Helen.

There was a large circle of people around the fire. It had always been like this for them for thousands of years, Helen knew. They could always make a fire, and there was always hot soup or tea. Then there would be meat, whatever meat there was, cooked by a woman with a proud smile on her lips. Almost instantly you would be dry and warm, as she was now, and everyone would be smoking all your cigarettes, if you had any cigarettes. But in this case the cigarettes were Eli's, and Max was having another one.

She looked at Max. He was as he had been in her vision, a brown face with a hawk-like profile in the firelight. His eyes were sad as he drew on the cigarette.

"I guess we'll be staying here tonight," he said.

"How did you spend last night? How did you spend the night before?"

"I made a fire," he said. "Sat here on a log and wished I was dead. Then I thought about you. Thought you were worrying."

"I was!" She laughed. "We all were. You can imagine how much."

"But where the hell are we going to stay?" he asked. "You—" He clarified it. "Where are you going to stay?"

237

"Do you think this is worse than Agaric's barn?" she demanded. "Besides, I'd spend the night under a spruce tree now that I know you are all right."

"You two got a problem?" Henry had overheard this exchange. "I can get you a tent."

They looked around. There were many tents. The rudimentary camp Helen had first glimpsed had sprung up into a small town. Lights were twinkling through the parted entrances of the white wall tents. At least fifty people were present, gathered around several fires; one by one, slowly, incessantly, they were coming over to shake Max's hand.

Henry began to make a speech in his language, the speech of an old-fashioned leader, lengthy and formal. Finally, he concluded:

"So we hope that he'll get the plane up in the air again and go on flyin' for us after break-up."

There were murmurs of assent and some applause.

Max had by now grasped that sometimes he had to make speeches. He said:

"Sorry I broke the plane. See what we can do, anyway. Pretty tired now. Thanks for coming. Thanks for getting Helen."

They were all clapping and laughing at his speech. Helen was glad he had admitted it was his fault. No one here held that against him. The people who might, she realized with a sinking heart, were their own people, in Ottawa, or Winnipeg.

She began wishing desperately that they could be alone. Looking around at the ring of dark, smiling faces in the firelight, she could see the odds weren't great.

"God, I'm tired," murmured Max.

"Oh yeah," said Henry. He began making another speech in the language and everyone was laughing. It was a dirty joke, obviously. Henry was looking at her out of the corner of his eye. He seemed to expect her to understand. Helen smiled politely, unamused.

"What's it all about?" whispered Max. He was leaning on her quite heavily and she felt his weariness. If only they could be alone, where he could lie down.

A moment later Henry was escorting them uphill and pushing them into the nearest tent. There was a blast of heat as he opened the flap. A woman who had been kneeling before the gas drum stove, putting in an armload of wood, got up and smiled at them, then exited hastily with a squawk at Henry, who was going out right behind her.

The floor was covered with spruce boughs, roughly and hastily cut, but laid down in a thick mat. A sleeping bag was spread out on one side. The warmth from the red hot stove was almost overwhelming.

"My sleeping bag," mumbled Max.

"My goodness." Helen was astonished. Henry was a very clever man. He couldn't organize his own private life very well, but he was good at arranging everybody else's.

Max had thrown himself face down on the sleeping bag without even taking off his parka or boots. He was going to be asleep in a moment. Helen considered him as she sat down beside his feet to unlace his boots. There were many questions that she needed to ask him about what was going to happen.

But Helen was very tired herself. And as she worked the stiff, frozen boots off his feet, she rejoiced to see him lying there, alive and sleeping.

CHAPTER FORTY-SIX
The Fatal Allure of Jewels

IT WAS cold again, and they had a much easier time travelling the next day. There were also many more of them, a long cavalcade of skidoos and sleds. Many people were going back to town.

First they went out on the lake to bid a ceremonial farewell to the plane.

It leaned crazily over on one wing, one side of the landing gear broken and askew. The wingtip was crumpled and the skin of the wing wrinkled nearly halfway up its length.

Max jumped off the back of the skidoo he was riding on and went over to stand beside the plane. Helen trudged over more slowly in his tracks.

"It can be fixed, can't it?"

"Sure. If we had the money to get an engineer."

"What about the insurance company?"

"Out here, at this time of year? They'll think it's a write-off."

"What about the insurance money?"

"The Holy-bolies get it. Plane's registered to them."

"Don't they have to pay Agaric?"

"Think they will? Think he's going to pay us?" Max shrugged. "Anyway, she'll be on the bottom of the lake by the time we finish arguing about it."

Almost as an ironic comment on their conversation, a small plane, a white one with candy stripes, came over the pale horizon and circled overhead. It dove down for an even closer look and Helen caught sight of Brutson's red face smiling broadly, while the two spotters, Freddy and Mickey, waved frantically from behind. The plane rose again and made off in the direction of Island Crossing, with a triumphant farewell waggle of its wings.

Max lit a cigarette.

"I can start driving a truck again," he said. "But what are you going to do?"

He thought they had lost everything.

She saw that he was afraid they might lose each other.

The cavalcade had started up again and they went back to their skidoos, Max riding behind Henry, and Helen behind Eli or Abe.

*

Missy hugged Max.

"I wished you were dead often enough, but now I don't know!"

"What happened, Dad?"

Max sat down. Freddy immediately handed him Mickey's cigarettes. He began telling them about the accident.

"What'd you think when she was going over?"

"What'd I think? I thought, Whoops!" said Max.

Missy's lips twisted into an ironic smile. Helen knew that Missy liked Max saying Whoops! about as much as Helen had liked him saying he needed a bandaid. Male bravado was really very annoying. And they taught their boy children things like that too; he was teaching his.

Helen went out to find Brutson. She wanted to say thank you. And she was also wondering whether, like everyone else in town, they owed him a lot of money.

She found him at the airport.

He was sitting in the cockpit, running up his engine. When he noticed her, he shut it off and got out.

"I came to say thank you," Helen panted.

He shrugged.

"It was my old lady, really," he said. "Told me I had to do something."

"You tried to look. And you helped me so much. I didn't know what to do."

"He can walk, can he?"

"Yes, he's fine."

"Too bad." Brutson lit one of his cigars. "If the sucker can walk, I guess he can still fly."

"We owe you something, I think."

"Sure. I'll send you the bill," he snarled. He got back in the cockpit and began to close the door. "Just kiddin'," he said, opening it up again. "The old lady would kill me if I did that. You don't owe me nothing."

"Well—thanks!"

"Yeah, but don't thank me. And anyway, you'll probably be hearing from her. She says she can write a letter as good as that frigging $100-an-hour lawyer any day."

"I'm sure she can," agreed Helen.

Brutson glowered at her briefly. "Yeah, well, deregulation is coming," he said. "Things are going to be pretty different around here when that happens."

Helen briefly contemplated a deregulated aviation with people like Brutson and Garuluk running amok in it. She smiled sweetly at him, then sat down on a gas barrel as he taxied out and took off.

A moment later Paul stepped out of the bush.

"So he-man showed up, did he?" he asked.

Helen looked at him with impatience. She had so much on her mind at present; he had become merely an annoying side issue.

"You know, this stuff is quite good," he was saying.

"What stuff?'

"I think I've got a Ph.D in these notes, that's all."

He was looking shaggy and strung out. Three weeks in a tent had taken their toll on his preppy camping clothes.

"Well, bully for you," she said absently.

There seemed to be a plane approaching. She was puzzled by the direction of the noise. Was Brutson returning? But she was certain it was not his Cessna. It sounded heavier.

It was a Piper Cub on skis.

It glided down the runway and came to a stand beside the gas barrels. A moment later she realized she was looking at Agaric. He seemed very out of place here.

He opened the door and unfolded himself from the tiny cockpit, his long skinny legs in their usual striped overalls, a tattered parka on his upper body, his chicken neck sticking out at the top.

He looked at Helen. Then he looked at Paul. Paul was still flipping the pages of his notebook, preparing to read Helen something.

"Where is he?" Agaric asked.

"Max?" she said. "At home. You'd better come with me."

"Who's this?" Agaric was glaring at Paul. Paul closed his notebook and glared back. He had been interrupted. Then he began putting the notebook away inside his kangaroo pocket. Agaric was not a person one would waste anthropology on.

"What happened? Where is she?" Agaric was saying, meaning the plane as usual. Of course he would have heard about the accident from Search and Rescue.

Helen beckoned him to follow her.

Paul hesitated a moment and then came along as well. She supposed it must have been rather boring for him in camp, even though he had his notes.

They passed the community hall, which was being heated for the dance that night. There seemed to be an enormous party going on all over town already.

At home Max was still talking to his boys.

"... forces her into a ground loop because she can't really go over forward. Not on skis," he was saying.

Agaric brushed past her as she paused to take off her boots.

"Tell me. Do you think this is really for you?" Paul asked her.

"Oh, for God's sake," she said. "What do you mean, Paul?"

"The guy just wrecked an airplane. Can't you see why I'm wondering?"

She hurried in, pausing only to shake her head impatiently at his question.

When she got to the kitchen she found Agaric goggling at Missy and the boys. Max was standing in front of the picture window, his arms folded, looking annoyed.

"Want me to apologize, Agaric? It was my own damn fault. "

"My plane?"

"*Our* plane," said Helen coldly.

"And we'll just be leavin' it out there too, you and me. Ha! Ha!" said Agaric. His eyes shifted from Helen to Missy, then back to Helen. He looked as though he were getting a headache.

"It could be salvaged. Max thinks so," said Helen.

"Well now, that'll be up to the insurance company. And the church. But I guess they'd probably like the money better, don't you think, Freddy? Maybe they'll put up a plaque to me by the altar. Call it a donation."

Max shrugged.

Agaric cackled.

"You know, I'm glad to see you, Freddy, my boy, in spite of all our little disagreements." He was enjoying himself, she could tell. "Nice to see you got the family up here too."

"Garuluk, you are a crook. I don't mind saying it to your face either." Missy spoke from her corner.

"Crook?" He looked at her wide-eyed. "Why, I just got a little payment you may not know about from Freddy here, and as far as I'm concerned, him and me are square. There's no crookedness in it, and now I'm out of the charter business, I don't need no plane, neither."

"But we need one!" cried Helen. "We're getting a charter license, maybe even this month. And we have to have that plane!"

"Well now, if you had just a little more money to ante up, we could talk about salvage," remarked Agaric. He looked at Max. "No? Well, that's too bad then."

Max turned away angrily.

Henry came in through the porch door, which was still open.

"We're havin' a party," He said to Max. "You're the guest of honour." He was holding a white enamel cup in his hand, and he pressed it upon Max. "Better have some of this. It's old and wise. The wife made it two weeks ago."

The room was beginning to fill with Island Crossing people.

"Hey, Helen! Remember when you two got married?"

"When's the kid coming?"

In fact the party had started in the bush the other day and just moved to Island Crossing.

"We found him."

"You better believe it!"

"He just went to the wrong lake, that was all."

Henry was doling more homebrew out of a pot with his mug. Helen could hear the sound of drums in the dance hall and smell the fire used to warm them. More people crowded in.

She was pushed over by the window with Agaric. He seemed to be trying to communicate, so she turned to him. Everyone was very loud.

"What?"

"I said, how in tarnation did you do this?"

Garuluk was pointing a yellowed fingernail at the heart on the window.

"With this." Helen showed him the pendant. "Max gave it to me for Christmas."

Garuluk looked at the ruby for a moment, then turned in protest to the window. He lingered over the heart for a moment, then came back, disbelieving, to the necklace. Jewellery seemed to evoke this this kind of response in men. But Helen had thought of something.

"He bought it from a pilot who claimed he was hauling drugs for the United States government." she said. "Max spent a lot on it. But that fellow's employer just told me it's worth $8,000."

244

She watched Garuluk's face carefully. It was very interesting. Hauling drugs, expensive jewellery; it was romance, almost better than money. It attracted them all, even this old farmer and religious nut, credulous and crooked to the bone.

"You like it?"

He liked it, she could see.

He was an aircraft engineer, she recalled; or at least nobody knew he wasn't.

She looked around. Where was Max? Everyone else in Island Crossing was in her house, even Paul, who was over in a corner talking to Dallas and Marion. He was probably going to read to them out of his notes.

Helen needed Max badly. There was something she had to tell him. But he was nowhere to be seen.

She put on her boots and went outside. He was not in the yard. Then she spotted his tracks leading along the lakeshore path. He probably needed desperately to be alone and she wondered whether she should follow him. She knew something he didn't, however.

It was cold, and she zipped her parka all the way up and put on her mittens as she ran along the path. As she came around the curve of the shore she caught sight of Max on the village dock.

He stooped and picked up something off the boards, then skimmed it out over the lake ice. He was throwing pebbles.

The violence with which he wound up for the throw told her he was full of self-disgust. He needed to hear what she had to say.

"Max!"

He looked around, hesitated, then threw the last pebble in his hand. By the time she arrived on the dock he was looking moodily downwards.

"Couldn't stand it in there. Agaric. Booze. Henry making me into a local hero. I didn't feel like celebrating," said Max. He turned his back on her and looked out over the lake.

It was chilly and dark beyond their bay and the clouds rolled overhead in a bleak promise of snow.

"Snow, not rain, thank God," said Helen.

She sat down on a gas barrel.

"Max, you remember when we were at Agaric's place in October and you told me to think of something, and I thought of the lien on the plane?"

He put his hands in his pockets, not turning around. He had none of his usual winter equipment, only boots and a parka.

245

"You said the right person can always think of something."

"Yeah, but now there's nothing to think about. I wrecked the plane. We spent all the money."

"Yes, but I am the right person," said Helen, her voice trembling a little at her temerity.

"I know you are. That's the trouble. I screwed it all up."

He kept his back to her.

"I haven't got anything," he said.

Helen took off her necklace.

"Yes, you have," she said, the tremble in her voice becoming laughter.

He turned around and she held the pendant out in her upturned hand. A snowflake landed and perched like a tiny star on the point of one of the diamonds.

"You paid $4,000 for this?"

"He said it was worth twice that."

Helen nodded and he looked up from the necklace to her face.

"I don't know that we could sell it."

"No, but I think there's someone we could give it to. Someone who could fix the plane. I mean Agaric."

"Agaric!"

"I just showed it to him. He—he liked it," she said, on another bubble of laughter.

"But I gave it to you."

"Oh yes," Helen agreed. "I'm not trying to give it back, Max." She put her arms around his neck. "I'm just trying to start a charter airline."

And as they embraced there in the falling snow, she gazed over his shoulder at the ruby that represented the promise and uncertainty of what lay ahead: long Northern nights and days, more airplanes, and perhaps moderate wealth, a happy marriage, and little children, all things that she knew she wanted to have.